a really terrible book, but you'll recognize all the settings!

ISLA
ICE

**Dazzle, Danger and Deceit
in the Caribbean**

Feb 2010

*a bad book about a great place!
Does the publisher not have an editor?*

B.D. ANDERSON

Outskirts Press, Inc.
Denver, Colorado

Outskirts Press, Inc.
http://www.outskirtspress.com

ISBN: 978-1-4327-4002-3

Library of Congress Control Number: 2009934018

Outskirts Press and the "OP" logo are trademarks belonging to Outskirts Press, Inc.

PRINTED IN THE UNITED STATES OF AMERICA

"Excellent Book-Super Reading. I could not put it down. Makes you want to apply for a passport."

----Paula L, Oakridge, Oregon

"I read your first book while in St. Maarten. It was great! I'll probably read it again this winter when I am missing the warm sunshine."

---PreK, Massachusetts

Dedication

To *Al and Margaret Ascherl with love,*

*Who believed in and encouraged our Caribbean
Adventure*

Chapter 1

Home Sweet Home: St. Maarten

Miguel adjusted his head higher with a pillow in the king-sized bed and looked down at the beautiful woman's back in the soft moonlight filtering into the room. Brown, muscular and sexy, the skin on her shoulder was splashed with her long, curly black hair. After two wild sexual episodes had taken them both to exhaustion, she had been sleeping on his chest as he laid there smiling up at the ceiling of the master bedroom. The home belonged to her husband Bart, and their two children were sleeping down the hall in a shared bedroom. Desiree was his 29-year old co-worker at *Island Ice* and married to a 40-something police captain whose elite paramilitary squad dressed in full riot gear and trained at odd hours and often off-island. The husband's police trip to the island of Curacao this week for a training seminar meant he would not be back to St. Maarten for at least 4 days and Desiree wanted them to make the most of his absence.

When summoned, he would come to her house around 10 PM or so after her 4 and 6-year olds had collapsed into bed. Mom always picked the nights when the children would be the most tired and quick to fall asleep. Tonight was no exception. Miguel had slipped in the back door with a bottle of her favorite champagne, chocolates, and a very strong libido. Always cautious about leaving any kind of trail, she made him drink from the same glass as her during their nocturnal escapades. They only spoke to each other when safely behind the closed bedroom door and Miguel was not allowed to bring any personal items. Anything that didn't fit in his pockets had to be left in his car, which she insisted was never parked closer than a five minute walk.

Desiree was quick to defend her trysting with Miguel by rationalizing that her husband visited the whore houses with his friends on Sunday mornings while she was busy taking the kids to Sunday school and Church. She'd made it clear to Miguel that theirs was not a relationship that would ever break up her marriage. She was not interested in him for anything other than wild sex. Miguel had agreed with enthusiasm.

Desiree's close friends were another matter. Her girlfriends often teased and tried to provoke her with stories of Mirabel, a Jamaican hooker who reserved her entire Sunday mornings for Bart's regular weekly visit. Cautious with her true feelings, Desiree refused to bite. She dismissed their gossipy comments and assured them that her husband was a family man and totally committed to their marriage. No one, especially Bart, suspected that she was enjoying regular rounds of these extra-marital relations with Miguel. At work in *Island Ice*, they rarely spoke or acknowledged each other. When they met outside the store, both drove separately and, unless someone had the ability to wire tap their cell phone conversations, there was no traceable communication between them. They used pre-paid cell phones without the tell tale monthly printed list of calls. In addition, text messages were still a mystery to Bart who hated computers and new technology. Desiree knew how to use the delete function for additional privacy.

Miguel adjusted the pillow behind him again

and began to stroke her hair. Stirring slightly, she reached down and lightly caressed his penis. He assumed that she was deep in sleep. Wrong. This remarkably sex-hungry woman was obviously ready for more fun. Wrapping her legs around his, she moaned and took him into her mouth. Miguel surprised himself with another erection and began gently thrusting his hips in rhythm with her motions.

A soft metallic clack distracted his attention for a moment. He paused with a primal feeling of danger. Desiree seemed unaffected by the sound so he returned his focus to enjoying the feel of her soft lips moving up and down his firm penis. A moment later the interruption of someone knocking on the foyer door frame and rattling the front door stopped them cold. Two more knocks and another rattling, this time more incessant, made Desiree almost skyrocket off the bed in alarm as if shot from a carnival cannon.

"Holy Shit! My husband's home," the young beauty whispered to the room as if she were talking to herself in disbelief. Then she turned around once trying to collect her wits. Naked, she grabbed their clothes where they'd been dropped around the bed and bundled them in her arms. "Get under the bed! Now…quick!"

Miguel stared at her. "How can you be so sure? The island of Curacao is miles away. He's out playing soldier. Relax. It may be a horny neighbor hoping you're tired of being alone."

"Don't be so fucking stupid. I heard a key in the lock. Only Bartholomew has a key. Thank God I locked the top and bottom security bolts on the door. He's not tapping too hard because he doesn't want to wake the children."

After switching on the nightstand light, she grabbed her perfumed powder container and began to shake its contents on the sheets to obliterate the muskiness that would reveal the evening's activities. "Now get under the damn bed!" She hissed as she grabbed a robe from the bathroom door and put it on.

Seeing that there would be no negotiating with her, Miguel rolled over and wriggled under the bed. The floor was dusty and there were a few children's toys scattered about, but he had room to stretch out and could still see under the less than one inch space between the bed's comforter and the floor. He adjusted his body and remained still for the moment. The fact that he was naked made him shiver, despite the warm temperature of the room and he began to feel a cough forming in his throat. He watched Desiree's feet moving around the bed fluffing the sheets and cover. Then he saw her walk to the window, open it, and drop all of their clothes into the yard. He wondered if she'd also found his sandals and dropped them too. Moving quickly, she lit candles on the nightstands and pulled a vibrator from the drawer in the one on her side of the bed and placed it on her pillow before scurrying out of the room without saying another word. Cocking his head to the side so that his ear was close to the small opening, Miguel could hear her sliding back the pair of steel bolts securing the front door. Next he heard a muffled greeting between husband and wife. Their footsteps then led to the kitchen, followed by the pop of a beer being opened and its cap clattering as it hit the counter. Miguel briefly considered standing and trying to slip out the window, but oddly wanted to stay and spy on his wild lover and her husband.

"Big Bart! Honey! My love! I missed you so much! Thank goodness you came home early. I had to use a vibrator and play with myself tonight when I started thinking about you." Desiree moved close to her husband and rubbed his shoulders. She looked directly into his eyes and then closed them with a sensuous pout. Bart took a deep breath and grinned broadly. Then the proud man in army camouflage embraced his wife and ran his strong hands down her back to her buttocks.

"I love to watch you touch yourself, Baby. I wish I had been home to see it. They surprised us in Curacao yesterday and staged a mock rescue on St. Maarten. We were flown here 16 hours ago and sent to the old hotel hurricane ruins in Mullet Bay. We spent the entire time trying to find our rescue target and being shot at with paint ball guns by hostile looters."

Bart grunted softly with happiness as he opened the front of his wife's robe and ran his hands down over her hips before sliding them up to caress her firm, full breasts. Desiree arched her back and purred. "So, did you win?" Bart watched in awe as his wife's nipples became hard under his touch.

Husband and wife separated by a few inches. "Of course. We were given two bottles of water each, but no rations to make the exercise as real as possible. My men were eager to finish up and go home, so they kicked ass with lightning speed." He gulped his beer then pulled his wife to him once again and kissed her passionately.

Desiree purred and made eye contact, "I am so proud of you." Quickly she dropped to her knees in front of him and deftly unzipped his army fatigues.

"Hold it, Baby." Bart moaned as he reached under her arms and lifted her back to her feet. "I need a shower first. Jungle grunge and lots of sweat in these pants."

"Well then, let me run you a bath. You get another beer and meet me in the bathroom, Big Boy. Oh, and you can take off the boots, but let me take off all the rest. Okay?"

"Damn woman, I love you." Bart took another swig to finish his beer and burped. "How are my children?"

"I sold them at a yard sale to buy a new diamond ring since you forgot my birthday last year" she answered as she walked back towards the master bedroom, dropping her robe on the kitchen floor with her exit.

Still hiding under the bed, Miguel could hear her bare footsteps in the hall and her return to the bedroom. "Stay quiet, okay? You can sneak out after I put him in the bath" she murmured softly as if speaking to herself. She disappeared into the master bath and switched on the light and exhaust fan. Shortly Miguel heard Bart walk down the hall and check on the children and then saw a large pair of military boots approach the edge of the bed inches from his head. A belt unsnapped and a leather holster with its 9 mm pistol dropped on the nightstand. Now Miguel felt even more vulnerable and his nerves were rattled at the heavy clunk of the weapon banging down on the wood. He knew that if he were discovered hiding under this *particular* bed the newspaper would report a police shooting with a "service weapon". There would be no reference to it as "the murder weapon". Guns carried by law enforcement officers were always called "Service Revolvers" by the media around the world and this island was no different.

The large man sat on the mattress and began unlacing the heavy combat foot gear. In his home country, Miguel had seen men kicked to death by boots like these. They were caked with smelly mud that made Miguel's nose itch. As he rubbed his nose, he prayed he wouldn't sneeze. The tiny space under the bed was beginning to feel as confining as a coffin. He twitched uncomfortably as he responded to the growing sensation of claustrophobia. Sweat poured from his forehead and back. The man's weight just inches above made the mattress creak and groan near his now burning ears. He prayed that the conversation between the husband and wife would resume, giving him a slight cover of background noise.

"Baby, I am running a bath for you...come get in the hot, steamy water," called Desiree from the bathroom.

Miguel made the sign of the cross on his chest.

"Okay, but remember you promised to undress me."

"Then get your big ass in here, Captain!" she teased back.

Miguel wanted to throw up. He watched the boots and socks drop on the floor and the man's bare feet head to the bathroom. Then he could hear Desiree's moans as zippers and snaps opened. Next came the sounds of a body relaxing into warm water. Splashing sounds followed with her voice. He heard more noise of water sloshing as it was pulled from the bath tub by a washcloth.

Realizing this might be his opportunity to escape; Miguel squirmed from under the bed and stood by the window. Immediately disappointed, he found the window open but covered by security bars held in place with a large shiny lock. There was plenty of room for Desiree to drop the clothes outside, but none for a man to fit through. He pulled on the bars in frustration. It was no use. Dropping to a crawl, he moved past the open bathroom door and saw the nude Desiree kneeling by the bathtub. Husband and wife were kissing passionately and her hands were moving under the bath water. Bart stretched back in the tub to allow her to lather his erect penis with soap and stroke it. Staring in disbelief, Miguel's emotions crashed over him with the force of a wild ocean wave.

"Is he getting mine... or am I getting his?" he wondered almost forgetting his need to flee. Jealous rage flared in his brain and he felt his face flush. For a moment, he considered charging the man in his bathroom. Then reason prevailed. Bart was approximately six feet tall, two hundred pounds and a combat-trained military man and police officer. Although a good 10 years younger, the Colombian quickly considered the odds. His one hundred fifty pounds of out of shape physique and six inch height disadvantage would not fare well in a fist fight against this man even with the element of surprise. Naked and without options, Miguel crawled away in frustration to seek an exit into the night.

Turning away from the lighted bath, he peered down the hallway allowing his eyes to adjust to the darkness, and then froze. Standing in the corridor about 8 feet away was a 4-year old child in pajamas rubbing his eyes and looking wobbly from sleep.

"Momma, who da man?" the child whined, his voice small and groggy sounding, "Momma!"

Keeping his head down, Miguel stayed still and away from the light spilling out of the master bedroom and bath. Trapped, his brain whirled with feelings of hopelessness with his mounting terror of envisioning 9mm bullets crashing into his back at any moment. With the distance between them, the child could run if he tried to crawl forward to silence him. If he tried to get up, the child might start screaming louder, a reaction guaranteed to trigger the father's investigation. There seemed no way out. He had no choice but to remain motionless.

Desiree appeared at the doorway carrying an empty beer bottle in a planned trip to the kitchen. Instantly sizing up the situation, she hurried past Miguel and without breaking stride quickly scooped the boy into her arms and, turning his head away from the naked man on the floor, headed swiftly back down the hallway. Miguel watched in bewildered amazement, his heart pounding like a trip hammer, as the nude woman removed her yawning child from the scene. Once again, Miguel made the sign of the cross.

"Oh darlin', you're just having a bad dream. Let's get back to bed. Daddy will be here tomorrow and we'll go to the zoo!" he heard her say as mother and child disappeared into one of the bedrooms. Miguel did not need another scare. He leaped to his feet and padded silently across the tile floors, gently opened the front door and stepped out. As he circled the house to retrieve his discarded clothing, his heart was still racing. There were no outside lights on to betray his presence but the moonlight concerned him. Several houses in the area had a clear view of the yard and it would take just one insomniac or nosey neighbor to sound an alarm. Nearby, a dog started to bark. Miguel could not see him and he wondered if the animal had sensed his fear in the darkness. The wonderful sex fest of earlier had become a nightmare. He stubbed his toe on a rock and momentarily stumbled forward, his bare chest brushing against a mature bougainvillea plant. The thorns drew blood. "Fuck!" Miguel muttered. He had to find his shirt and pants. Darting his head from side to side, his eyes focused on lumps ahead. The light in the master bathroom, continued to glow, which gave him a beacon for finding the scattered clothes. He didn't wear underwear tonight so his search was limited to only a few items. He separated his clothes from hers and dressed quickly in the dark. Using her soft, sheer thong panties as a swab, he wiped away the blood on his chest to protect his shirt from a stain and then dropped them absentmindedly. He knew he would be walking barefooted for several blocks to his car since his sandals were not among the items she threw out the window. It didn't bother him at all; he was used to island living. Next time she would probably make him come over without shoes, anyway. As he turned to leave, he remembered that Desiree would not be able to retrieve her clothes easily from the yard if he left them behind, so he rolled them up and tucked them under his arm. With his confidence returning, he thought about the drama tomorrow in the couple's house and smiled wickedly. Desiree would have a hard job hiding his sandals and remaining on guard in the morning should her child remember and begin relating his "dream" of a strange man in the hall. *The cheating bitch deserves it.* Miguel could hear their voices in the bedroom. For a fleeting moment, he considered moving closer and raising his head enough to look inside at the couple, but decided he'd pressed his luck enough for one night. A light came on in the house just behind the rear fence and a car turned down the road passing the property. Another dog barked in the distance. Without another moment's hesitation, Miguel moved away from the house and entered the street in a brisk trot which took him into the anonymity of the darkness.

Chapter 2

The Drop

Half asleep, Chad drove his small sedan down Front Street in the island's tourist district just after 7:30 on Sunday morning towards his reserved parking spot on the roof of the St. Rose shopping complex. Some large trucks slowed his progress as they took advantage of the early morning quiet to drop off deliveries and pick up stock to transfer to other locations, but for the most part he was delighted by the absence of traffic. Slowing for a speed bump in the street, Chad, a barrel shaped man with a playful smile admired himself momentarily in the sun visor mirror and blew himself a kiss. Fortunately, there was no one close by that might be offended or curious about his uninhibited display of self-love. Tourists were nonexistent in town at this hour because most stores would not open until 10 AM or later. In fact, early morning appearances at the store were out of character for Chad. As a top sales person, nothing was ever said by the owners or manager of his rather flexible work schedule. He avoided the usual routine of opening procedures and cleaning, often not arriving until after 10:30 when the tourists began to fill the streets from the cruise ships. His co-workers openly showed their resentment, but no one was able to match his performance on the sales floor. This day, unable to sleep soundly the night before, Chad decided to spend a few hours in his office at the jewelry store "Island Ice" before the other employees arrived. Born on the island, Chad's real name was Chester Johnson but he considered it too dull for his top producer status on the stage of jewelry sales. Competition was fierce and many stores would drop prices quickly to save a sale before the customer walked out. *Island Ice* was unique. First, they were the only store that specialized in selling high quality synthetic diamonds and gem stones. At roughly one fourth of the cost of mined diamonds and even less for many fine stones, the prices of the jewelry using the CVD lab grown diamonds became the talk of the cruise ship crowd, hotel guests and locals. Special care

and expense had been taken by the owners to provide an environment of upscale appointments in
the store as well as "must see" landmark displays.
Using technology worthy of Hollywood's best
stage sets, illusions were created with laser projec-
tors that actually changed the entire wall scenes
in the store. Eye popping lighting graced the entire sales floor. Using light-emitting diodes, colors
pulsated and danced with energy saving efficiency.
Shoppers entered through a special foyer accented
with an ice waterfall. Even the most skeptical visitors flocked with movie cameras in hand to experience the shopping theatre. However, these visual
fantasies also set the stage for criticism. Whenever
the store or its merchandise was tagged as "fabulous fakes" by competitor briefed customers, Chad
would instantly correct them and briefly explain the
process that produced the stones. He assured them
that he was not selling cut glass. The diamonds and
other gems were man-made, but very real nevertheless. With the same properties of stones that
were mined from the earth, without the flaws or
expense, the jewelry pieces took on a new light in
the minds of the shoppers after an educational
sales presentation. Chad loved the challenge and
used it to close the sale, especially if the couple in

front of him consisted of a woman sporting a pair of newly enhanced breasts. With a wink of the eye, he would ogle the low cut top on the woman in front of him and coo, "Sometimes man made can be even better, don't you agree, Sweetie?" It was good to be gay when using harmless flirtation to close the sale. His outrageous flaunting somehow put the men at ease and they reveled in his compliments when directed towards their wife or girlfriend with several thousand dollars worth of new boobs. Chad thought that it must be akin to having someone drool over their newly purchased sports car or a set of high end golf clubs.

In addition to his sales position, he functioned as the store Assistant Manager with many administrative duties to fill the slow traffic periods common in the retail world. He hated paperwork and reports but they came with the job and the end of the month was near. Besides, part time management offered him a private office in the back and a place to find refuge when he needed time away from the demands of the sales floor. Often hot tempered with peers, he suspected that the top management gave him this job to remove him from agitating the other staff during the breaks in crowds. His flamboyant approach and theatrical

mannerisms may have been a hit with the customers, but not with those who had to bear his humor
and often pointed remarks on a daily basis. One
of the older and very religious women on staff
had remarked that more than eight hours of non-
stop Chad would drive her to drink or possibly,
homicide.

The chain had several stores throughout the
Caribbean and the Headquarters in St. Thomas
would be nagging him any day now for the daily
traffic counts, records of ship sales, and projections
of needed inventory. This rare case of insomnia
and the lack of a partner in bed last night triggered
his early morning trip. He planned to get the paperwork out of the way and head to a remote nude
beach by mid afternoon. Chad's uninterrupted ride
through town came to a quick stop when he found
that his car was blocked by a large van. One man,
obviously working alone, unloaded 5 gallon bottles
of water at a classic "island time" pace.

Chad muttered under this breath to the muscular brown male body working in front of him.
"Hey pretty boy…hurry up! Move yo ass" he said
under his breath, "One night with this flame and
you'll never go back to a bitch."

In a world of his own, the young man failed to

notice Chad tapping his steering wheel impatiently or to show any concerns about blocking the small car behind him. The Front Street renovation of expanded walkways and palm trees in the town's main tourist shopping area was not without adjustment for the merchants. The single narrow lane created for vehicular traffic prevented any passing. During the day, tourists appreciated the emphasis on foot traffic and impatient motorists quickly learned to avoid the route. Scanning the street to break the monotony of the wait, he could see the local drunk, Fernando, crossing the street just ahead. Dressed in his usual uniform of jeans, a clean T-shirt, and tennis shoes, he always seemed to start the day looking normal. Fernando was actually a reliable courier from 8 AM to Noon offering his services to the businesses. He was related in some way to most of the women in the utility and government offices and could get in to pay a bill without the agony of waiting in long lines. The trick was to catch him before he began collecting payments in cash for his deliveries. By midday he would be on his 6th or 7th beer and then disappear to a side street. By then his clothing would become dirty and his hair disheveled. Occasionally he would resurface during the afternoons and become sexually aggressive with local women embarrassing or frightening the tourists. However, all in all, he was harmless and tolerated by most of the merchants and visitors.

Chad started to honk and wave to Fernando but was distracted by the thumping of a loud bass speaker in a low slung car just ahead on the right. The sporty Honda two door was a favorite choice among young men on St. Martin. The driver had pulled into one of the many alleys that fed Front Street and allowed direct access to Back Street or the Beach. The noise from the car shook the metal security shutters of stores and made Chad's teeth hurt. The dark tinted windows and windshield prevented Chad from being able to tell if the car was occupied and the sinister appearance of the vehicle's custom wheels, candy red paint job, and low-rider suspension system told him that the owner was probably mixed up in the drug trade or other bad things. A lot of money was spent on extras for that car and the sound system was probably powerful enough to use in a movie theater. Chad had learned long ago to avoid people like this whenever possible. It was best to sit quietly and wait for the van to move so that he could pass the Honda without a confrontation over the awful noise. He pushed the button to roll up his driver's side window and tried to tune out the disturbance. He shook his head in frustration at the impossible task as his glass continued to rattle with the beat of the music.

In his line of sight, Chad saw the door open on the passenger side of the parked hip hop concert as the blaring music momentarily increased and a man exited quickly and slammed the door. Chad was shocked to recognize him as one of his fellow co-workers, a Colombian man. Dressed casually, Miguel Martinez, who was one of the store's vault managers darted across the street carrying the shiny bag of a well known perfume shop, Senses. Miguel gazed briefly at the van and the water bottles on the sidewalk then hurried to *Island Ice* without noticing Chad's car or looking back. It was obvious that he was on a mission. Chad suddenly felt uncomfortable for no reason. He lowered his window and leaned his head enough to see down the sidewalk. Miguel was now standing in front of their store, using his key to disarm the outside alarm station and then opening the bars that protected the outside foyer. In a flash he disappeared inside.

"What the hell?" Chad murmured aloud. With sudden paranoia, he raised his window and slid down into his seat. Hiding in a small sedan was not easy for a man of his height and weight. He squirmed, afraid of being noticed by Miguel or the driver in the Honda. His instincts told him that it was best not to be exposed as a witness to this strange off hour's entrance into the store. While Miguel had enough seniority to carry a front door key and open the store, there were strict procedures. He was not top management; he was only allowed to enter in the presence of another employee and not before 30 minutes of the scheduled opening time. Chad felt sweat break out on his forehead. He had seen something at this early hour that obviously he should not have.

In just minutes, Miguel was back out on the street and his hands were empty. Scanning the street briefly, he locked the store, the security bars, and set the alarm. With one swift move, he turned and walked away in the opposite direction without acknowledging the driver in the Honda. In front of Chad, the worker who was blocking the street with his water bottle delivery loaded the last one into his vehicle, then sauntered to the driver's door, slipped inside and started the motor after taking a drink from a McDonald's paper cup. Chad fidgeted in his seat not wanting to move into view. With the delivery truck gone he would be in the open. As the van in front of Chad's car began to move forward slowly, Chad squirmed in his seat again and rocked his large belly in fear. With a quick reflex motion he grabbed candied nuts from an open bag on the passenger seat and stuck a handful in his mouth. Suddenly the van was blocked by the Honda as it backed into the street and took the position in front. Chad breathed a sigh of relief knowing that he would not have to drive past the parked Honda or risk being seen by its driver. Brushing his hands to remove the food residue, he picked up his cell phone from the center console and dialed the home of the Store Manager. After a long series of rings, the phone was answered by a woman's voice. Chad drove forward slowly and approached the ramp which would lead him to the private parking area.

"Hey Boss. It's me" he said as he reached for more goodies from the bag.

"Good morning Chad. Don't tell me that you are holed up with some pretty young thing and want to avoid your end of the month reports. You promised me yesterday on the phone that you would work today."

He swallowed hard and cleared his throat. "You

won't believe it. I'm already at the store. In fact, I was just sitting in my car outside the front" answered Chad trying to sound serious. "I'm calling because I saw something happen that you should know about."

There was no immediate response on the phone. Then after a long pause the store Manager questioned the strange announcement. "You, early? You haven't been to work early since I moved here."

Chad pulled into his parking space and shut off the engine. "Do you hear what I'm saying? I just saw the strangest thing and I thought that you should know." Chad began to tense and feel some irritation with his boss's relaxed approach.

The tone of Chad's voice was not alarming to his boss. "Okay, I'm listening" She had gotten used to her Assistant's ranting and raving, often on unimportant subjects or events. "Was Fernando wearing a suit and walking into church this morning?"

"Shit, not unless they are using beer for communion" replied Chad quickly feeling a little less uncomfortable. "It was probably nothing. But..."

Over the phone, he could hear dishes rattle and a liquid being poured as his boss waited for the news. "I have a fresh cup of coffee and I am ready. Spit it out. What did you see this early Sunday morning that is concerning you?"

Chad scanned the parking lot suspiciously and checked his door locks before he spoke. "I saw Miguel get out of one of those druggie cars and take a bag into *Island Ice*. He went in alone and only stayed a few minutes. Then he came out without the bag and walked away without getting back into the car."

"So? What kind of a bag? A backpack? A grocery bag? Maybe he was going to get breakfast and did not want to carry anything bulky or heavy to Burger King and back. After all, I think that he is scheduled to open the shop today and he does not have either of the combinations to the safe. What could he do in there alone, anyway?"

Chad answered with a grunt of disapproval. "It was a bag from one of the perfume shops."

His boss continued as if thinking out loud. "Yes, Miguel violated procedure. He should not enter the store alone and certainly not at this hour... but I don't follow your upset about a shopping bag that we see by the hundreds on any given day."

"Let me be honest with you, Judith. I don't think that anyone was supposed to see this visit.

The driver of the car he was in waited for him to put the bag inside and they did not wave goodbye to each other when he finished. It looked like a drop to me. I almost peed in my pants! Something bad is going on here."

"Let's stay calm. Tell me about the bag." Judith was beginning to share her Assistant's concerns. During the pause in their conversation she tried to remember if Miguel was even scheduled to work today.

"It was one of those expensive perfume bags with the red glossy finish and a gold handle on top."

A sigh on the other end of the phone was the only response. Chad started to feel foolish and he wondered if his lack of sleep last night was affecting his judgment.

"Sorry I called." Chad's voice sounded weak.

"No. Don't think that for a moment. Are any perfume shops open early on Sunday morning? Of course not. I am just processing the information. You did the right thing. Now I want to ask you to do something else."

"What? Call the police?" he said with a tinge of excitement.

"Not yet. First, please go into the store. Cut

on all the lights in the back offices just like normal. Then go to my office and lock the door behind you. Review the security recording of this morning. Once you find the place where he enters the store write down the exact times and then call me back with what you see on the cameras. I doubt that anyone else will come to work early, so you should be alone for the next hour. Okay? Are you comfortable with doing that?"

"Oh yes, Dumplin', I am. Chad's Investigative Services at your command. Now I feel like a private dick!" he roared.

With the conversation over, Chad walked down from the parking garage and scanned the street before crossing. Since it was still early for a Sunday, the other shops remained closed and pedestrian activity remained quiet. Two more delivery trucks passed and one driver recognized him and beeped the horn once. With a quick wave in return, Chad relaxed and entered the darkened store relocking the front entrance behind him. He cut on a row of lights then crossed the familiar sales floor to pass through the doorway marked "Private, Employees Only." Nothing was different and for all purposes everything he inspected looked exactly the same as any other morning. He entered the long hallway leading past the employee kitchen and turned on every light switch as he checked the rooms and hall. After turning on the lights in the Manager's office and his own, he returned to the kitchen and poured himself a large glass of filtered water from the cooler. The water tasted cold and he gulped it down. Realizing that he was perspiring heavily he refilled the glass. He needed to sip this one and calm down. Shaking off the jitters, he returned to the Manager's office and shut the door. An entire wall across from her desk held several flat screen monitors that showed 6 scenes per screen of the entrance, the delivery bay, sales floor, hallways, and display cases. The entire security system was state of the art with a large digital recorder capable of holding over three weeks of data in beautiful crisp color images. Unfortunately, there was no off premises monitoring or internet access to the machine. That left Chad to play detective and try to figure out the reason for Miguel's strange visit and quick exit.

A sudden bumping noise made Chad freeze. Feeling like his heart had stopped; he held his own chest with an open hand. Then the bumping sounds became more constant as an air conditioner choked itself to life and the sound of air came through the nearest ceiling vent. Looking down, he realized that he had been clutching his cell phone with the other hand. He placed it on a small conference table and pulled a chair close to the screen that showed the front entrance and cash register counter. He used his management keys, unlocked the cabinet to gain access to the recorder controls and found the remote. Backing up the action to the approximate time that he first drove near the store, he settled comfortably to watch the darkened and empty room as the counter moved forward second by second and minute by minute. Becoming bored he started to scan the other monitor scenes when a flash of light from the front door caught his attention again. At exactly 7:41 he saw Miguel enter the main sales floor without turning on any lights, move quickly to the cash counter, and grab a stapler. He used it to secure the top of the bag with two passes of staples, then dropped to his hands and knees and crawled under the counter. When he backed out his hands were empty. He sat back and checked his concealment of the bag, then stood. Seconds passed before he spun around and headed out the door. Chad was amazed at the speed of the exit. He pushed the pause button to consider the scene he had just witnessed. Employees were each given a personal locker in the back hall way and could secure their valuables there. Why was Miguel crawling around under the front desk? Why did the driver wait outside and watch the store, but then the two men did not acknowledge each other when Miguel left? What could be in the bag now hidden in a very public area of the store? Chad pulled a phone toward him from the across the conference table and dialed his boss again at home.

She answered on the first ring this time. "Hello?"

"Boss, it's me again. He hid the bag under the front cash counter."

"That doesn't make sense, Chad. We have private lockers for employees to secure belongings. You know that."

"Damn right, I do. This bag is meant for easy access and removal from the store later."

"Why do you say that?"

"Simple, if the person who places the bag is not supposed to be the same person who retrieves it, then a drop point makes sense."

There was another long pause while Judith, the Manager, considered the events as reported to her. Chad waited squirming in his seat and reaching for an open bag of chips that had been left on the table.

"Chad, I was going to call you at a later hour this morning anyway. I received an email on my Blackberry earlier telling me that the scheduled ship for today was re-routed due to a seriously ill passenger." Judith paused so that Chad could assimilate the information. "We need to call the scheduled employees and tell them that the store will remain closed today."

"Holy shit! You are leaving me alone here with this drop bag to be tortured and murdered?"

"No Chad. I will be there to meet you. Together we will figure this out and decide what to do next. Relax, okay? Some private dick you are!"

Her reminder of his earlier boastful statement brought a grin back to Chad's face and he dropped the bag of chips on the conference table. "Damn right, Judith. You got me. But what do I do now? I sure as hell ain't gonna wait in this office like a duck in a barrel." With caution, Chad sat up in the chair and examined the room carefully as if some-one might be listening or hiding in a corner.

Thinking about fish in a barrel, Judith decided not to correct her crazy and emotional co-worker. "No, I want you to give me the names of employees on the schedule today. I will make the calls to them from home. Then I need a little over an hour to dress. I will call your cell phone when we can meet. For now, get the bag and lock it in the office safe. Once you do, get out of the store and wait for me…"

Chad was relieved but still felt vulnerable. "I'll do it, Judith. I'll go visit a friend close by and wait for your call."

"And Chad. One more thing. Not a word of this to anyone…do you understand?"

Chad feigned surprise. "Me? Of course not, Boss. My lips are sealed" he said as the thrill of his excitement grew. He knew that now he had a riveting story to share.

Chapter 3

The Bag

Instead of driving to a friend's house, Chad left the store with his cell phone in hand and headed out to the new boardwalk on the Philipsburg beach. His first stop was the Pasanggrahan Hotel but the two waitresses on duty were too busy with breakfast customers to sit and hear his tale of adventure. Hungry for an audience, Chad continued to seek a friendly confidant, bored bartender or tourist killing time as the morning came alive. Hiking briskly back to the walkway, he turned west in search of more businesses opening for the Sunday beach goers. He passed several downtown residents during his search, but all seemed content with their morning strolls, and no one paused beyond a nod and the traditional greeting of "Good Morning."

He noted the absence of an arriving cruise

ship and remembered Judith's phone calls to staff which would cancel the store opening. He wondered how Miguel would react. Miguel was not expecting Chad or Judith to show up today at the store on a one ship day, so he must have had a plan for the mystery bag.

The sun was high in the sky now and the bay water was calm and clear. Several workers raked sand and moved beach chairs and umbrellas into place in front of hotels and beach bars. Chad felt more excitement knowing that he was holding a secret unknown to the people he passed. Seeing a friend from his neighborhood take a seat outside of a coffee shop, Chad quickened his pace in anticipation of blurting out his clandestine incident. Steps from joining the man and interrupting his coffee break, Chad's cell phone ringing stopped him in his tracks.

"Hello" he answered fecling a slight twinge of guilt.

"Chad, it's Judith" the familiar female voice said unnecessarily. "I just parked on the roof next to your car and I'll be at the store in minutes. Can you meet me?"

"Yes, I am on the Boardwalk near the Court House Square."

"Good. Let's go in together. When I talked with Miguel, he argued that he needed to work today because Friday's shipment had to be checked in. After several protests he had to accept my decision that the store would remain closed today, but he did not like it. I am sure of that."

Judith, a petite brunette whose passion for dressy flip flop sandals was well known in the retail community, waved to Chad as soon as they approached each other. Given the purpose of the visit to the store, she had dressed sensibly this morning in cargo pants with a layered series of conservative tops. Chad zeroed in on her as he noticed her tennis shoes.

"Running shoes, not sandals today?" he smirked.

She passed him, heading in the direction of *Island Ice* without comment. Chad followed.

As they walked along Front Street to the store's front entrance, both Chad and Judith scanned other stores in search of friendly faces. News of the cancelled ship had spread quickly that morning thanks to email, so most stores were shut tight with security bars. A few of the diehard merchants who sold souvenirs and confectionary items were opening in hopes of beach traffic, but all of the major retailers remained closed. Chad peered down the length of the narrow street and thought that he saw a candy red hood sticking out of an alley. Squinting his eyes for a better look, he still could not be sure. As Judith opened the store's doors he shook off his paranoia and followed her through the entrance. Without cutting on lights, they passed the empty display cases and moved through the door leading to the management offices, safe, and stock vault.

"Did you stash the bag in the safe?"

"You can bet your ass, I did. Then I got the hell out of here. Never even peeked in the damn thing to see the booty" boasted Chad still riding the roller coaster of emotion from fear to excitement.

Judith turned the top dial of the safe to set the opening code, and then she leaned down to do the same for the bottom dial.

With a loud click, the lever on the 6 foot tall safe moved and Chad pulled the heavy door open for her. They bumped into each other as they stooped over to examine the bag at the same time.

"Sorry, Boss. Go head" Chad apologized and stepped back to move out of her way.

"Don't call me a Goat Head" joked Judith hoping to defuse the tension in the air. It didn't work. Both managers had heartbeats that were racing.

She pulled out the easily recognized perfume bag and took it over to a nearby table. Using a staple remover, she released the seal Miguel had added when stashing the bag out front and carefully unfolded the opening.

Chad stood beside her and squealed in satisfaction, "I knew it! Cash, the bag is full of cash! I told you so! I told you so!"

Judith emptied the stacks of bills on the table. All neatly bound in thick bundles, the bills were US hundreds. Judith winced and mentally estimated the total without breaking any open to count.

"Not bad carry around money for a guy who makes less money than I do working in a vault warehouse! There must be over 10 Grand there" Chad declared to the room as if it was necessary.

"Chad, I never doubted you. Okay? You caught me off guard this morning with the call, that's all" she said as she put the money back into the bag and walked over to the safe. Placing the loot inside, she closed the safe and turned back to her Assistant. "Now we have more detective work to do."

"How so?"

She held her chin with her left hand and pointed to the door with her other. "Think about it.

Miguel wanted to be in the store today something terrible. The money under the front counter was not his focus when he talked to me. He rattled on about checking in the order from Friday. Let's start there. Something is behind this money."

Chad agreed. "Yep and I bet ya it is spelled d, r, u, g, s with a capital D."

Judith looked around deep in thought seeming to ignore his hypothesis. "My brain is racing. Most of our customers use credit cards. Our cash sales balance perfectly everyday. Theft is almost impossible with our full tray presentations in locked glass cases and inventories at the beginning and end of each day. Every sold item is replaced in minutes after the transaction is completed. What am I missing?"

"You're not listening to me. The money has nothing to do with *Island Ice*. We're obviously a drop point. Theft in our store is not behind the money" insisted the burly man.

"Well, I am still having trouble wrapping my head around this situation. Let's go see what we can find in the vault."

Chapter 4

Working on Sunday

On Sunday morning Andy was enjoying a quick nap on the outside terrace sofa at home when Dana entered and said, "Honey, have you seen my glasses? Andy was jolted awake and his eyes opened suddenly. She paused, and cast a quick glare at Andy as he peered at her with sleepy eyes. "Oh, sorry. Did I wake you?"

Andy stirred more from side to side, rubbed his eyes and looked directly at his wife with a sarcastic smile. "I am having a Zen moment. Give me some privacy. The knowledge I am about to uncover could help the world." Closing his eyes again, he crossed his arms over his chest.

"Sure. And what did you learn from the Universe, my teacher?"

"If you must know my little grasshopper, I

learned that I can transform the small object in my pants into a power tool." Andy smiled smirking in self satisfaction and the joy of spontaneous male adolescent humor.

Dana put her hands on her hips and said, "Andy, you're reading too many of the porno spam emails we receive. Now answer my damn question. Have you seen my glasses or can you ask the cosmos to help me find them?"

Owners of the Former Life Bar at the Chill Grill, Andy and Dana had spent the last couple of years working seven days a week during high season to build the business. Because St. Maarten is shared by a Dutch side and a French side, currency values had had a strong influence on business success. With the current weak dollar and the strong Euro, the majority of tourists from the USA had restricted most of their spending to the Dutch side because of local currency being tied to the US dollar. Andy and Dana were benefiting from location, location, location plus good ole American hard working values. The beach bar was located just a few minutes from town by car, the water was spectacular, and the food was good. Andy had used several unusual marketing programs including free family days at the beach for taxi drivers to encourage them to bring visitors to the beach. He purchased advertising on the cruise lines and made sure that every tourist magazine had a colorful ad with a coupon for a free drink. The growth in business was far beyond the original business plan, and profits were beginning to appear. Product sales of souvenir items that branded the beach and restaurant were also beyond expectations, and they had to build on to the deck area to accommodate a larger retail sales floor for sunscreen, T-shirts, and other paraphernalia. Growth meant more expenses, but the future was bright. Regardless of the restaurant's demands, the couple still enjoyed their time at home alone. Dana had taken up a new habit of watching the food channel on cable, and Andy enjoyed watching Dana.

Giving up on her question for locating her missing eye glasses, Dana turned her attention to her new purchase. "Honey, do I look fat in this bathing suit?" she continued.

"Dana, why do women ask men questions that could possibly result in the poor man's death?"

"I just want your opinion…this is a new suit."

Dana twirled around and waited for her husband's comments on her choice. "Do you like this one better than the black one?"

"Look at the time…I am on duty in just 10 minutes at the bar…got to run!" Andy stood and smiled in triumph.

"Chicken shit!" was his wife's humorous good bye that he heard as he hurried out of the house.

Sundays were one of the couple's favorite times to work because of the groups of locals as well as tourists who would frequent the beach and restaurant. Andy and Dana loved to play hosts and greet friends by name. Also, by local labor laws, the wages for those who worked on Sundays were double the usual rate. Two owners on the schedule helped to keep the business profitable. However, Dana often packed a swimsuit just in case the beach called out to her.

Andy arrived in his 5 year old Suzuki jeep and found the parking lot starting to fill as he selected a space as far away from the restaurant as possible. He believed that it was always best to save the places by the door for his customers. He exited his vehicle and paused to collect some paper trash and discarded cups on his way to the restaurant back door. The smell of the sea was invigorating and he listened momentarily for the sound of the waves softly crashing on the beach. A small car entered the lot behind him and the driver dropped off two of his kitchen workers. After the traditional greetings of "Good Morning" Andy opened the door with his key and held it for his employees to pass. Inside, two other employees were already busy cleaning tables and chairs in preparation for the opening. Andy moved about unlocking the bolts on the heavy wooden shutters and pushed open the windows to let sun and breezes fill the rooms. Once finished, he moved behind the bar since he was alone on the schedule until afternoon when the crowds would come looking for cold drinks to take out on the beach. His routine of setting up the bottles and cleaning consumed the quiet hours, and the morning passed quickly.

Late morning brought several taxis to the beach, rental cars and jeeps plus one tour bus from a large Simpson Bay hotel. Happy vacationers were everywhere and Andy welcomed the arrival of two young waitresses to help him with the growing bar crowd and requests to take drinks out to the beach.

Someday we'll have the extra money to add beach waiters and waitresses, Andy thought to himself. He and Dana made a large investment in comfortable lounge chairs last year with soft cushions and over sized umbrellas which had required hiring two additional staff to set up, rent and take down the equipment. The absence of competition on the beach gave him some additional time to consider adding more staff. For now, everyone walked up when thirsty or hungry. His "Former Life" theme with mannequins dressed in various career uniforms such as a nurse, an airline pilot, and even a former porn star guaranteed souvenir photos and the purchase of hats, T-shirts and ladies apparel with the destination's logo.

Dana had arrived and joined the kitchen staff to help. Without needing to direct the well trained and enthusiastic cook, she fell into place to assist where necessary. While the menu had been Dana's creation, the local man jumped into his job with such enthusiasm and dedication that the couple rewarded him with profit sharing after his first three months. Raymond Cannegieter had trained to be a computer programmer and graphic designer but instead found that cooking behind the open kitchen counter at the Chill Grill was more to his liking. Dana quickly nicknamed him "Chef Ramón" and pronounced it with an exaggerated French accent which further delighted the young man.

Andy had just placed more cold Carib beers on the bar for his waitresses to deliver to the dining area when a familiar hulk of a man entered the bar. Dressed in long pants and a black Tommy Bahama button up island shirt, Chad looked like someone with a story to tell. Well known by Andy and his staff for dramatic behavior, the gay man was an island treasure of entertainment, gossip, and outrageous one liners that brought laughter from everyone. Even the most homophobic and up tight tourist who avoided Chad on first sight would warm up to his performance after one drink at the bar.

Today, however, was different. Chad walked in with a tale of danger and intrigue. Whispering to Andy as he leaned over the bar and swearing Andy to secrecy about the facts, he gained Andy's attention.

"Chad, so you are telling me that this employee entered your store early in the morning without permission, hid a bag full of money and rushed away?" asked Andy from behind the shiny wooden bar counter. Two large flat screen TV's in each corner showed continuous DVD's of snow storms complete with cars sliding into each other and frustrated motorists examining damage. Under each screen was a sign, "Ice belongs in a rum and coke. Not under your tires or your feet."

Obviously shaken and still upset, he stirred the bloody Mary in front of him with a stalk of celery and bobbed his head in agreement. "Yeh, it scared me to fucking death. There I was, caught in the street with nowhere to go and these Colombians were just feet ahead of me. God knows what they would have done to me if they knew that I witnessed the drop. Oh my God in heaven, I am still shaking." He raised his arms in submission and turmoil as he turned his head upward.

"Chad my friend, you do seem to be a bit over the top at times. Except for breaking company policy and coming in without another employee, having money is not a crime, is it? Don't be outrageous." Andy wiped the counter and polished the salt and pepper shakers nonchalantly.

"Anyone can be outrageous. However, few can burst into flames. It is a gift that I have." Chad chomped on the celery and picked up the Old Bay shaker. After adding an enormous amount of the spicy powder to his drink, he gulped half of the colorful liquid. He leaned forward and grabbed the pepper shaker. "You know Andy, life is meant to be spicy. Not boring. Mordacious! Just call me Mord. Shit, you should have a mannequin of me here, not just army uniforms, business people and a porn star!"

"Chad, we want you in the present. Not in our former life. You are too good a friend and bring us joy with every visit. Just don't expect drinks for free!"

"Well, at least name a drink after me. How about Pink Paradise or the Flaming Volcano?"

Andy acknowledged the humor with a quick smile. "Back to the crime, my flaming friend. What did you find when your boss joined you to inspect the store?"

A young Asian man, barefooted and in swim trunks, entered the bar from the beach with a broad grin. Pausing to examine the topless former Porn star display, he turned to Andy and saw the TV shows. "Ah, man. That's cruel. I'm from Buffalo, New York, and we have to go home in three days. Yesterday my mom called and said that it was 14 degrees. Oh, shit."

Andy cocked his head with an "Oh well" gesture and said, "We hope you remember this day and tell your friends to come to St. Martin soon. What would you like Sir?"

"Other than wishing that my wife had tits like your Former Porn star, after seeing your videos of snow storms I have no choice but to order a rum and coke. Also, one of those Guavaberry frozen drinks for my lady, please."

"You got it, coming right up. Also our kitchen is open all afternoon for lunch so if you get the munchies in the late afternoon, just come back."

As Andy turned to make the drinks, Chad leaned back in his bar stool to admire the younger man's rear end. The swimsuit clad man was aware of Chad scoping him out and immediately moved further down the bar.

"Here you are!" Andy signaled with two drinks in hand. "Do you want to pay now or start a tab? We accept all the major credit cards."

The man handed over a shiny Visa card and took the drinks. "I'll be back soon, just keep the card in the register. We want to buy some of your hats and ladies thongs to take home. They'll remind us of St. Martin all winter!"

Chad watched the man walk away and sighed, "Why are all the pretty ones married and straight?"

Andy chuckled and shook his head from side to side. "Yes, you do have the gift of bursting into flames! Now my friend, let's return to the subject at hand. Explain your voyeuristic adventure from this morning to Dr. Phil."

Two young women walked by the bar entrance without pausing then continued to the beach. Andy grinned as they simultaneously removed their bathing suit tops and spun them in the air to greet friends near the water's edge. Uninterested, Chad drained his glass with a slurping sound and put both of his hands in the air.

"I'm telling you, Andy. There is some serious shit going down in town. Probably smuggling, drugs, and even Voodoo rituals going on near my store every night. Danger is everywhere! I just can't believe it." His voice raised an octave and he rolled his eyes up dramatically. Andy stood behind the bar and feigned concern.

"Would you like another drink?" was all that Andy could think of saying at the moment. Chad needed to vent.

"Not now, I need to keep my wits. If someone saw me this morning witnessing the drop, I might be on a hit list already."

"Did your boss talk to Miguel yet about the money?"

"Not as far I know, she didn't." Chad replied with another wave of his arms in the air. "Sunday is her regular day off, and we still have the money in our safe so she will probably decide what to do on Monday. Hopefully I will still be alive to find out."

"Does this mean you will start a diet and exercise program, and take a medication to lower your cholesterol?"

Chad dismissed Andy's black humor with a wave of his arm. "No, you know what I am talking about. This guy, Miguel, was upset with Judith when she decided to keep the store closed today. He claimed that he needed to work in the vault to check in a shipment from Friday.

"Did you guys look in the vault?"

"Exactly. Judith went over everything carefully."

"What did you find? Any inventory missing? Any bundles of white powder? Any evidence of Haitian Voodoo Rituals? Any bags of bones or dead chickens and goats?"

Chad attempted to take another drink from his empty glass and instead sucked on the ice. "I'll have another, Mr. Bartender! No, all cases were perfect and the back stock was in place. We opened the new shipment and checked that too. No problems. In fact, there was an extra package of new jewelry pieces that we did not expect. Someone must have added it at the last moment and forgot to give Judith a heads up. There was a separate invoice for it. But everything checked out."

Andy finished making Chad's drink, he switched the full glass for the empty one. "Okay. That means there was more merchandise in the vault than you expected instead of a shortage. Sounds like the guy is innocent to me! Most of us who run or own a business find stock missing from time to time."

An attractive couple in bathing suits entered the bar from the beach. "Hey Mister! We hope that you're Andy" the man bellowed to the room.

"Yes! Welcome to the Former Life Bar."

"We saw the sign out front. Is it true?" the sun-tanned man asked with a mischievous grin.

Andy and Chad looked at each other with some uncertainty. Andy was first to get it. His welcome sign had become so popular that they now sold a T-shirt with the script on the back:

> Please check at the door:
> Firearms
> Bad attitudes
> Regrets and disappointments
> Demanding "I'm on vacation" behavior
> Demanding "I'm a local" behavior
> Dysfunctional families
> Bitchy Ex-wives
> Jealous or stupid Ex-husbands

Whining children (We love 'em, they taste like chicken)

And, of course, anything that might disturb our relaxed island life

All major credit cards accepted
Your dog or cat is welcome, just please take them when you leave.
No shirt, no shoes…you know why you're here!
Topless women drink free at the Former Life Bar when Andy bartends.

And please remember, "Chill" is our name.

"I'll have a Carib beer and my wife, Cheri, will have a frozen Margarita!" continued the laughing man. He untied the back of the woman's top and held it high in the air.

Andy shrugged, smiled and said, "Coming up, you party animals." He paused to admire her for an extra second or two before reaching for the blender.

Drinks in hand, they left three dollars on the bar to pay for the beer and headed back to the beach. As they paused at the door, the man turned back to the bar and said, "We'll be back in a few to take photos for our website, so save some time for Tony and Cheri before you leave."

Andy put the money in the register, waved in acknowledgement to the couple and said, "I love my job." Then he thought *Maybe we don't need beach waiters after all.* He turned back around and saw Chad stand and stretch. "Oh, are you still here?"

Chad sat back down. "Very funny. We were talking about the extra jewelry…nothing unusual. Just great looking stuff that we did not already have in stock. No duplicates either. Must be a new design and the buyers at Corporate sent previews. So I tagged them and moved several to the first trays to be pulled for the cases in the morning. New stock gets sales people motivated to sell more."

Andy gazed upward thoughtfully then nodded his head in agreement, "You know Chad, the new stock that I see in front of this bar motivates me too!"

"Yeh, but you are talking about tits. I am serious, we really got some winners in this shipment."

"Aren't most of your pieces fake?"

Chat straightened up and began his usual sales lesson on laboratory made stones and diamonds. "Andy, my friend, most of the fabulous tits you ogle from behind your bar are surgically enhanced. Our jewelry on the other hand is real. All gold or platinum, with stones that are flawless. But they are not pulled from a dirty and dusty mine. They are created perfectly in a laboratory for a small fraction of the cost of what you are calling real jewelry."

"Did I hear the word jewelry?" Dana called to the two men as she entered the bar area. Dressed casually in her signature string top T-shirt with Chill Grill on the front, a pair of sexy white shorts, and 2 inch flip flop sandals, Dana could easily pass for a woman half her age as she crossed the room and went behind the bar to kiss her husband. "How are you, Chad?"

Before Chad could answer, Andy jumped into the conversation. "He is recuperating from a morning of his usual secret agent activities...chasing drug smugglers, catching jewelry thieves, and making the world safe for democracy."

Dana considered Andy's playful statement with some puzzlement. "What?"

"Oh Dana" Chad wailed moving his arms and swaying his head dramatically. "I could have been killed this morning! I saw a cash drop. If the perpetrators find out about my ability to testify against them, I am a doomed man."

Expressionless, Andy deadpanned Chad then turned his head and stared into Dana's eyes. "Many drama queens can flame, but only the chosen few can catch fire" he said dryly.

"Pleeese. That is my line!" Chad responded. "Bartender, I need another drink. Dana, will you please join me in libation to help sooth my shattered nerves?"

"Sure will. The staff just ordered me out of the kitchen. I'm off for the rest of today! I'm ready for a day on the beach." Dana said as she held up her small beach bag. "Bartender, one Chardonnay in a chilled glass, please!"

All three of them laughed as Andy poured wine for Dana. She pulled herself up on a stool next to Chad and coyly leaned over to the large man. "So, Mr. Bond, what about the jewelry you and my husband were discussing on my arrival."

"Oh my god, girl. You won't believe the new diamonds we just received. I have them tagged and on trays for Monday's opening. There are some obscenely beautiful items to die for! You must be my first customer of the day." Chad's delight in talking about his newly found stock items quickly diverted the conversation's focus from the cash bag that

Miguel had hidden in the store.

"I do love bling. Even your fake pieces are stunning, I will admit."

"Madam" Chad replied with his hands on his hips for extra emphasis. "Only the uneducated call them fake. They are laboratory produced stones of the highest quality. You will be able to have a wonderful ring for only a few thousand dollars that would cost in the tens of thousands if the rock had been pulled from some dusty old hole in the ground by unpaid and abused workers in sordid areas of the world by oppressors that use the money to finance horrible and unspeakable deeds."

As soon as Chad's tirade was over, Andy gazed at his friend with continued amusement, "Wow, how do you really feel?"

Chapter 5

Monday morning at *Island Ice*

With a blank expression on his face, Miguel sat across from Judith at the desk in her office. The door was closed. She had arrived early expecting that he would be one of the first to unlock the store. She was correct. This time he followed procedure and opened the door with another employee exactly 30 minutes prior to the scheduled time for work. Judith exchanged the pleasant greetings for the morning with them and asked Miguel to come directly to her office.

Judith leaned forward on her desk and clasped her hands together. "Miguel, we need to talk about the bag you placed under the cash counter early yesterday morning."

"I don't know what you mean." His accent was

Spanish but his English was excellent.

Judith reached for her DVR remote and pushed the play button. The large screen just to the side of her desk came alive with a scene from early Sunday morning showing a darkened sales floor empty of any people. As the counter clicked off the seconds and minutes, a light from the door area broke the monotony of viewing and Miguel walked across the floor to the cash counter, bag in hand. Judith remained silent as they both watched the entire episode in full color and sharp focus. Once Miguel left the store on the recording, Judith pushed pause and stared at her employee. He averted his eyes and remained motionless in his chair.

"I need you to tell me about the bag."

Miguel shifted slightly and tapped his feet on the floor softly. "Do you think I do dirty business?" he asked.

"Miguel, you brought a lot of cash into this store and hid it under a sales floor cash counter. What am I supposed to think? Then you got very upset when we did not open yesterday. I need the truth."

"It's my money." Miguel's eyes flashed upward and he straightened his body in his chair. "I needed it bad, so I got a loan. My family in Colombia is having financial trouble and I am going to send it home to help them. I did not want to come to the company for it. That is why I needed to work overtime Sunday. I must make payments."

"It is your money? You borrowed it?" Judith raised her eyebrows clearly showing her skepticism.

"Yes, yes, I did." He replied weakly.

"How much money is in the bag?" Judith said as she considered his story.

"About eight thousand dollars..." Miguel held his palms up as if displaying the cash.

"How did you plan to get the money to your family?"

"I...I have a cousin who is traveling back next week. He is going to take the money with him."

"Miguel, you have been an excellent employee. Your work in the vault with stock is accurate and dependable and everyone here likes you. I want to believe your story. But you have to understand that bringing in large amounts of cash puts everyone who works here at risk. If someone lent you the money, then someone knows you have it. That is the kind of cash that people come to steal. Why did you leave it in the front instead of asking us to lock it in the safe?"

"I was ashamed. I am sorry." He put his head into his hands and started to sob softly.

Used to her employee's emotional outbursts, Judith sat in her chair without comment and continued to consider her vault worker's story. It was true that he had been a model employee. He frequently worked overtime whenever a new shipment had arrived that needed to be processed quickly for busy ship days. He had even come to work on his day off if a surprise shipment had appeared. Shrinkage from the vault was non-existent, and he was tireless when it came to checking the sales floor for the needed restocking during the day. All jewelry trays were closely supervised by Miguel and the sales people loved his constant attention to detail. Sales were never lost because a desired item could not be found. Miguel had made sure of it. Precious time away from the customers was never wasted by sales people searching in the vault for stock. Miguel was truly a one man show and a tremendous contributor to the store's success.

After about 30 seconds of silence, he spoke. "May I return to work now, please? I have to finish the new shipment that I was supposed to complete yesterday."

"Not to worry, Miguel" Judith replied.

"Company policy requires management to perform a security check as soon as possible in the vault whenever an incident like this one occurs. Chad and I spent time Sunday when the store was closed and checked in that shipment. I am please to say that our entire inventory was accounted for and we even found that extra package and added skus to the merchandise. Everything is out and ready for sale this morning."

Miguel's expression turned to panic. "What? I…"

Misunderstanding his reaction as genuine concern for work, she rushed to say, "Don't worry. We won't take over your job. It is just that some of the pieces we discovered were very unique and Chad was anxious to get them on the floor today since we have six ships in port. We wondered if they were previews of next fall's line. I expect a follow up survey from the Purchasing Department."

"But, I…" Miguel stammered and gazed down at the floor as if confused.

Judith stood and walked around the desk. "Miguel, please. If this morning has been too upsetting for you, take a paid day off and go home. We can start fresh again on Tuesday."

Miguel was on his feet in an instant. "No" he

whispered as he pointed to the door. "I just need some water."

"That is fine. I have your promise that large amounts of money will never be brought into this store again, don't I?" Judith extended her hand shake and the bag.

Miguel avoided her hand at first, then quickly grabbed it and shook it. "Yes, yes." He tucked the perfume shop bag with the cash into his backpack.

As he exited and her door closed, Judith took a deep breath and wiped the wetness from his palm on her slacks.

Chapter 6
Monday on the Sales Floor

As customers strolled about in the refreshing air conditioning of the jewelry store a few minutes after the doors opened, Chad once again cleaned the glass over the diamond ring tray. He had taken extra pride in stocking for today's business, using several items from the new shipment discovered in Sunday's vault audit. His co-workers had teased him about his unexpected arrival for work, but when they noticed Miguel being called into the Manager's office the moment he arrived, they sensed that Chad's early showing today was probably required because of his Assistant Manager responsibilities. Something unusual was going on. No one on staff wanted to open any more discussions after seeing the very serious look on

Judith's face as she ushered the young Colombian into her office and shut the door.

Chad looked up and saw a familiar face enter the store and pass the security guard. Marta, a large woman, elegantly dressed compared to most tourists and wearing a dramatic and brightly colored straw hat, held a similar position to Chad's in a jewelry store on the island of St. Thomas. She was the top sales person and her reputation for being eccentric and outrageous met or exceeded his. Always dripping in diamonds and lots of bling, she carried the most expensive Fendi and Gucci handbags, wore custom made Gucci shoes, and her dresses and skirts were of the finest silk. Never seen without makeup or in casual clothes, few of her colleagues could guess her age. She did not socialize outside of work with her co-workers and no one from work had ever been invited to her home. Most learned to deal with her like any prima donna, stepping aside and allowing her to command the sales floor. Her success offered her the special status. She was well liked by her base of repeat and referral customers and the management had even added her to the store's web page. What was unknown to everyone on St. Thomas was that Marta took frequent trips to St. Maarten to buy her diamonds, stones and jewelry from *Island Ice*.

"Chester, my boy! How are you, Darlin'?" she yelled to the entire room as she floated across the carpet. Marta knew that she could get away with calling Chad by his real name.

A huge smile appeared on Chad's face as he greeted her. She was one of his best customers. He had learned years ago that sales to Marta would always be confidential and that merchandise would be delivered quietly to her room at the nearby Divi Resort after work hours. She would make a show of shopping the competition as she called it, always waving off the merchandise in the event anyone recognized her. Whenever she decided on an item, she would tap twice on the piece that she wanted to purchase. Chad had a file of her ring sizes and she would pull on the finger that she had selected for the size adjustment. This discreet yet theatrical approach to every transaction was a perfect fit for two people cut from the same cloth.

Running out from behind the glass case, Chad danced on tiptoes and giggled like a girl as he wrapped his arms around Marta. "How are ya girl friend?" he boomed so that those in close proximity could hear. "Come over to my case so that I can pretend to be working."

Marta followed him and was momentarily taken back by a large canary diamond ring in the tray directly under where Chad was standing. The center stone alone had to be close to five carats, the setting was stunning and it screamed Marta's name. It was hard for her to hide her enthusiasm. Chad noticed her attachment to the piece, and seized the moment.

"I know you need to waste a little time, so why not try on one of these new pieces we just received. I unpacked the shipment and brought them out just a few minutes ago."

Marta tried to remain cool. "You, boyfriend, worked in the vault? Are you feeling okay?"

"Of course, I feel fine. I feel marvelous, darling" He lowered his head for dramatic effect. "I do more around here then you realize, and today is your lucky day since we didn't even expect these to arrive Friday." Chad whispered as he pulled the tray out of the case and selected the ring that Marta was intently studying. "Just for the hell of it, try this one on to see what you think."

Marta slipped on the magnificent ring and sighed with admiration at the exquisite piece. It looked far more wonderful on her hand than it had in the case. "Only $6800 for this one?" she said without thinking of being discreet.

"You know it. A ring like that in your shop would be at least 60 grand." Chad tried to keep his voice down.

"Boyfriend, a ring like this might bring as much as 100 grand in the right upscale store location. Just give me a horny rich guy, a babe with new tits, and a half an hour to offer champagne in crystal goblets" Marta laughed. "But not today" she said as she handed back the ring and tapped it twice in Chad's hand. Then she handed him a credit card wrapped in a napkin from her purse. "Please drop this in the trash, won't you love?"

Chad smiled and put both the ring and the credit card in the top drawer under his glass display with one smooth movement. Within a few seconds, another customer approached them. It was Dana from the Former Life Bar.

"Hey Dana! Meet my friend from St. Thomas, the one and only Marta! She owes all of her sales success to me."

Dana extended her hand to Chad's friend and stepped forward. "Good to meet you Marta. Are you shopping today?" The two women were now just inches from each other by the glass case.

The larger woman sized up Dana with a friendly

smile. "No, I work in retail on the other island and I just like to stop in and see Chad goofing off when I visit St. Maarten."

"Well, me too, I'm here to window shop! Chad worked me over on Sunday with his sales pitch of a new shipment containing to die-for-rings. I fought all the traffic on a busy ship day to see what he was talking about. And to dream. My husband and I have a restaurant and bar, so jewelry is not on the priority list right now like a new freezer, a new ice maker, and a better security system, I'm afraid."

Chad nodded but quickly ignored her protest. "Dana, honey, this one is beyond bling. This one says that Andy would want you to have it." He raised his hand from the case and laid a stunning diamond solitaire mounted in platinum on a dark blue presentation pad. "Just try it on, for me."

"Oh my god, it fits perfectly!" Dana stretched out her arms and admired the fire in the diamond at maximum arms length. "How much is it?"

"For you, only $4900 with no tax and no duty."

Marta gave them both an exasperated look and chimed in first, "Geez, everyone knows that there is no tax or duty on this island."

"Five thousand dollars! Andy would kill me."

Dana said as she shrugged her shoulders and removed the ring.

"I am not feeling the love here." Chad replied. "A ring like this in her store would cost you five times this amount. Or more. You deserve it. You and Andy have been working 6 and 7 days a week making that business grow. Now you have an opportunity that I can't offer everyday. Put the ring back on, Dana. Let's call Andy."

Most of the sales people on the floor were used to Chad's loud sales techniques and tried not to take notice, but today the new stock was obviously worth a look-see once he moved away from the case. Desiree was working in the bracelet section nearby and she craned her neck to view the display.

"Dana, we just met. But since I am in the business, I will tell you that Chad is right. That ring in another store would cost at least five times or more." Marta whispered to Dana so that others would not hear her endorsement of a competitor's product.

Dana felt torn. "I don't know, let me think about it." She once again removed the ring and tried to hand it back to Chad.

Chad put his hand up to block the return. "No!

If I put that bargain back in this case it will be sold in another hour. Give me a credit card. Go home. If Andy knows what is good for him, he'll agree. Besides, we have a 30 day no questions asked return policy. Right? Now go. Go."

Dana was an easy sell. She slipped the ring back on and turned to shake Marta's hand again. "Nice to meet you Marta. My death will now be on your conscious forever. My husband is bound to kill me for spending this money when we need some much new restaurant equipment."

Both woman gazed warmly at each other and held the goodbye gesture for another moment as Chad moved down the cases to greet an older couple examining earrings. As they walked out the door, Chad called out to Marta "Sweetheart, order a bottle of nice wine for later. I'll stop by your hotel on my way home after work." Then he turned to the couple and said, "Aren't you the stars from the Young and Restless?"

From the window in the *Employees Only* hall door leading back to the vault, Miguel watched with a pained expression on his face. Since Chad was now busy with customers in another part of the store, Miguel seized the opportunity to hurry to the case and retrieve the tray with

Friday's unexpected merchandise. Before he could reach the display, Desiree stepped up and used her key to open the sliding door of the glass case. Smiling with achievement, she grabbed a third ring out. Frustrated, Miguel stopped in his tracks and examined other cases pretending that he was looking for possible restocking needs. Kesia, a single employee who had tried on several occasions to attract Miguel's interest, caught his eye and moved close to him. She was local, very attractive and in her early 20's. Her light brown skin reminded him of coco. Ignoring her striking appearance had been difficult for him in the work place. However, Desiree was sure to object if he showed any interest to another woman. As Kesia reached out to touch his shoulder lightly, Miguel knew for the moment he was trapped. He wanted to bolt, but could not. Instead he greeted her with a small grin.

After a few minutes of polite conversation with Kesia, Miguel was rescued. Several female customers wearing bathing suit cover-ups, sandals and an assortment of souvenir hats surrounded her area and Kesia was forced to divert her attention away from Miguel. Once again, he saw the new tray unattended so he worked his way through the now crowded store to check for restock. Quickly he removed two trays, sealed the tops as was store procedure, and carried them to the vault. After pressing his security code into the pad for access, he stepped inside and breathed a sigh of relief as he placed them on the counter and closed the door. Moving the regular stock tray to the left, he gazed in horror at the tray containing the extra shipment items. Now another one of the rings was gone! Chad must have sold all three of them. With no time to waste, Miguel plucked out 7 of the remaining rings, dropped them into the front pocket of his pants and restocked both trays with regular merchandise. Then he returned to the sales floor entrance door and peered through the small window.

On the floor, Desiree was showing Chad the ring that she had decided to purchase with her employee discount. "Here, Chad. Please hold this at the register so that I can pay after we close for the day. I love it."

"Are you sure that your policeman husband won't scream when he finds out you spent $4200 on a ring today?"

Desiree replied coyly. "I have my own money, you know. And my own credit cards. Besides,

I can always charm Bart."

"Yeh, yeh. That is what most island woman say before they show up at the shelter with a black eye."

Desiree put her hands on her hips in defiance."Fuck you, Chad. You just don't want me to take something new that you want to sell. I like it. I want it. And I am gonna have it."

Chad threw his arms up in surrender and put the ring in his management drawer and locked it.

Again from the *Employees Only* door Miguel watched and wrung his hands in frustration. He knew that Chad had just agreed to an employee purchase and was holding the third missing ring for payment. *Fuck!* Today was not going his way, that was for damn sure.

Chapter 7

Happy Hour

Just after 6 PM the first cruise ship ready to depart the harbor sounded three blasts on their horn signaling that the boat was in reverse. A Disney ship berthed next to the departing vessel returned the signal with the beginning notes of "When you wish upon a star" to the delight of tourists and locals alike. On shore by the beach at the Get Wet Beach Bar overlooking the Philipsburg Bay, Miguel was in no mood for childish music or fantasies. He grabbed the Heineken beer in front of him and took a long swig emptying the bottle without stopping. Phil, one of the owners, stepped up and wiped the moisture from the wooden counter. "Need another, friend?"

Without any conversation or eye contact with the man in front of him, Miguel nodded "Yes."

Then he continued to look down intensely at the brightly painted bar's simple exterior and remained deep in thought. *How could this have happened? Why did they have to go to the store on Sunday? What the fuck? Now everything is ruined. Sunday has always been my private day in the vault. Chad screwed up everything. I need to get those rings. Mother fuck. Desiree even has one. Fuck! Thank God that Chad sold several big ticket necklaces this afternoon and didn't come back to the ring case and get suspicious. I have enough to worry about...*

Another ship sounded the signal of departure, then another. Before long, Miguel had four empty bottles in front of him and he was no closer to figuring out a solution to his problem. He felt a body slide onto the bar stool next to him and touch his leg. It was Kesia.

"Hi Miguel" she said softly. "Can I buy you a beer?" Glancing down to his left, he saw that her skirt was pulled up over her knees exposing a lot of her thigh. While he watched, she removed her work jacket revealing a low cut and tight fitting silky top. He noticed that her make up was fresh and her lips much redder than her normal appearance at work. He suddenly felt like prey.

"Whatever" he answered sullenly. "You buy, I drink."

She leaned forward and caught his eyes before he could look away. "I hope you will do more than drink with me, Miguel."

Phil the bartender saw his new customer arrive and hurried over to ask for an order. Before he could speak, Kesia placed a fifty dollar bill on the bar and said, "I'll have a Guavaberry colada and he'll have another beer, please. I hope this covers his tab so far."

Phil made a quick appraisal of the couple and suddenly felt like a third wheel. "Yes, ma'am…coming right up." Instinctively he knew it would be a great time for him to disappear into the shadows.

Miguel refused to bite. His relationship with Desiree was dangerous enough. If he brought in another woman, especially one who worked at the store, his sex life with Desiree would be over and he knew it.

"Kesia, don't take this wrong. You're an attractive woman, but I'm not looking right now."

She turned and flashed more thigh and touched his leg with hers. "Why not? No one has seen you with a date." She rubbed his arm. "You're not gay are you?"

"Do I look gay? Chad looks gay. Chad acts gay." Miguel was annoyed by her question.

She felt his mood change. "So why not me? You know that I'm interested."

Phil returned with the drinks and quickly disappeared pretending not to overhear any of the couple's conversation.

"Kesia, the girl I love is in Colombia" he lied. At the same time he pushed against her leg for emphasis. It probably sent the wrong signal to her.

"Some of the sales women say you have eyes for Desiree, but she's married and her husband is a policeman. I don't think you are that crazy."

They sipped the drinks in silence and turned to watch the sun disappear over the hill in the west. Miguel felt her hand rub his shoulder. The ache of today's missing rings had produced tension knots in his muscles and her touch felt good. Damn good.

She moved close to his ear and whispered. "If you did not have someone special at home in your country, would you want me?"

Miguel spoke without thinking. "Yes."

"Then for now, we can be together. I will not ask you to give up your love in Colombia. But now, we are here. Come to my apartment. We can take a bath, relax, eat, and forget the day." Her legs were now separated and clasping his knee. "I make amazing Mexican and Cuban food. How about Arroz con Pollo? I also make the most delicious fried plantains you have ever had. What would you like?" Her hand moved from his shoulder to the back of his head and she stroked his neck.

Miguel felt defeated. His failed obligation today to produce the jewelry as scheduled from the extra shipment to the man in the red Honda was overwhelming. He felt confused. He needed time to sort things out. The safe haven Kesia offered was a life raft in a growing storm. Desiree would not find out if he went for a drink and some dinner. He was so tired.

"Yes, I'll come. You must promise never to tell anyone. It could mean trouble for us at work. Do you understand?" He studied her eyes and hoped she would buy his story.

With her heart in her throat, Kesia beamed. "I promise. Come and follow me in your car. I parked on the Pond near the electric company." She squeezed his knee once again with her legs. As she turned to exit the bar stool, she hiked her skirt up more for Miguel to admire her legs. "Here is my cell phone number in case you get lost following me or delayed."

"You go to your car now. I'll call later. I will be

on the road in about five minutes. The men here cannot see us leave together. They will think bad things...like I am picking you up. Your reputation will be hurt. Now tell me that I am an asshole so that everyone can hear."

Understanding his point, she took the clue and raised her voice, "You asshole. You let me buy the drinks and I get no dinner? Just go and fuck yourself!"

Miguel watched as she walked away in a huff. He appreciated her ability to adjust to the situation. Too bad for her that Desiree had come first. He would have enjoyed this one. She had spunk. Desiree had never invited him for dinner, either.

"Can I get you another?" asked Phil.

Miguel held his beer bottle up to the light and then drained the last drop of liquid. "Okay, looks like I won't get any of that tonight."

"Too bad, my friend. She is a real looker. She obviously likes you. But not that I noticed."

Miguel turned with a feeling of accomplishment and handed the empty bottle to Phil. Now he was feeling better. The day could turn out okay after all. Phil returned with a cold beer and passed it to him. "On the house."

Miguel waved a thank you and walked up

the ally to Front Street. His car was parked two blocks away on the salt pond. He walked with a new purpose and rubbed his crotch absentmind-edly with anticipation. After turning into an alley he stopped to urinate against a building. Relieved, he continued to the next block and entered a dark passageway. Just ahead, he thought that he could see a red Honda. He slowed his pace to avoid run-ning into it. Suddenly from behind, a strong hand pushed him to the left as a blow from the side hit him in the ribs. He crumpled to the ground in pain. His eyes focused and he saw the legs of two men. When he looked up, one of the men smashed his chest with a fist and then kicked him in the abdo-men as he fell backwards.

Both men leaned over and glared at him. "Where da shipment, Miguel? You know da rules. We get our stuff today. You got the money Sunday. You didn't call. What's up?"

Miguel coughed. "Give me some time. There was a problem. I'll get you the stuff. I promise."

The larger of the men spoke forcefully, "Ya worthless fuck. We need dem jewels now, not when dey ain't no ships on this island. Everyday we lose money. Where da fucking rings?"

Miguel reached into his pants and produced the

ones that he took from the tray. "Here are most of them, Mr. Bucket. Tell Mr. G that I am trying to get the others."

The big man sneered and showed some gold fillings as he grabbed the jewelry. "Where da fuck da rest?"

"There are just three missing. I had problems, okay? I'll get them. They were sold by accident."

"Shit! Cruise ship people? What ya gonna do, asswipe? Swim out to them in the harbor? Dey leaving now."

Miguel shook his head back and forth rapidly. "No, no...local sales. I can get them."

Bucket leaned over and slapped Miguel in the back of the head. Then he grabbed him by the hair. "Listen boy. What chew tink? Ya better get dat ice back now. If ya fuck up again, ya pay with ya worthless weasel life. Call da voice mail number for da pick up. Understand?"

Without waiting for his answer, they slipped away and left him on the ground sobbing. The three rings would not be easy to retrieve. Except now, he had the motivation to try anything to get them back. Sitting up and breathing heavily, he saw Chad walk past the alley with an *Island Ice* package. Chad did not see Miguel.

Of course...that fat woman always gets a delivery from Chad when she buys our stuff!

He composed himself and called Kesia on his cell phone to explain that he would have to take a rain check on the dinner plans.

Chapter 8
Marta's Hotel Suite

Elegantly dressed in a flowing silk multi-colored robe, Marta relaxed on the terrace of her hotel and watched the setting sun slowly turning the sky to golden hues against the lacy white clouds. With a glass of crisp white wine on the table next to her chair, she epitomized the happy tourist with nothing to do but enjoy the sights and sounds of a Caribbean island. Even though she had lived on a nearby island for many years and worked continuously in the jewelry business, she always looked forward to a few days of solitude on St. Maarten, peppered with some retail therapy, of course. The suite had full kitchen facilities, so many times on her visits she would grocery shop and stay at the hotel rather than venture out alone for dinner. Being alone was her preference. She had never married, but had taken both male and female lovers over the years. She usually grew disconnected from their lives and bored with the companionship. A good vibrator was her constant bed mate and she liked it that way. No bitching to put up with, no whining about the relationship not going forward, and no extra expenses to bear except for buying batteries which she kept in abundance. Not bothering to turn on music or the television, she savored the sound of the lapping water on the shore a few feet from her room. She always requested the ground floor. So many travelers sought a view from a higher vantage point and they paid extra for it. Not Marta, she loved to walk as quickly as possible into the sand and hear the ocean when possible.

She checked her watch in anticipation of Chad's delivery visit. Chad never stayed for a drink, but he always made a show of asking in the store so that his visit to her could be easily explained. *Island Ice* was a competitor, and she did not want to be seen purchasing the faux stones. To her, wearing jewelry was as important to her customers as wearing clothes. She liked to sparkle and the more bling she piled on, the more she could encourage others to spend, spend, spend. Plus it made her feel good.

She didn't give a damn if the stuff was made by man. She wanted it to look good and leave plenty of cash to stash in her 401 account at the end of every quarter.

"Here you are. I have been knocking on your door for over twenty minutes, damn it." Chad greeted her from the beach.

"Like I believe that.. You don't have twenty minutes worth of patience. You probably knocked once, almost peed your pants in anticipation, then came around to the beach hoping to see some newly wed husband walking around with a towel around his buns."

"Well it would have made my day." Chad walked onto the terrace and looked down. His shoes had tracked water and mud from the garden along with sand onto the tile surface. "Sorry. I didn't watch were I was walking."

"Hard to do when you can't look down and see your feet!" Marta cackled. "But not to worry. They clean this room everyday. Where is my package?" Marta stood and pulled open the door to the room. "Let's go inside."

Chad followed dutifully and produced a small ring box and her credit card and receipt. "Here you go..."

"You outdid yourself this time, Chad, my boy. Look at this beauty. The boys in the lab are good. I would swear that I can see some imperfections.

"Damn, your eyes are good. I struggle most days reading sales slips and credit card numbers without my reading glasses."

"I forgot my manners in the excitement of getting this delivery. Would you like a glass of wine?"

Chad shook his head and answered as usual, "No, thank you. I am having dinner with some guys at a friend's house where we watch adult videos, play Wii, and bitch about equal rights for all people. I need to get home first for a hot shower, walk the pets, and water the plants."

Marta slipped on the new ring and admired it in a large mirror on the wall of the dining area. "Chad, please straighten that mirror for me before you go. It is messing up my feng shui."

He stepped over and moved the mirror with both hands lightly touching the glass with both thumbs. "Shit, now you will have finger smudges. This could be an endless process."

"Yes it could. The maid will come in the morning and put it out of whack cleaning it. It is a housekeeping thing. Maids all over the world learn it."

They laughed together and Chad turned to exit the way he had come into the suite. Marta followed and picked up her almost full wine glass from the table. "Thanks again, Sweetheart. Be sure to call me when you receive another shipment like this one."

Chad hurried off the terrace and into the sand. "Will do, but I suspect that those are samples and next month we will have ten of that ring in different sizes."

She called back to him as he disappeared around the corner. "I doubt it." Marta was sure that Chad did not hear her.

With the sun gone from the horizon, the garden lights were on and the night creatures began to chirp. Marta adjusted her chair so that the light from inside her room fell on her new ring and she continued to admire its brilliance even in the low light. She sipped her wine a few times then stretched and closed her eyes for a moment. Listening to the soft sound of the surf, she caught herself nodding off. After placing the wine glass on the table next to her, she once again reclined to a comfortable position and reveled in the joy of the moment. Within seconds she was asleep.

The man in the shadows approached Marta's

beach entrance and moved with care while scanning the other rooms for anyone who might appear outside. There were no other vacationers sitting on their terraces. Softly crunching in the sand, his tennis shoes made little noise to draw attention. In his hand was a common hammer handle without the head. It was not much of a weapon but it was the best he could do with such little preparation time. After watching Chad's car leave, he had crossed the parking lot with a group of strangers and had walked as if he had been traveling with them. A security guard had been talking to the front desk attendant in the open air reception desk but neither had looked up at him. Just to be safe, he concealed the hammer handle in his back pocket under his T-shirt until he rounded the corner to Marta's room. He tapped his front pockets to check the large cable ties he brought in case he needed to tie his victim to a chair while he escaped. Expecting to find her inside with lights on, he almost tripped over her napping on the terrace. The opportunity was right and he seized the moment. With one quick swing, he hit her head several times with the blunt stick and watched her body fall forward to her knees, then slump over into a heap. He grabbed her left arm first and pulled it away from her torso. The ring was on her middle finger. He wiggled it off, then took the other two rings she wore on that hand for good measure. This needed to appear like any common robbery and he would discard the other jewelry later. He could also see a diamond pendant on a gold chain plus several other chains around her neck, so he pulled her hair back in an attempt to find the clasps. His touch near her face seemed to revive her and he pulled his hands back. She stirred slightly and groaned. Quickly he pulled her other hand away from her body and started to remove her watch and rings when suddenly her eyes popped open.

"Let go of me!" She spit out. "You! I know you! You're the little asshole from the vault at Chad's store. Get out of here."

Feeling trapped, Miguel raised the wood to hit her again on the head but this time she fought back. She grabbed his hip hop jeans and jerked them below his hips. Off balance with his pants down and his underwear showing, he dropped the rings. Spreading his feet apart to steady himself, he hit her three more times and she released him. He hit her again and she fell unconscious.

Panicked by the recognition and her ability to fight back, Miguel pulled his jeans up, then found the large cable ties in the pocket and wrapped one around her neck. With a wild motion he pulled the loose end as tight as he could until the plastic cut into her skin. Her body twitched and then became lifeless. He stepped back, out of breath and with wide eyes. It took a few moments for his heart beat to calm down. He blinked, and then closed his eyes to collect himself. Remembering the dropped rings, he squatted and felt the tile floor around her chair. Nothing. Bile rose in his throat and he coughed to clear the foul taste. Crawling about madly on his hands and knees, he moved purposely from one end of the terrace to the other until he found them. Relieved, he stood and listened to see if anyone had heard the struggle and might be coming to investigate. The only sound was the chirping of insects in the night. With a sigh of relief, he put her jewelry into his right front pocket, and then returned the wooden handle to his rear pocket. After straightening his shirt and hair, he walked calmly onto the passageway of the hotel's tropical garden.

Chapter 9

The Immigration Sweep

L ater that afternoon Dana returned from her shopping spree at *Island Ice* relieved to find that Andy was not at home. It was not unusual during the course of the business day for him to stop by the house and let their dog, Coby, out for a run in the yard. She wasn't ready at the moment to explain her impulse purchase. While the business was doing well, what they were lacking was new equipment for cooking and refrigeration. Capital was needed to purchase several upgrades and a personal expense at this time was a bit off the wall and outside the business plan. When she approached the front door and pulled out her keys, the noise alerted the dog and he barked happily in anticipation from inside the foyer. Dana stepped inside, flipped the deadbolt lock with her key and placed her handbag on the table under a mirror. She had already decided that the discussion of new jewelry was best handled after a nice dinner, a bottle of wine and in candle light. She entered the kitchen, flipped on the flat screen TV to the Food Network channel and reached for a bottle of Pinot Grigio. Coby sat impatiently at her feet. Feeling guilty, she put the bottle on the counter and reached down to touch the dog.

"Sorry Bo," she said as she patted his head. "You need to go outside, don't you?"

Crossing the room to the back terrace over-looking the swimming pool, she pulled open the sliding door and watched as the dog disappeared into the garden. A bark or two told her that Coby had found something to occupy his time for now. She returned to the kitchen and poured the wine, flipped through her recipe book for a suitable healthy and gourmet dinner, then shrugged. *Why aren't there any special dinners for telling your husband that you just blew 5 grand on new jewelry?*

The house phone rang. She picked up the cord-less extension and headed to the outside terrace.

"Good Afternoon, this is Dana."

"Hey Baby. Good. You're home. I was afraid that I would have to drive over to your boyfriend's house to find you" Andy teased.

"I just got here, how was your day?" Dana hoped to avoid a discussion of her shopping trip.

"Fine, I went to the Chamber of Commerce to pay our dues and get a fresh extraction for renewing the business license, had lunch with Jack Donnelly, and then went back to the restaurant to work on payroll. How was yours?"

Dana took a breath. "Is Jack any closer to getting his residency permit?"

"No, it is difficult. Even though he gives free advice to the St. Maarten police force and the head of the Detective Squad is his friend, he lives on the French side and it makes the whole process a mess. I keep urging him to move to the Dutch side but it is hard to get him off those topless beaches. Being the dirty old man that he is…"

"Stop. You are worse with your free drinks at the bar for topless women when you bartend."

"Touché" he admitted happily. "Guilty as charged."

"Well, you two adolescents enjoy the beach tits while your eye sight lasts. You aren't getting any younger, that's for sure. When are you coming home? I am planning a special dinner"

"Are you cooking topless?"

"It can be arranged."

"I am on my way to meet Jack again at the Get Wet bar for a follow up to our lunch conversation. I was going to ask him to join us for dinner at home, however given the nakedness of the cook I think he'll have to fend for himself tonight."

"You mean you are headed to have a few beers with him to avoid helping with the cooking."

"Well, that too, but…"

Dana felt relieved and guilty at the same time. "Have fun, don't drink too much, and get your ass home before my wonderful dinner is put away or given to the dog."

"I don't think that I have to worry. For a dog that was rescued on Orient Beach, he certainly has a remarkable diet. Expensive veterinary dog food and ground turkey prepared especially for him. I'm the one who gets the tacos and chicken wings."

Looking out the window, Dana saw Coby cross the pool area and disappear again into the garden. "Call before you leave the bar so that I can gauge the time for dinner."

"Will do. I love you. But if you don't mind, let's eat a bit later. I probably won't leave Jack until around 7:30 or so."

"And I love you too, Andy. No problem on the

time, I was planning on a dinner time after 8 anyway. Bye." Dana hung up the phone, found her cookbook, and continued to search for a special dinner recipe.

After closing his cell phone, Andy walked down the alley from Front Street towards the beachfront and the Get Wet Beach Bar. He passed the Hot Dog man packing his cart and attaching the trailer to his truck which signaled the end of the business day. As he got closer, Andy saw what appeared to be a group of uniformed police officers in paramilitary camouflage mulling about with automatic weapons at their sides. Groups of men and women who appeared to be hanging around for the after work happy hour were in discussions with the stern looking officials. Andy could see several of the customers producing ID's and paperwork. He scanned the group for his friend, Jack Donnelly, but did not see him.

Suddenly a large woman in a standard police uniform stepped in front of him. "May I see your papers, please?" Her stance was all business and she did not smile.

Momentarily caught off guard, Andy stared for a split second at her without comment. Then he reached into his pocket and produced his St.

Maarten census office ID card and handed it to her.

She examined the ID card. "Do you have your residency permit?"

"Yes, there is a copy in my car and a copy of my work permit and business license."

Quickly losing interest in him, she handed back the card and motioned him away. Andy continued to the bar and took a seat near the bartender. "When did this start."

The bartender shrugged and polished a glass. "Just about ten minutes ago. Most tourists have returned to the ships or hotels, so we mainly had a local group enjoying after work drinks. They already took away 3 people in handcuffs when they couldn't produce paperwork."

Andy searched the area nonchalantly for his friend. "Any chance you saw a fifty something retired American police detective here waiting for me to buy him a beer?"

Phil, the owner, joined Andy on the customer side of the bar and sat next to him. "I'm sorry to tell you this. They took your friend."

"What?"

"Yep. They also took two other customers. One was that Canadian guy who was working at the T-shirt stand down the street and the other was that young woman who worked part time with him. I think she is Dominican, but I'm not sure."

"All in handcuffs?" Andy waved at the bartender. "I think I need a beer."

"Most of the Immigration Officers are from Curacao. They come here to make the raids. It's been quite a show. Your friend may be on the front page of the newspaper tomorrow. I saw photographers out front."

"Crap. Do you think that I can get him out of that jail cell tonight?"

"Not likely. Unless he has papers you can take to the jail showing legal residency. They looked at his passport and saw that he entered the country 7 months ago. My guess is that they will keep him there and force him to buy a ticket back to the USA." Phil waved his empty beer bottle at the bartender.

Andy watched as the group of police moved down the board walk and away from the Get Wet bar. The bartender put two cold beers in front of him and Phil, then turned away. Andy picked up his beer first and guzzled almost half of the contents.

"Phil, I would toast first but this pisses me off.

Can you imagine how a New York City detective feels being thrown into a Caribbean slammer when his only crime is feeding the tourist economy?"

"I know. No one wants to see a friend hauled off like a common criminal. Immigration laws are harsh. For example, I'm pretty sure that that Canadian guy has a work permit. He just didn't have a copy with him."

"What will they do with him?"

"Probably leave him in the jail for a day or so, then escort him to his house and let him produce the work permit. Then they will parade him back to work in handcuffs."

"You're kidding." Andy took another sip and stared at his Carib beer bottle. He continued to shake his head in disbelief.

"Seen it before. Last month an Indian jewelry store manager who had worked here for over 10 years was locked up. His boss was on the phone all day assuring the police that his work permit was up to date. They finally let him go home in handcuffs with a fully armed police escort to retrieve his original paperwork. They would not accept the copy his boss had in the store."

Andy glared at the police group now further down the boardwalk. "Were they satisfied when they saw the original documents?"

Phil thought for a moment. "Yes and No. They acknowledged the authenticity, but then took him back to work in handcuffs. It was unbelievable. They walked him past locals and tourists on Front Street in the middle of the day. The guy was completely innocent of any wrong doing. But the show must go on."

"I guess the apology for making a mistake was issued personally to him by the Chief of Police."

Phil roared with laughter. "Bartender! Two more beers, please. And his tab is on the house. I need more friends who were just born yesterday."

Chapter 10

One Down, Two to Go

After Miguel left Marta's lifeless body on the terrace and moved quickly through the cover of the thick tropical gardens toward the front entrance of the hotel property, his first goal was to remain unnoticed. So far, so good…passing the main guard house near the road as he exited went without incident. He kept his head down and avoided the field of vision covered by the security camera. The twilight was working in his favor. He just needed to remain calm. He knew that running would only call attention to him, so he pretended to be taking a brisk walk for good health like the many tourists who passed him in both directions. He timed his movement out the long private driveway just as two cars approached to further avoid being noticed by security. The focus of the guard would be on those entering, not leaving. The walkers and joggers he saw were women and all were heading back to the resort now that darkness was fast approaching. He avoided all eye contact. The hill ahead was steep and the extra effort helped to steady his nerves even though he was sweating profusely. After work, he had changed into a St. Maarten souvenir T-shirt which was very common and sold at three for ten dollars on most street corners. Jeans were jeans, but wearing his normal logo shirt from *Island Ice* would have been stupid. The shirt he was currently wearing was going into the garbage when he passed the first dumpster on the side of the road. He doubted that anyone was studying the security camera, but...you never know.

As he began the descent to the nearby Bel Air Hotel and his parked car, a police vehicle slowed as it approached. *Fuck me.* His eyes darted from side to side and searched for a quick exit from the roadway. The cliffs were too steep. There was no escape, so he continued to walk forward. Suddenly a young black woman in shorts and a running bra came into view as he rounded the bend. *Those horny bastards, no wonder they slowed down.* She ran by Miguel going in the opposite direction just as the police car moved past and over the hill. *They sure as hell didn't look at my ass.* Feeling that his luck was beginning to change, he almost laughed out loud.

Miguel reached his car in the nearly vacant lot and suddenly felt ill. He had purposely parked his car on the far corner of the lot away from the lights. Looking for the darkest spot possible he rushed over to the nearest flower bed, fell to his knees on the walkway and threw up. Shaking, he composed himself and stood up. The dizziness was horrible. He knelt down again as another wave of nausea hit him. A loud clunk sounded behind him and he froze. The hammer handle had fallen out of his rear pocket and had bounced on the concrete side-walk behind him. He turned and saw blood on the handle. With one quick swoop he retrieved it and put it back under his shirt in his jeans. Breaking out in a cold sweat, he began to shake uncontrollably.

"Are you all right, son?" a man asked as he and a woman approached Miguel. The man's accent sounded Dutch. He was dressed in long pants with a flowered shirt and the woman at his side was black and wearing a low cut evening dress. The low illumination from the distant security lights made it difficult for Miguel to guess their ages so he hoped that they could not see him clearly either. With some effort, he stood and composed himself.

Miguel chose his words carefully but his Colombian accent was pronounced. "I'm fine. Thank you. I had too much to drink on the beach earlier. I play too much on vacation."

The couple watched as Miguel brushed off his jeans at the knees and flipped his hair to straighten it. "We know the feeling. Fun, alcohol and sun will get you every time. Where are you from, fellow?"

He stumbled for an answer. "Costa Rica. Have you been there? We have beautiful beaches also."

"No, but maybe next year." The man looked at the woman. She smiled lovingly back.

Feeling less nauseous, Miguel took a breath and cleared his throat. "When you see it, you will love my country. Try it sometime...I must go. A pretty lady invited me to her apartment for a special dinner. I am late." Without any other platitudes, he turned and walked to his car, jumped in, and drove away. Bits of gravel shot from his rear tires.

Surprised by the abrupt exit, the couple watched without comment. The woman finally spoke. "He didn't have much in the way of social graces, did he?"

The man took her hand. "No, but then again cultures are different around the world. Don't judge him too quickly. He may have been some-what embarrassed by puking in the parking lot. He wasn't a kid. Besides, did you see the blood and dirt stains on his T-shirt? He must have been caught with another man's wife. Someone worked him over. " Then the man put his arm around her waist and pulled her close. "Let's stop at the Casino before we go to Peg Leg's for steaks. I'm feeling very lucky!"

The woman agreed by taking her partner's hand but remained focused on the Costa Rican's exit. "I doubt that he was telling us the truth. He probably is not on holiday. Did you notice that he was not driving a rental car? His car had local plates."

Chapter 11

Jack in jail

Tuesday morning following the surprise evening Immigration sweep on the Boardwalk, a patient but angry Jack Donnelly found himself sweating as the sun came up. Confined to a five by eight foot cell, he sat across from another man who had also been arrested on an Immigration violation. The other man was from Trinidad. His family owned an interest in retail stores on the island. He had come to assume management duties in St. Maarten but had not completed the necessary paperwork for a work permit. Just like Jack his lack of papers landed him in handcuffs and in a van with armed officers who took him quickly to the lockup. Their cell consisted of an open toilet, a sink, and several simple wooden benches that lined the walls. Jack and the Trinidadian had spent the night dozing on and off while sitting up against the rough concrete wall. They had been given a dinner of bottled water and stale crackers. There was an open window covered with bars about eight feet above which provided the only ventilation. No ceiling fan circulated the stale and sour smells of the cell block. Both men had shared basic personal information on arrival. They were friendly towards each other, but distant. Neither had any idea what would happen to them, so they avoided unnecessary conversation or complaints. Waiting quietly seemed to be their best option. Their mutual relief was in not having a crack addict or dangerous street criminal sharing the confined space. Both were known for a lack of personal hygiene. The noises in the cell block brought back many memories of Jack's life as a police officer in New York City. An occasional inmate screamed in anger. Someone from time to time was yelling passages from the bible and a weaker voice begged for a beer or a joint. Never having been arrested before, the Trinidadian was alarmed by the constant cries, and watched his cellmate carefully for any reactions. Jack remained aloof, which seem to comfort the younger man. Truthfully, Jack could not often even distinguish male from female voices. This contrast to incarceration in the states gave him pause. No guards had passed the cell during the last six hours or so. Jack was used to sending bad people to jail but he had escaped spending the night in one. Once in New York, he had been sent to jail by an upset female judge and was placed in a holding cell. Then he was released in two hours. This jail was in a foreign country and this experience was totally different. No one offered the prisoners a telephone for one call after being taken into custody. No one stopped to check on their health or needs once the dinner had been left under the bars. No one had discussed assigning an attorney if they could not afford one.

From somewhere down the hall, Jack heard foot steps approach and then watched as a group of scantily dressed blond women were ushered past and into a room at the end of the cell block. Four uniformed male officers followed them and closed the door.

"What was that about?" the younger man asked as he jumped to his feet after the unusual parade passed. He grabbed the bars and tried to see down the corridor.

Jack walked to the bars and held them. "My guess would be another work permit raid that nabbed some Eastern European prostitutes or exotic dancers."

"Holy Shit. Some of them looked like movie stars!"

"Let's just say that I have never seen any of those girls down at the Rainbow building picking up work permits."

"What do you think is going on in that room?"

Jack looked at the young man and made a how the hell would I know gesture.

Both men laughed then fell silent as another set of footsteps echoed in the hall. These feet had a purpose and they sounded heavy as if the owner's were wearing boots and uniforms. Jack sat down and the Trinidadian man followed suit. The young man took a deep breath and held his hands in his lap as he watched and waited. Jack stayed unemotional and listened carefully as the steps grew near them. Unexpectedly, a familiar figure to Jack appeared and stopped in front of their cell bars. It was J.R. Holiday, head of the Detective Division and a friend.

He signaled relief to his cell mate and acknowledged the visitor. "Good morning, J.R."

Without formalities, Holiday motioned to a

guard that had followed and asked him to open the cell door.

"Follow me, Mr. Donnelly."

Jack gazed with some guilt at his cell mate and said, "Talk to you later, good luck."

Jack and Holiday walked through a series of corridors until they reached a small interrogation room. Holiday opened the door and waved Jack inside. With the door closed, he finally seemed to be himself. "Sorry about your hotel accommodations, Jack. You were just in the wrong place at the wrong time yesterday. Can I get you anything?"

The room was plain but cool and clean. Jack took a seat and let out a breath of air as he enjoyed the padded desk chair and the soft hum of the air conditioning. "Yes, breakfast from Baywatch, a spicy Bloody Mary garnished with steamed shrimp, and a key to the front door."

J.R. Holiday picked up the wall phone receiver and pushed a button. "Denise, can you bring me two cups of coffee and several of those ham and egg biscuits from across the street, please? There is some cash in my desk drawer. Thank you. Oh, and please get whatever you would like for yourself. Also ask Thomas if he wants something." He hung up the phone and pulled out a chair for himself across the table from Jack. "Your unfortunate arrest was well timed because I needed to see you this morning."

Jack stretched in the chair and felt the aches of stiff muscles caused by his night of discomfort in captivity. Not wanting to appear weak, he shook it off and continued to make light of his situation with his police friend. "Hopefully you need me to go into that room with those young ladies that I saw brought into the jail a few minutes ago."

"I wish it was that simple." Holiday remained calm and focused on his words. He paused again to emphasize the serious nature of his information. "A housekeeper at the hotel just outside of town found a woman's body on a room's sun terrace this morning. She was a registered guest at the hotel. She checked in yesterday, alone. I just left the scene. I called your cell phone and one of my men in the property room answered it. I had no idea you had been picked up yesterday evening. Sorry."

Jack ignored the news about a dead woman. "Apology accepted. After all, I am the illegal. Not you. And they didn't exactly give me an option of making a phone call to you from the slammer. Was I on the front page of the newspaper today? It seemed that there were several photographers following the raid."

"No, the front page photo showed scruffy looking Haitian men being led away. No old white guys."

Jack laughed in agreement, "Hey, I resemble that remark." This was a morning when he definitely felt over fifty years of age. "Am I to assume that the death is a murder?"

"Yes. Having you give me your perspective on this woman's attack would be most appreciated. When I found out you were in the jail, I called around and was told about the Immigration sweep yesterday. Frankly, I'm not sure some of my Federal colleagues assigned to Immigration appreciate your contribution to our department as much as I do. As a tourist over staying your visa, you become a political target..."

The door opened and a sharply dressed police woman in a crisp uniform entered and placed two bags on the table. Jack smelled freshly brewed coffee and warm breakfast biscuits. His stomach growled and he felt like tearing apart the bags.

"Would you Gentlemen like anything else?" she asked as she surveyed Jack's disheveled appearance. She kept a polite distance from him in anticipation of the usual foul jail house body odor common on prisoners in the building.

Jack noticed that her uniform was beautifully tailored to accent her shapely and athletic figure. As she turned away, he felt a passing lustful desire as he admired her body and imagined her in a bathing suit at the beach. *One night in jail didn't break my spirit...do policewomen like to go topless?*

Watching his friend's eyes on the woman, Holiday cleared his throat loudly. "Thank you. I do need Mr. Donnelly's personal items from the property room. Could you please bring them after you have a chance to enjoy your breakfast?"

Without turning again to face Jack, the woman nodded her head in agreement to the Detective and exited the room. Jack opened the bag with the coffee cups and placed one in front of the police detective. Then he spread the coffee cream and sugar containers out on the table between them. Holiday opened a coffee and sipped it black. Jack savored the smell of the steam rising from the food and didn't wait to find any condiment packages to add to the sandwich. He grabbed his and took a large bite.

Not waiting to finish chewing and swallowing the food, Jack motioned with a wave of his hand towards the door. "Nice ass. I bet you don't mind office hours around here."

"Easy Jack. Talk like that often gets your American Congressmen, Senators and even an occasional judge in a shit load of trouble."

"Yeh, and I also know that the number one match making activity in the civilized world is work. Think about it. Most men and women look their best at work. Especially in a formal office environment. Then mix in the jungle rules of human behavior and the result is physical attraction."

"Socially and politically unacceptable in these days and times, Jack."

"Sure." Jack pulled another biscuit out of the bag and quickly unwrapped it. "That is why it never happens anymore."

Several moments passed without further discussion. Both men ate and sipped the hot coffee. Finally, Jack spoke, "Let's talk about the body. Any chance that it was a heart attack or other collapse from natural causes? Many times people push themselves too hard on vacation."

"Not unless this woman put a cable tie around her own neck, pulled it hard enough to strangle herself after beating herself with a blunt object. Of course, we won't know the official cause of death until they do an autopsy in Curacao."

"A woman? Traveling alone? That is unusual.

I see more men traveling alone than women. Was she here on business or was she a tourist?"

"We have her USA passport and her St. Thomas driver's license. The business cards in her purse identify her as a salesperson with Diamonds in Paradise, a jewelry chain with stores all over the Caribbean. She worked on St. Thomas. As we speak my men are investigating the few leads that we have so far. One detective is headed downtown and the other is on the phone trying to reach the manager in St. Thomas. From the number of St. Maarten immigration stamps in her passport, she visited our island 3 or 4 times every year. The front desk staff at the hotel knew her well and insured that she always had a ground floor beach access room for her frequent visits." J.R. stirred his coffee with a small plastic straw.

Jack took the last bite of his biscuit and folded the paper. He gazed around the small room for a trash can, but the only items in the room were two industrial office chairs, the table, and the phone on the wall. "Was this a robbery, an attempted rape, or a crime of passion?"

"Good question but we have no answers yet. She was wearing jewelry, basically dripping with diamonds as my investigators put it, and her purse was on the table inside the suite in plain sight. It was full of cash and credit cards, plus there was no sign of a struggle except for some expected sand and blood on the terrace."

Jack crossed his arms and leaned back. "Do you have your notes from this morning?"

"Sure, in my coat pocket." J.R. reached inside his blazer and produced a small spiral bound pad.

"Tell me everything you wrote down and add anything you remember."

"Here is what I saw. A mature and slightly heavy woman lying crumpled on the outside terrace of her hotel room facing the beach. Besides the beating I mentioned and the cable tie around her neck, I didn't see any apparent gun shot wounds. She was dressed. On her right hand there were two colored stone rings possibly rubies, a Rolex watch and a diamond bracelet. Oddly her left hand was bare. Around her neck there was a heavy gold chain necklace with pendant bent by the cable tie during strangulation. There were some other gold chains. Her earrings were large stud diamonds. It appeared that she had changed into comfortable clothes and was wearing a silk lounge dress. It was not torn but was soiled by blood, sand and dirt. Her bra was on and seemingly undisturbed but she was not wearing underpants. The cable tie was the large variety commonly used for electrical wires and is available at any hardware store. We estimate the time of death long before midnight."

Jack scratched his head. "Shit, we're talking about the kind of cable pull ties that most of us use on our stereo and TV wires to keep the mess behind our entertainment center organized?"

J.R. drew a visual picture of a two foot length by moving his hands apart in the air. "Exactly, but the large ones are at least this long and they are strong. You probably used less than six inch lengths to keep speaker wires under control."

Jack considered the image of the plastic tie then asked, "If I had two or three of them in my pocket now, would you be able to see them?"

"I doubt it. They are easy to carry, light, and are the favorites of kidnappers in the high crime areas like Trinidad and Colombia. Great for quickly securing the hands and feet of a victim, then all you need is some duct tape to silence the person."

"So they are not usually used for killing?"

Holiday knew that Jack was on to something. "No, kidnap victims that do not survive are usually shot. It is quick and less personal. I don't remember any killer using the ties to strangle someone."

"Like the old saying," Jack paused. "Silence is golden but duct tape is silver. Any duct tape found?"

"No. We didn't. I assume that beating and strangling her was the approach to silencing her." Holiday stood and stretched. Then he paced in the small area across from Jack. "Strangulation is a hell of a way for anyone to die. Given the lack of a witness to a struggle or cries for help, we suspect that she was overtaken while dozing off on the terrace. There was an open bottle of wine and most of it was gone."

"So she never saw the attack coming." Jack looked up. "We still need a motive. What else was in her purse or found inside the hotel room?"

"The usual for a traveler. Her luggage. Some clothes hanging in the bedroom closet...two more bottles of wine and a container of half and half in the refrigerator. She had purchased some books at the Shipwreck shop on Front Street. One was a self help diet book for controlling cholesterol and the other was a popular beach novel called *Wet Feet*. There was a receipt from the jewelry store *Island Ice* in Philipsburg for a ring and her credit card was next to it. It appeared to have been processed after normal store hours since the receipt shows time and date. She must have been the last customer of the day."

"The receipt and credit card were not in her wallet?"

"No, my investigators found them on the table just inside the door. Now that you mention it, why wouldn't they be in her wallet?"

Jack was lost in thought for a moment. "You just told me that she worked in a major jewelry store in St. Thomas. *Island Ice* sells that faux stuff, don't they? Why would she be shopping at a competitor? Especially at a store known for less expensive merchandise. Her discount at work had to be a good one. She could buy the real thing for a great price, couldn't she? By the way, have you talked to the clerk who rang up that sale at *Island Ice*?"

Detective Holiday shifted in place and suddenly appeared uncomfortable. "I was hoping to do that with you after I spring you from the pokey. You and I both know the guy." He pulled out his chair and sat back down.

"I've never been in that jewelry store in my life. Have you noticed that since me wife died, I shop at bars now? I buy Carib beer, not carats. How in the hell would I know the sales clerk?"

Holiday leaned forward on the table. "It was

Chad, or Chester Johnson, which is his real name. The receipt identifies him and the front desk receptionist remembered giving him the dead woman's room number around sunset. I have known him, his mother and grandmother all of my life. You know him because of his friendship with Andy and Dana. He goes to their restaurant quite often since it is so close to town"

"The big gay guy? Come on. He wouldn't hurt a fly. If anything, he is one of the kindest and most gentle souls on this rock. He loves to be outrageous, but anyone can see through that act."

J.R. sighed. "I agree. But we need to start with the last person we can place at the murder scene and work forward from there. And we need to move fast."

"How so?" Jack rubbed his day old beard and felt the need for a hot shower after spending the night in a bare cell. "Is the political heat rising because of the bad press of a tourist murder?"

"No. We are releasing to the press that a visitor from another island was found beaten outside of a hotel. There will be no mention that she has died. And there will be no mention that a cable tie was used to strangle her."

Jack understood. "I see, and you need to notify her next of kin."

"That too, but we are hoping that the killer will be watching the paper and we hope to convince him or her that the woman survived the attack. If she might be able to identify her attacker, then a second attack might occur. We have checked a police woman into the hospital as a patient, well bandaged to hide her identify and registered her in the dead woman's name."

"You think that will work?"

"I need to give it a try. My time spent on this investigation has to be focused on the next two days. I only have a budget to give round the clock protection for my officer at the hospital for the next 48 hours. Plus I need to get as much help from you as I can before you leave, Jack." Holiday stood and motioned for Jack to follow. "Let's go pick up your personal items from property and drive over to your house so that you can clean up. Where did you leave your jeep?"

"My car is on the Salt Pond road." Jack stood and followed him out of the room then stopped as he realized what the Detective had just said. "What do you mean before I leave?"

Holiday turned and looked into his friends eyes. "To get you out of jail, I had to promise the Commissioner of Immigration to put you on a plane for the USA within 48 hours."

Chapter 12

Give It Up

Miguel sat nursing a beer at the bar of the Poor Man's whorehouse behind the Government dump site. Several of the working women approached and tried to persuade him to spend twenty dollars on a blow job, but he simply waved them away with a flip of his hand. He had urgent matters to deal with before pleasure. That ass-hole who worked for Mr. G was sure to beat the crap out of him if he failed to deliver the rest of the stuff quickly. *If it had not been for that dumb fuck Chad finding the package and selling three on the first day.* The rings were real, stolen in the states then sent to the island as costume jewelry. The process was simple. Miguel's role in the fencing process assured the delivery without arousing suspicion of the merchandise's origin. The profit margin was high when sold in the jewelry store down the street. Missing items meant lost sales, so his life was still on the line. The men in the alley would stop at nothing. He tapped his pocket again to feel the ring he took off that fat bitch that recognized him when she woke up. Too bad for her. It was all her fault. He didn't really intend to kill her. His plan had been to knock her out, tie her up and take all of the jewelry and cash in her hotel suite to make the attack appear to be a simple robbery. It just didn't work out as planned. *If only she had been in the shower and the jewelry on a table or on the bed.*

At least he had one of the three rings to give to that mean son-of-a-bitch, called Bucket. It would buy him some time. He needed to get the others. Luckily few shoppers paid cash. Just standing around after work as the register was balanced gave him the research he needed. He had the name from the second woman's credit card. It was Dana Parkerson, and he saw a local phone number on the receipt. He found an Andy and Dana Parkerson in the phone book with an address in Guana Bay. When he asked Chad about the day's business, the fat guy boasted about his sales especially the one to his friend Dana who also owned a bar. Things were falling into place. He knew Desiree had the third ring and he would be able to lift it during their next home sex adventure. She was always running into the bathroom after intercourse so he would grab the ring at the best moment. She would never suspect him of taking it. *That dumb bitch bought one of the rings! She deserved to lose it. In the future, she should let her policeman husband buy jewelry for her. Women should not shop for themselves.*

Miguel mulled over the details of his next robbery. This Dana woman had to be robbed without another murder. It should be easy. Kesia, a salesgirl and always eager to please, had rattled on and on about the locals who shopped in the store. She told him that this Dana and her husband were older Americans who lived alone and worked almost seven days a week at their business. No children or extended family in the house to worry about. He would be careful. No mistakes this time. If things got out of hand again, a shit storm could start. Once bodies started turning up on the Island, the Government would move quickly to protect its tourism reputation. They would ask for help from the Americans and the FBI might even enter the picture. This had to be kept simple. He would toss the house like any residential robbery. Happens all the time to business owners who might have large amounts of cash at home...he only needed to get the fucking ring back to save his skin and keep a good thing going.

The main area of the brothel was divided into a bar with fifteen or so tall stools, a game area with two pool tables and a dart board. Tired worn chairs and sofas faced the stage and the several brass polls. A few booths allowed for some privacy. The walls had been painted black. The lighting was kept low with the exception of a spot light on the center of the stage. Not all of the women danced in bright light. Blaring music played continuously but the CD player was hidden from customer access. The performing women and the bartender controlled the tunes. A 6 foot man who weighed at least 280 pounds sat on a stool by the door. He never cast a friendly glance at anyone. Next to the front entrance was a discreet door that led to an enclosed passageway to the rooms used for sex. No one passed with a girl without being approved by the bouncer. He knew the crazies and the non-pay guys. The girls were protected. This business was off the beaten path and almost never stumbled upon by a tourist. The parking lot contained dust or mud depending on the weather, there was no sign to advertise the name. Lighting on the street was non-existent. The women were a mix of Colombian, Jamaican and Haitian. All of the customers were black or Hispanic. Miguel felt completely at home.

The entrance door opened and two uniformed policemen walked inside. Miguel froze for a moment and lowered his head. They crossed the room and found a booth for themselves ignoring him, a few men playing pool, and one of the women who sauntered in front of them in a flimsy negligee. The bartender walked over and took their order. Miguel watched the conversation in the mirror over the bar and relaxed. It amazed him that men came to clubs like this to eat. He stuck with beer and avoided the food. Sensing someone near him, he felt a rude tap on his left shoulder. Bucket, the larger of Mr. G's men who had beaten him in the alley Monday after work sat down on the stool. Adjusting his seat, he bumped Miguel's stool with his on purpose and glared at him.

"Ya got da ice, fuck face?"

Before Miguel could answer, the bartender reappeared behind the bar. "What you want?" The bartender was also a huge man with massive arms who often doubled as a second bouncer when needed. He eyed the men with a casual but careful stare.

"Heineken and a shot of Jack Daniels."

Miguel sipped his warm beer and waited for the bartender to bring the order. No one spoke until the drinks were placed in front of Bucket.

"Six fifty" the bartender requested.

Bucket picked up the beer with one hand and the shot with the other. He pointed the drink at Miguel. "My Chicano friend is buying. Pay the man." Then he chugged the whiskey and slammed the shot glass on the bar. The beer was next. He drained half of the bottle then let out a loud belch.

Miguel fumbled in the front pocket of his jeans and produced a small amount of cash. As he opened his hand to count the money, he almost dropped the ring that he had taken from the dead woman's finger. The bartender pretended not to see. Closing his hand quickly, Miguel used his other hand to separate the money and threw a ten dollar bill down on the bar.

"Keep the change."

The bartender grabbed the money and turned away.

Miguel turned his attention back to the man next to him. "Tell Mr. G that I have one of the rings. I'll get the other two in just a few days. I promise. I want to keep the job. Tell him. This is the first problem in almost a full year of bringing in the stuff. We didn't get caught. It was just a screw up in the vault because I couldn't get to the shipment fast enough. Tell him…"

Miguel opened his hand and revealed the ring. He wrapped it in a bar napkin but did not have a chance to pass it before it was snatched from him by Bucket.

"Okay shit fer brains…you got one back. Where da other two?"

Miguel considered his options. If they knew all the details, they might not need him to collect the rings. He was scared.

"I…should have them in a few days."

"Not good 'nuff, asshole." Bucket squeezed his arm and popped the back of his head.

Embarrassed, Miguel squirmed to shake off the physical and psychological discomfort of the bullying. "No, really. I know. One ring was bought by a woman who lives in Guana Bay and the other by one of my co-workers."

"Yo know names? Talk…or we go outside now."

Miguel needed to buy time. "Really, I know a lot about them. Desiree Richardson, the salesperson at our store and Dana, an American, from the only bar in Guana Bay...the Former Life Bar in the Chill Grill Restaurant. I can take care of everything. You'll see."

Then the man leaned closer to Miguel and spat out the words, "Listen to me. Get dem udder rings back and don't fuck dis up. Ya know? It be an easy scam to run. Ya get da package in your normal shipment. Ya remove it before anyone else sees it. Ya bring us the jewelry. Simple. How you fucked up dis one is beyond us. Island Ice never misses inventory because the jewelry was never deirs to begin with. We sell da stuff. Everyone be happy."

"Everyone except the vic back in the states who had the stuff stolen from them" Miguel added before he knew what he was saying.

Rage filled the big man's eyes. He growled softly so that no one would overhear, "Shut yo fuckin' hole. Our suppliers ain't none yo business." He waved his empty bottle in the air and the bartender appeared with a fresh beer.

"Sorry" Miguel replied with quiet resignation as he looked meekly down at the bar top.

Once again, the man leaned in close to Miguel. His breath smelled like old meat and his voice dropped slightly to mute the sound. "Ya got two days. Get me the udder two rings or yo'll roll yourself to work for da next six months. Now pay da man for my beer." He turned, shook his head at the bartender and slapped Miguel on the back. "My friend is taking care of dis one too!" Before the bartender came back to collect, he was gone.

The music increased in volume as a dancer took the stage. Miguel reached into his pants for money to pay for the man's last beer and bumped the hand of a woman reaching for his right thigh from behind him. Turning quickly he looked into her probing brown eyes for a moment and then smiled. Her dark skin was shining in the reflected light from the mirror over the bar. The thin negligee she wore covered a near perfect shape. She was very young. She smelled good. She pushed her body against his seductively. She rubbed his leg from his knee to his crotch. With a knowing smile, he reached behind her and played with her ass. The thong bottom she was wearing exposed plenty of soft warm flesh. His hands lingered and she purred some words he did not hear clearly. He didn't care what she was saying; he was feeling strong again like a man should. With Bucket gone, it was time for cold beer and the companionship of a woman. He needed to relax. He could get the other two rings later.

From the booth on the opposite wall, the two policemen, now long forgotten by Miguel, pretended to watch the dancer on the stage.

Chapter 13
The Investigation Begins

Jack and J.R. Holiday drove in a police car over to the Salt Pond parking area where Jack had left his jeep the night before. The police car had several bashes on the sides. The ride was bumpy and the air conditioner did not work. Neither spoke. Before leaving the private area of the lock up, Holiday had insisted on putting handcuffs back on Jack just in case a political rival or a member of the Press happened to see them leave. As a former NYC police detective, Jack understood the game but was humiliated nevertheless. He would not sulk for long. After a night in jail, the sun appeared brighter and the palm trees more vivid to him. The beauty of the day underscored the joy of being free again. The first breeze that rustled his shirt reminded him of his need to take a morning shower and enjoy the sights and sounds of island living. At least for 48 hours, then he would be expatriated to the USA.

When the police car pulled up next to his jeep, Jack got out. He was still wearing the handcuffs with his hands in front of him. Holiday leaned across the passenger seat and looked up at his friend. "Jack, believe me. If I could avoid putting you on a plane you know that I would. Give me your hands" he said as he motioned keys towards the cuffs.

"I'm not sure what will hinder me more in helping you with the murder investigation. These fucking cuffs or my pending expulsion from St. Maarten." Jack leaned back into the car and extended his arms.

Without answering, Holiday reached over and unlocked the shiny bracelet of metal. Jack dropped the shackles on the passenger seat and tapped the top of the car absentmindedly. "Wait a minute. Didn't you tell me earlier that the murdered woman was dripping in diamonds, precious stones, gold and was wearing a Rolex watch?"

"Yes, I did."

"However, you said that her left hand was bare. That's weird, don't you think?"

Holiday held out his arms. "Not really, I have a wedding band on my left hand and a diving watch on my wrist but I have no jewelry on my other hand."

"You're a man. It is not that uncommon for men to limit jewelry to one hand. Not so for women. You probably never wear any jewelry on your right hand because you shoot a gun right handed. Am I correct?"

Nodding his head in agreement, J.R. thought about his wife and her lady friends. All of them wore rings and bracelets on both hands and wrists. Few of his police friends wore more than a watch and a wedding ring.

"This may have been a robbery gone bad, pure and simple." Jack hit the top of the car to punctuate his remarks.

"Then again Jack, she may have had a habit of leaving one hand without bling."

"No way." Jack stepped back and pulled his keys out of his pants pocket. Another gust of warm wind blew his hair askew. Self consciously he ran his hand over his head. "Wanna bet? I'll bet you a plane ticket back to this island that she was robbed and then killed by the perp. Follow me to my apartment so I can shower and change into clean clothes and we will go and talk with Chad. We need to find out everything that this lady did while on the island. By the way Detective, when did you start scuba diving? Nice watch."

J.R. looked puzzled for a second then glanced down at his large diving watch. "What are you talking about? I don't even swim. My wife just thinks it looks cool."

After they arrived at his Grand Case apartment, Jack fed his cat then went directly into the shower to remove the jail funk from his body. His home was one of several units in an older building on the sea. The owner and architect during the transformation of the original structure had been Italian. While they maximized the number of residential units upstairs and created two commercial spaces on the street level, no expense in design or quality had been spared. They loved creating unusual spaces that echoed the grand mansions of old Europe. Jack's home was a one bedroom, but the expansive French doors and windows facing the water made it feel large. His bathroom had once been a bedroom. The polished marble shower without the need for a shower curtain was completely open to the room, all floors and walls were tiled, and the double vanity sinks were handmade ceramic pots in antique wooden cabinets that once were washstands over 100 years ago in France. Because of the French influence and the tourist population, Jack expected to find a bidet in the room. There was none. Perhaps the owner was not expecting to rent to a woman. Even the toilet arrangement was bit unusual. It was located in a true water closet setup and entered from the hallway. It surprised Jack to see a bathroom without a toilet. He considered it very European, and sensible. The mix of warm wood, cool tiles, and bright sunlight flooding the bathroom were enough to convince Jack that he had found a perfect rental the moment he saw the property.

While Jack was showering, the police detective paced in the kitchen with his cell phone planted firmly against his head. Jack could hear one side of a continuous conversation as he dressed, but he could not hear enough to guess the content. He knew that Holiday was trying to get as much background information as possible before the two of them began a face to face investigation with Chad and any other people that the dead woman had had contact with the day before. Then Jack heard the words of the phone call coming to an end. Silence followed.

"Hey J.R." Jack called to his friend.

"Yeh"

"What was her name? Didn't you say that you had her passport and St. Thomas driver's license?"

"Marta James, born 1955, height 5 ft. 8 inches and 185 pounds" J.R. announced as he flipped through his notes.

Jack entered the living-kitchen area, opened the refrigerator and selected a cold bottle of water. "I see you found the coffee. You need to cut back on all that caffeine, you know. It is the police officer's curse."

"So are low wages, long hours and bad attitudes from seeing so many ugly aspects of life." Holiday responded. "Somehow you survived and prospered, Jack."

"Several years ago my wife and I inherited a little money. We bought some residential rental units and did the work necessary to keep them in good shape ourselves. She had a knack for design and I did the handiwork. After she died, I sold them while the market was hot. Lucky, I guess. She always wanted me to put the money into the stock market. I never learned what to do and could not really understand the system enough to trust our money to a big name investment firm. When everything crashed in 2008, I would have been wiped out. Retired police guys like me without resources have to find work where and when they can. The retirement pension is nice but it is not enough. Without the real estate investment, I would be a guard today at a Wal Mart or some big car lot."

"And here you are...an illegal being ejected from a Caribbean island. Congratulations." Holiday responded and allowed himself the quick jab at Jack's situation. Sensing his friends chagrin, he stood and slapped the counter. "Well you look ready to go. Let's head for Philipsburg and visit the *Island Ice* store."

"Every time I hear that name I think it's an Ice Cream store, for some strange reason." Jack grabbed his keys.

"If you lived with a woman, Jack, you would not only know the store well, you would love it. The stuff is spectacular and the prices are a fraction of the other jewelry stores."

The men walked out the kitchen doors onto the deck facing the water. Jack pulled his door shut and flipped the lock with his keys. "But the stuff is fake."

Holiday started down the stairs. "I wouldn't say that to Chad if I were you..."

Back in Philipsburg, Jack and J.R. Holiday sat in Chad's office waiting for him to finish a discussion with a salesperson in the hallway over a special order and shipping options. Neither spoke. When they asked to see him privately he was unconcerned and completely unaware of the serious nature of their visit. Finally he stepped inside and closed the door behind him. "Hello men. How can I help you today?" Chad flashed his bright teeth with a warm beam of recognition for the well known police officer.

Holiday spoke, "Thank you for seeing us. Unfortunately we are investigating an incident that happened last night and need to verify your whereabouts. Can you tell us where you were from the time that you left work last evening until to your return this morning?"

"Well, doesn't that make me important! I am not used to that question. Is there a jealous wife out there who lost her husband for a few hours last night?" he answered flippantly.

"No Chad." Holiday sounded stern. "Please don't play around with us. It is important that you answer completely and honestly without drama or jokes."

"Okay then. Let's see...I stayed a few minutes late to run a sale on a credit card for a special customer, then I stopped by her hotel to deliver the purchase, I went home after that, I showered and fed my pets, then I went to a private residence, had dinner with friends, drank too much and watched videos with them."

Ignoring the feeling of getting too much information, Jack interrupted. "What was the name of the special customer?"

Chad studied J.R.'s face before he spoke and waited for the police detective's nod that it was proper to answer the American guest. "Marta... Marta James. A friend and a good customer from St. Thomas. Why?"

"We will get to that later, for now, can we simply review the events of last night as you remember them?" Jack said in a matter of fact tone.

"Sure, I guess."

Holiday shifted in his chair. "Go on. How long did you stay with her after delivering the purchase?"

"Not long. We only socialize during lunches normally. When I delivered merchandise to her, it was all business. Oh, she would offer a glass of wine but I never took her up on it. She loves her time alone when on vacation."

"Go on." Holiday made a few notes.

"Like I said, I dropped off her purchase, left and went home. After showering and doing the chores, I drove to Mary's Fancy for dinner. I think I returned home, very drunk, around 4 AM."

"Can anyone verify your presence at the dinner?" Jack asked.

Chad roared with laughter. "Now I see. This must be some kind of a witch-hunt to find out where gay guys spend their personal time when not at home."

"No Chad. Jack and I are here because we need to know about your relationship with Marta James. The rest of the evening is only important to establish your alibi. Please help us here." Holiday pleaded for cooperation.

"Alibi? Alibi? What the hell do I need an alibi for? It is not a crime to be gay. Maybe you should leave." Chad stood and walked around his desk.

Jack and Holiday held their ground and remained seated. This was not going well.

"Look man, one of the men at the dinner last night is the Assistant Deputy Prosecutor. Call his office and ask him where I was last night."

Holiday jumped in to soften the tension that

was rapidly building in the room. "I believe you, Chad. I have known you all of your life. Relax, please."

Chad considered the statement for a moment then walked back to his chair and plopped down with a disgusted sigh. "I can't believe this shit. Excuse my French."

Holiday turned to Jack. "We need to tell him. Everything he remembers about yesterday could be very important."

Jack waved his hand in agreement to proceed.

"Tell me what? I don't have a clue what is going on here. You are expecting me to take a test without the benefit of a study guide."

"Chad..." Holiday began slowly, "It is important for you to tell us about last night because your friend, Marta, was hurt badly during the evening hours. A maid found her early this morning. Was she expecting anyone to come to visit after you? Was she upset? Did she argue with anyone yesterday? Anything you remember could help us."

Chad pounded his fist on his desk. "Wait a minute. A police investigator and a hot shot New York City guy don't come to question a fat boy because someone got in a fight or got hurt. You're not telling me something. I can feel it."

Jack realized that it was time to be blunt. "You're right. Marta James was found murdered this morning."

The shattered look on Chad's face was full of pain. He stood, put his hand over his mouth and ran from the room. The door opened across the hall and slammed behind him. As the two men waited and listened, the wailing sounds coming from behind the door reached dramatic levels. The minutes dragged by and finally Chad reappeared with a moist towel in his hand dabbing his red eyes.

"Are you sure she is dead? I can't believe it. There was nothing in the newspaper. I was just with her last evening. Oh my God!" He wept and his body shook. "I've never known anyone who was killed." Returning to his desk chair he began to rock his large frame back and forth and tap his feet nervously. Tears streamed down his cheeks.

Jack waited for Chad to regain composure then spoke first. "Chad, we understand. Now you can help find the person who did this. We need your cooperation and your absolute silence about what we have told you."

Holiday added to the speech. "Chad, for now very few people know that she died. When we removed the body from the hotel, we checked a policewoman into the hospital using her name."

"Why?" Chad gazed at the two men in front of him through blurry red eyes.

"So that we might have a chance to catch the killer. If she had any possibility of identifying her attacker, that person might come to the hospital to finish the job. You understand don't you? We also need to tell her next of kin once we run all of her background information."

Chad opened a drawer and reached for a tissue. After blowing his nose loudly, he started to cry again.

"How well did you really know her, Chad?" asked Jack.

"We...we had the same positions at different companies. She even tried to recruit me to her company a few years ago. Not in the same store, mind you. We would have killed each other."

Jack and J.R. straighten their backs simultaneously.

"Shit, I didn't mean that" Chad bellowed. "I meant..."

"It's okay Chad, we know that you were not speaking literally." Jack soothed him with his best psycho babble voice.

Chad breathed deeply and continued. "We were

like sisters. Always bitching about lovers, bitching about customers, bitching about co-workers...it was marvelous." He sobbed softly in disbelief.

"We have her personal belongings in my brief case. Can you take a moment and see if you recognize any clues?" J.R. did not wait for an answer. He reached down and pulled out three envelopes marked with Marta's name. The top of the desk in front of Chad was clear so Holiday opened one of the packages and spread out several rings, a bracelet and the Rolex watch. The package was marked "hand and wrist jewelry."

Chad leaned close to the items and said without hesitation, "Yep, that's my stock. I sold all of them to her. Except the Rolex, of course. We don't sell knock off products. She bought a real Rolex from Goldfingers on Front Street. I was with her that day. It was sometime last year. We had lunch at the Green House and walked over to the watch store afterward."

Jack sat up. "Wait a minute...you are sure that all of her jewelry comes from your store? These items are not real diamonds and stones?"

Before Chad could react, Holiday jumped in to sooth the insult. "What Jack meant is that we are surprised that she wore manufactured stones instead of the mined variety from her own place of employment. Certainly she could buy at a good employee discount. Right Jack?"

Jack retreated, nodding his head in agreement. "What do I know? I'm a dumb old white guy!"

The grieving man brushed off the comments with a wave of his hand and continued, "Marta was all about Marta. She told me many times that she was investing in real estate on St. Thomas with every extra dollar. The jewelry she wore was a part of the role she played as a salesperson. She loved the bling but she loved having investments more. She had a goal to retire at 65, live on rental income, and travel."

Holiday opened the other two packages and spread out the other personal items, her passport, her driver's license, credit cards, more jewelry, and sales receipts. The sales receipt with Chad's name as the cashier was on top. "See the receipt for the ring you sold her yesterday after closing hours."

"Yes. But she was long gone from the store by closing time. She left her charge card with me to avoid being seen buying from a notorious competitor. As usual, I would bring the merchandise to her hotel on my way home. That was the last time I saw her." He broke down again and started to weep uncontrollably.

"Well, for what is it worth, it doesn't appear that she was killed during a robbery. There must have been a different motive. She was wearing a lot of expensive jewelry when her body was found." Holiday conjectured.

"Why would someone kill her? Why? It doesn't make sense. Was she raped? Chad wiped his nose. "Yes, she was a bitch, but not enough of a bitch to deserve this."

Jack folded his arms and looked at Holiday then back at Chad. "I know that this is hard, but could anyone have followed you to her room? The front desk attendant only remembered you asking for her room number. They insist that no one is ever given a room number unless the guest requests it. Marta had notified them that she was expecting you."

"There were guests all over the grounds. Several people could have seen me. I walked directly to the row of suites, knocked on her door and then made my way around to the beach side when there was no reply at the main entrance. She loved the beach front rooms and often drank wine on the terrace as the sun set. She liked the ground floor. The sound of the sea comforted her, I guess. She never played music or the television when I was there."

B.D. ANDERSON

Holiday made a few notes and interrupted Jack as he started to ask another question. "How long were you there? ...Sorry for cutting you off, Jack."

Chad looked up in thought. "Probably not longer than twenty minutes or so, as I said before I had other plans. I need time. I need to think about this more. I don't know..."

Jack jumped back in, "Is there anything you remember about her plans for the evening? Did she mention any other visitors due to come later?"

Shaking his head no in frustration from his lack of being able to produce any clues, Chad carefully examined Marta's other items in front of him and began to push them around franticly. "Oh my God! It's not here! What's going on? What the fuck! Shit!" he whispered to the table.

There was a firm knock on the door and it opened. Officer Bart Richardson stepped into the room wearing his police uniform and holding his hat under his left arm with an air of formality. "Excuse me J.R., but I was sent to partner with you on this investigation. I assume that you heard. The Prosecutor called me about an hour ago. I have been calling your cell phone to join you, but it was turned off. Your office thought that I might find you here."

Despite his annoyed expression, Holiday remained calm. The obvious lack of communication within his chain of command was clear. He didn't mind working with Bart, but he would have postponed any changes in the probe's approach until after Jack left the island. "Jack, this is Bart. Bart, this is my friend from the US who is a retired New York City Detective. You may remember that he has assisted us, unofficially of course, on two other murders in the past."

Jack stood and shook the Officer's large hand. Bart wrapped his grasp around Jack's fingers and shook firmly. Jack felt like a little boy. The mere presence of this hefty and very physically fit man in Chad's small office suddenly made Jack wish that he had been going to one of the gyms on the island instead of hanging out at his favorite bars. "Nice to meet you Bart. Welcome aboard. Wish I had more time to get to know you, but it seems that I have been ordered to leave St. Maarten in two days."

Chad cleared his throat. "Hey guys, listen..."

Bart looked away from Jack and avoided Holiday's eyes with a slight show of contrition. "I know. Actually I am supposed to accompany you and Detective Holiday to the airport in addition to my duties as a partner in the murder investigation. I must confirm Jack's departure. Sorry, men. My orders. Okay?"

This announcement made Holiday more than upset. Silently seething, he did not stand. The latest news was more than awkward for the men. Both Bart and Jack were embarrassed. They remained on their feet hoping that the strained moment would pass.

Chad slammed his fist on the table to gain attention. "No one is listening to me, damn it! The ring! The fucking ring I sold to Marta yesterday is missing!"

Chapter 14
Girls' Lunch at Peg Leg Pub

Desiree adjusted her chair in the Peg Leg Pub and brushed her hair to the side as she reached for her purse. The familiar hum of the vibrating tone of her cell phone was not noticed by her two girlfriends, Trinity and Rosa, who were sitting across from her at the table. Casually she looked at the display and saw a text message. The other two women were busy with a conversation full of gossip and catty remarks about their attractive boss at one of the Government offices and neither were expecting Desiree to interrupt their fun.

"where r u? can i see u tonite?"

She knew that the message was from Miguel. An answer could wait. Besides, Bart had been assigned to a murder investigation just today and he would not be going anywhere for awhile. This stud would just have to cool off or play with himself this week. The phone shook again with the vibrating ring while still in her hand.

"plez. tonite?"

Desiree placed her napkin on the table and dropped her phone into her purse. "Excuse me, I need to go to the Ladies room." Before her friends replied, she stood and took her purse with her. The restaurant was filled with locals and tourists and the waitresses and waiters moved between the tables with pleasant efficiency. Desiree turned down the hall by one of the many Pirate decorations on the wall and found the door to the bathroom. She knocked to see if it was occupied. There was no answer. She wanted the privacy. When she stepped inside, she pulled her cell phone out and sent a quick reply to Miguel.

She typed *"no maybe next week."*

She placed the phone into her purse again, admired herself in the mirror and reached for her lipstick. The phone hummed again. *Another fucking text message.* Annoyed by his unusual insistence, she plucked the Nokia out again and glared at the screen almost dropping it into the wet sink. She could barely believe the message.

"im outside i saw your car."

Now she was more than annoyed. She was royally pissed off. This broke all of the rules of their arrangement. That dumb fuck of a boyfriend was never supposed to seek her out in public or even to acknowledge her if they ran into each other accidently. Had he followed her from work when she left for lunch? If so, that could be even worse. Anyone could have seen him stalk her. She had even talked to Bart about her lunch plans on the phone while driving from Philipsburg to Union Road and the Port de Plaisance location of the Pub. She made it a practice of reporting to Bart regularly when she left the store whenever possible. It helped to build trust. Bart seemed to like the constant flow of information on his wife's whereabouts. Besides, the resort also had a casino and hotel rooms. If word that her car was parked here without his knowledge ever made its way to Bart, he would be furious...especially since all the police knew her car well and they were everywhere on patrol. Keeping Bart informed of her movements when she was out on her own was just plain smart.

Another buzz from a text message appeared

on her phone... *"come out pleeze"*

Determined to avoid Miguel, Desiree returned to her table as her friends looked up with envy. Rosa, the youngest in the group, pointed her finger at the new ring on Desiree's right hand. "So girlfriend, what wild sex act with Bart convinced the policeman to mortgage his children's future for that beautiful diamond?"

Coyly Desiree slipped into her seat. "My husband does not pay for sex."

"At least not with you" Rosa countered smugly.

All three of the women chuckled and Desiree dismissed the challenge. "I bought this ring with my own money, using my employee discount at *Island Ice* yesterday. It was not expensive. Do you like it?" she presented her hand dramatically like a newly engaged woman.

Rosa grabbed the extended hand and examined the ring carefully. "Holy shit! That looks like an estate piece. I thought most of your fakes had ten copies just like them in the vault."

Trinity, the other girl nodded her head in agreement. "I want one like that. Could you buy me one with your discount?"

Desiree shook her head from side to side. "I

wish I could, but we are required to sign a purchase sheet identifying the item for our personal use or for a gift to a family member. It is a requirement in our employment contract. And even if I could, I only saw three unusual rings in the case and all of them sold. Chad told me that they must have been previews of new stock sent out for market testing. Just after we opened a woman had Chad hold one, another local lady bought one almost at the same time, and I scooped up the third one when I noticed the attention that Chad had given the tray. I have no training in gemology, but it sure looks fabulous. All of our stuff is nice and the prices are wonderful, but this one was calling my name!"

Trinity sipped her wine and put the glass down. "Well even if I spent my own money, my husband would have pitched a fit when he saw that rock on my hand. He watches every dollar I spend."

Desiree winked with a show of mischief, "Bart first saw it while my hand jerked on his dick during a blow job last night. I think he only said something like Oh Baby."

Rosa blurted out, "I knew it! Sex and jewelry. It is like bacon and eggs, salt and pepper, new shoes and a new bag...some things are just meant to go together."

Their laughter at the table was now louder than the television monitors playing over the bar, and one of the owners, Jack, walked over. "Is this a special day, ladies? Could I offer a birthday cake and candle?"

"Only if you bring it in your birthday suit with a diamond in the center instead of a candle" Rosa teased the host.

The proprietor was never caught off guard by lusty remarks. With a theme of "Surrender the Booty" on the walls, on souvenirs, and even on women's thong underwear hanging on display in the restaurant, sexual innuendoes were a part of the Pub's culture.

With a sign of mock embarrassment, Jack flirted back at Rosa. "Now you know how I asked Linda to marry me! Of course, two wives are not a bad idea! I have a cake in the back room. I just need a diamond."

All four of them continued to snicker and giggle when Trinity motioned towards the bar. "Desiree, isn't that one of the guys from your store that works in the back? Let's see if he can suggest an appropriate diamond for Jack's next anniversary."

Desiree stared in disbelief. The dumb fuck had actually come into the restaurant. She would kill him. Rage filled her eyes.

"Desiree, are you okay?" Rosa asked. "You are staring at us strangely."

Jack, Trinity and Rosa fixed their attention on Desiree as she felt her face flush from anger. Luckily the low lighting in the restaurant was appropriate for the dark and cozy atmosphere of a pub setting and no one noticed her face change. She quickly composed herself and tried to hide her irritation, "I'm fine. I was just thinking about Jack's proposal to Linda. My proposal from Bart was the same with one exception. I was the one who was naked, not Bart!"

"Tits and ass get the diamond every time!" howled Rosa.

Jack bowed out. "I think my wife is calling me from the kitchen. Gotta go, Ladies!"

The women finished their lunches and Desiree forced the conversation to other subjects of current gossip hoping that Miguel's name or presence at the bar would not reenter the dialogue. She was successful and much relieved. Her friends seemed to have forgotten the man. When the check arrived each woman dutifully divided the total by three and produced the share owed. Before the wallets were put away, Trinity spoke up with a reminder, "This owner does not have the usual 15% gratuity on his checks. See, it says NO DEAD WOOD HERE in bold letters at the bottom. Let's each throw in another four bucks."

"That is a bit strong. We weren't exactly a demanding or drunken group of college kids to wait on..." Rosa protested.

Trinity stood firm. "We come here all the time. I don't want to be known as cheap."

Desiree opened her purse again. "You go girl. I am adding more money."

"Hell, I want to open a restaurant with you, girl" quipped Rosa as she watched a young male waiter walk past. "I just want to interview the new hires. Take a look at that great ass."

Trinity groaned loudly. With the check and gratuity paid, the three women walked outside the restaurant and air kissed each other goodbye. Checking the parking lot over her friends shoulders, Desiree saw Miguel standing by his car just off to the right of the casino entrance. She tapped her head. "Oh, I forgot my sunglasses. Bye. I'll call you both later. Drive carefully."

After waiting a minute or two inside the foyer and pretending to examine the logo clothing for sale in the display cases, Desiree walked outside.

She looked to her right and Miguel's car was in the same spot, but he was nowhere to be seen. She stood still for a moment letting her eyes adjust to the bright sunlight and then walked forward. She knew all along that her sunglasses were in her car. She had parked near the entrance but slightly out of sight under a tree to provide shade and keep the car cool. As she held her car keys and pushed the green feature button on the remote, she heard the loud click of the front doors being unlocked. Holding the door handle, she once again gazed around casually. Satisfied that she was alone, she opened the door and got in. Before she put her key in the ignition, the passenger door opened and Miguel joined her. She turned to her right and saw his smooth smile and curly black hair.

"Hey Baby! Did you get my text?" He reached over and felt her thigh through her skirt. She tensed and brought her legs together as he moved his hand up and down the fabric with a sly smirk on his face.

Desiree held the steering wheel with a determined grip. "What in the hell are you doing?" she hissed. "We had an agreement. No contact unless I initiate it. You were recognized at the bar. You'll fuck up everything, you idiot! Now take your goddamn hand off me."

Miguel removed his hand and slumped forward. With a smooth voice he pleaded, "I'm sorry... I screwed up. Something has happened and I'm in trouble. I need your help."

"I can't help you. We don't really know each other, remember? You have risked exposure by coming here."

Miguel was quiet. Then he rubbed his own legs and leaned forward. "The ring you bought from Chad. I told a guy about it and he wants it for his girlfriend. He was supposed to come into the store and buy it that morning but he partied all night and slept until noon. By the time he came to the store in mid afternoon, you had it. He wants it."

Desiree admired her new purchase. "Well, then tell him to go fuck himself. I like this ring."

"I know. But I owe him money. Lots of money. I owe him favors, too. He has men that will hurt me. I need that ring."

"No, Miguel."

"He offered eight thousand dollars for it. I have the money in my car. Cash. You'll make a great profit for one day. Please?"

"Get out of my car! I don't know what kind of deep doo doo you are in and I don't give a shit.

I like this ring. You are the problem. You never should have come here. Don't ever speak to me again. Don't text me. Don't even look at me."

"I love you." Miguel gave his best puppy dog expression. "I need your help. Please. We are special together."

"Then you are dumb as shit. I told you. This was for sex. I can get sex anytime I want. Now leave me alone or I will tell Bart that a nut case at work is bothering me. You are scared of the other guy who wants my ring? Well, wait until Bart finds your sorry ass. Sharks will feast on your balls. Out! Get the fuck out! Now!"

Defeated and with no other plan, Miguel stepped out of the car and watched as she drove away. Slowly he walked back to his car and slumped behind the wheel. On the other side of the parking area near a large dumpster, a police car with a single man inside behind the wheel started the engine. It remained still until Miguel had driven away. After moving a few feet, the patrol car stopped and remained at idle. Inside, Bart Richardson was having problems controlling his rage. As he choked the steering wheel with his massive hands, a tear rolled down his cheek.

Chapter 15
Dana's Garden

Today was Dana's scheduled day off from the restaurant. Since neither the gardener nor the housekeeper worked at their home in Guana Bay on Wednesdays, she used it to schedule an appointment with herself. Andy stayed away. She would get her nails done, have lunch with girlfriends, or just putter around the house and do almost nothing. Today was a near perfect day for staying home. The temperature was holding in the mid 80's with few clouds in the sky. A soft breeze would make working in the garden a pleasure. After checking her email and reading a few recipes on the Food Channel website, she stood and stretched. Their home office, adjacent to the open kitchen and living room, had the same expansive view of the pool and the ocean at the bottom of the hill. She could see Coby sleeping on his back in the bright sunshine near the edge of the terrace.

Weird dog...he likes to sun bathe.

She walked into the master bedroom, opened a drawer and selected a bathing suit bottom. Stripping off her usual at home uniform of shorts and a cotton top, she put on the bikini and started applying sun screen to her arms, face and chest. Picking up her cell phone, she walked through the laundry room, selected a garden spade and slipped on a pair of old sandals she used for working in the yard. The high walls and lush tropical plantings around the house offered complete privacy from neighbors or passing cars so Dana preferred to remain topless even when she was not at the pool. She took the theme from the Club Orient towels "Happiness is no tan lines" seriously. With a watering can, the spade and her cell phone she walked out the side door and surveyed her palm trees, bougainvilleas and fichus plants along the century old wall that framed the property. Most of the wall consisted of old stones put into place by hand. Locals called the structures slave walls. Around the island, developers had been stopped when clearing land for construction projects that uncovered the historical fences of the past. Historical groups had worked hard to convince the French and Dutch Governments to preserve the past. The old walls were a major part of the attraction that Andy and Dana felt when they found the house. She was glad that no one had destroyed them over the years.

Her phone rang and played an island steel band tune. "Good Morning, this is Dana."

"Hey Sexy, are you naked?" Andy teased.

"No, topless in the garden but not naked. Sorry..." Dana swatted a passing bee away from her face and squatted down to examine some new plantings from her attempts to propagate a vine that produced beautiful yellow flowers. They had taken root and showed signs of new growth. She grinned with the accomplishment.

"I have news. Jack got out of the jail yesterday. I called his cell phone again this morning and he was with his friend from the police force, Detective Holiday. He put me off saying that he couldn't talk at the moment, but he would call us tonight."

"Was he pissed off?"

"No, just guarded. He mentioned that there had been an incident and he was helping out with the investigation. He didn't give me any other details."

Dana watered a yellow flowering vine and moved some dirt around the nearby plants to hold the moisture. "Invite him to dinner. Since I am home today, I'll marinate some steaks and pull three lobster tails out of the freezer."

Andy agreed. "After spending time in that jail, I'm sure Jack would appreciate one of your special dinners. Can we pick up any additions to the menu?"

Dana thought for a moment. "No, the last time you and Jack went out to get me buttermilk for a recipe you returned three hours later, drunk, and carrying that stupid Carib beer bar furniture for the pool. You didn't even remember to get my buttermilk! I could have killed you both."

"Hey, I love that bar. It is a genuine work of art. We tried to buy the matching chairs but ran out of cash."

"Thank goodness for small favors."

"Something else came up. I just got off the phone with Carl. He and Lisa want to charter a boat again and revisit the British Virgin Islands. Would you like to go again? We are checking availability and may be able to charter for a week as early as next month."

"Do you think Carl is planning any more death defying free dives under the boat with a cutlass in his mouth?"

"Geez Dana, it was a kitchen knife and he was just trying to free an obstruction on one of the props. Don't be so dramatic."

"Yeh, well let me be honest. He has a wife and two young children and he scared the hell out of us when he jumped overboard on the last trip."

"You had fun, admit it."

Dana leaned forward to rest more comfortably on her knees. "Then there was the fishing episode. He pulled that barracuda out of the water and the damn monster chewed through the line to free itself. It almost landed in the boat at my feet. I could have lost a toe."

"Well, it does add to the adventure of the vacation. Besides it was probably only fourteen inches long or so...hardly a monster. You and Lisa had your moments too. I remember when you girls were swimming off the anchorage and those young guys in a catamaran sailed over to pick you up!"

Dana broke into a giggle from the memory. "Yes, they did and they asked if you and Carl were our fathers!"

"Ha, ha. Very funny. I guess you needed that thrill." Andy said dryly.

"Lisa and I only need the thrill of finding a new dress shop on Tortola or St. John. And we can find plenty of fish at the restaurants."

"Sounds like a plan...I can tell you're excited." Andy closed the sale. "I'll let you know what dates we have as options later today."

"Do you think Jack would mind staying at our house while we are gone? I feel better when we don't have to board Coby."

"Good idea. Let's ask him at dinner after he has had a few rum and Cokes. It will be easier to get a commitment from him! It's not like he has a busy social agenda these days."

"I love you, Andy." Dana said into the phone. "I'm glad that you and I have a busy social agenda."

"And I love you, hot stuff. Have fun today. I'll call you later."

Dana put her cell phone on the ground and returned to tending the plants in front of her. During the phone conversation she never heard the foot steps behind her or sensed the presence of anyone near her until she saw a shadow on the ground. It was too late. A swishing sound was followed by a thud against her head and she toppled forward crushing her new plants.

Miguel crouched down over the attractive woman who lay unconscious at his feet. He had taken the day off with the excuse that the weekend ship schedule would require working on both Saturday and Sunday. After driving past the house with a sign naming it "Villa Dana" he parked his car at the bottom of the hill, put on another one of the generic three for ten dollar souvenir T-shirts and walked back to the driveway. There were no vehicles on the stone paved lot, which was a good sign. He pulled his ball cap low to hide his face and kept his eyes to the ground. Without a locked gate, his entrance onto the property was simple. This had to be the place. He expected that the couple would be at work and breaking into the house would be his best bet now for recovering the ring. He was better prepared this time. With an old backpack over his shoulder, he appeared to be a gardener headed to find work in the neighborhood. Inside the pack, he brought a large screwdriver, duct tape, a knife and cable ties. Under his shirt and in the waist band of his jeans, he had tucked the hammer handle. He walked inside the front courtyard as if reporting for work and searched the windows for any signs of a housekeeper. All seemed quiet, so he continued around the corner of the building to find a point of entry. As he slipped quietly into the side garden, he heard the woman's voice and saw her on the ground with her back to him. She had a cell phone in her hand and was completely engrossed in the conversation. He could not have been luckier. As soon as she hung up, he moved forward silently and hit her with one strong blow. She had collapsed easily and he did not have to pound her repeatedly with the stick like he did with that fat woman at the hotel.

That last bitch woke up and saw me. I need to get the duct tape on this one fast.

Reaching into his back pack, Miguel pulled out the duct tape, knife and cable ties. Crouching beside her, he cut off a long piece of tape and wrapped it around her head to create a blindfold. Then he cut off another piece and stuck it lower to cover her mouth and silence any attempts to scream if she woke up. He was careful to leave her nose unobstructed.

This bitch can't die.

Now he turned her over and gazed at her body.

Nice tits. Too bad I'm not here to play with 'em.

Ignoring his feelings of lust, he pulled her arms over her stomach and searched for the ring. She wore no jewelry but that did not surprise him. It was sure to be in the house, hopefully on her bathroom counter. She was, after all, working in the yard...topless and wearing a bikini bottom but still gardening in dirt. Her jewelry would be left inside. He selected two plastic cable ties and wrapped them around her wrists to handcuff her, and then he pushed her legs together and did the same with her ankles. She stirred and moaned softly but did not seem to be awake. She made no attempt to struggle or sit up. Standing and feeling powerful, he dropped the burglar tools, hammer handle and tape into the back pack and brushed off the legs and knees of his jeans. A low and unexpected sound caught his attention. Turning his head slightly, he was surprised to see a dog flying through the air toward his chest. The creature had never barked. Instead the dog had run at full speed with almost no sound coming out of his mouth except heavy breathing and a low and determined growl. The dog hit him with full force and the back pack went flying. He felt his butt bone hit the ground and the air escape from his lungs. Without a weapon, Miguel could only bring his arms up to prevent the dog from tearing at his neck. The angry creature's snarling jaw and big sharp teeth seemed to be larger than life. Miguel's skin was punctured by teeth as the animal held his forearm in a vise-like grip. Blood streamed down the front of his white T-shirt. Thrashing about wildly, he could only keep the weight of the dog off of him. No matter how hard he fought the dog, he could not get to his feet. He rolled from side to side to break the bite. Every time Miguel managed to shake off the angry beast, the dog lunged again and took another chomp of Miguel's flesh.

Miguel screamed and looked over at the woman for help. Blindfolded, gagged and tied up, she had somehow managed to sit and was shaking her head from side to side as if trying to wake after a long nap. The dog saw the woman moving and immediately lost focus on his prey. Miguel felt the jaw relax on his arm and watched the animal rush over to the woman's side. It was all that he needed. He grabbed his backpack and hat, then ran to the rear of the house as fast as he could. Pausing at the back terrace by the pool, he considered entering the house to search for the ring until he looked at the gashes in his arms and the amount of blood on his shirt. If the dog followed, he was not sure if he could survive another attack. His mind was made up when he heard an automobile horn out in front of the house, and the dog began to bark loudly.

Oh shit...company. I'm getting the fuck out of here.

He turned and continued down the hill behind the house and out of sight. As soon as he passed the first tree, he broke into a desperate run.

In the garden, Dana was having brief moments of consciousness. She couldn't see light or talk, because something was wrapped around her eyes and mouth. Her hands and feet were bound with something and they hurt. She wanted to lay back and go to sleep but Coby was barking. It was annoying. Why wouldn't he let her sleep? Then she heard a man's voice.

"It's okay. It's okay, Coby. Let me near your mom."

She felt the dog's fur next to her legs. He stopped barking and licked her face.

"Dana, can you hear me? It's Chad. Don't try to speak. Someone has put duct tape around your head. I can't pull it off without tearing your hair, so wait for me to find some scissors in the house. Okay? Just nod yes for me."

Dana nodded in agreement.

"I would carry you into the house but we need to find out if you have any broken bones before trying to move you. Stay still. I'll be right back."

Coby did not follow Chad. He sat next to her and whined as he licked the duct tape. Next Dana heard her friend return and pet the upset dog.

"There, it's okay, it's okay, Coby." Watching the dog carefully, Chad snipped the plastic cord on her wrists and moved down to her ankles to free them before working on her face. "Dana, pet the dog so that I can remove this tape."

Dana felt for Coby's head and rubbed him. Touching her chin, Chad cut the tape at each side of her mouth and gently pulled it off.

Dana licked her dry lips and said, "Thank you."

"Now let's uncover your eyes. Hold still."

Dana felt the tape pull her eye brows and she winced. As her vision returned the sight of her dog and her big friend made her eyes swell with tears.

Chad made a funny face. "Wow. You're a mess girl. Let's call an ambulance."

Dana rubbed her eyes and felt the remaining tape in her hair. She started to pull it then stopped as it held tightly to her skull. "No, call Andy. My cell is here on the ground somewhere."

Chad looked to the side and saw it. While he reached for her phone, Dana stood and felt a tremendous throbbing in her head. Nausea passed over her like a huge ocean wave and she staggered like a drunken person. Chad caught sight of her awkward movements and moved close to her. Catching her in his arms he whispered, "Come on Dana, let's go inside and I'll call Andy from there."

When Jack and Detective Holiday arrived in Jack's jeep, Chad's car, Andy's jeep, a doctor's car, an ambulance and a police car were already in the courtyard driveway. Two uniformed police officers were walking in the side yard and two paramedics were leaning against the waiting vehicles.

Holiday waved acknowledgement to the men and women as he and Jack walked briskly to the front door. Jack knocked then opened the door and walked in without waiting for a reply.

"Where's the dog?" asked Holiday before following his American colleague into the house.

"No need to worry, Detective." Andy stepped into the foyer from the kitchen and greeted the men. "My wife is lying down with a cold pack on her head and the dog is in the room with her. Welcome back."

Holiday reached for Andy's handshake and said glibly, "At least this time I found you at home. The last visit you went missing, as I remember."

Andy raised an eyebrow but did not respond to the policeman. Instead, he embraced Jack. All three men remembered that once Andy had run from Holiday to avoid being questioned about the murder of a man who had once been his business associate. There was no need to open the old wound.

"How is she?" Jack asked. He gazed quickly over Andy's shoulder and saw Chad sitting out on the terrace staring pensively at the ocean view. Once again, the emotions of the experience had upset the big man and he needed time to collect himself.

"Okay and stubborn as ever. She won't go to the hospital. She was basically unharmed except for a terrible bump on the head. She has a few cuts and bruises that you would expect, she looks fine. Even though she was topless in the garden, there was nothing to indicate that anyone tried to rape her. The doctor won't give her any pain medicine because of a possible concussion so we have her resting. It looks like an ice pack will be her only relief for a few days. I'd like to find the son-of-a-bitch that did this." Andy gestured upward as he rambled. Jack and Holiday understood his need to vent and speculate on revenge.

Holiday opened his notebook. "What does she know about her attacker?"

Andy shrugged and gave the men a blank and frustrated look. "Nothing. At least nothing she remembers. Before it happened, we had talked on the phone while she was working in her garden, then someone must have clubbed her from behind. Chad came by the house unexpectedly and found her on the ground. There was blood in the dirt but it didn't come from her. We think the dog chased the attacker off. The policemen who are here have walked the whole property, but they haven't found anyone or any weapons. When I got here everything in the house was normal. I doubt that the attacker was ever inside, even though the terrace doors by the pool were unlocked and open."

Holiday made a few notes. "Have there been any recent threats to you or Dana?"

"No."

"Have there been any disagreements with friends or employees?"

"No."

"Where were you this afternoon, Andy?"

Angered by the question, Andy moved forward with clenched fists as Jack stepped between the two men. "Andy, relax. J.R. has to ask these questions. You understand, don't you? It comes with the job... especially in a macho culture where women are often beaten by husbands or boyfriends."

Remembering a murder in the Oyster Pond area the previous year that was committed by the husband, Andy held up his hands in surrender. "I get it. Sorry, but I'm angry as hell right now. I want to find this asshole. I want to understand what happened to my wife. I want to know why she was a target. We should wait and talk about this in a day or two. When I'm not so fucking upset! All right? "

Jack and Holiday exchanged glances. Holiday closed his notebook. "Perhaps I can catch a ride back to the station with my officers and leave you men to attend to Dana."

"What J.R. means, is that my time on the island is limited. I am supposed to be deported. So I may not be around in a few days to talk about this attack. He is leaving us alone to speak more comfortably."

Andy examined his friend's face and could see that Jack was not fooling. "Why?"

Holiday spoke. "We have a new and aggressive Head Immigration Officer on the island who is responding to the usual public outcry against illegals. In addition we have a press seeking Prosecutor that agrees. My hands are tied. Jack does not have a residency permit."

"But he lives on the French side of the island."

"That doesn't create any exemption. The two Governments are supposed to cooperate in matters of this kind. That's why we have no boarder controls. He doesn't have residency on that side of the island either" Holiday responded. "He was picked up in that raid Monday evening and all hell broke loose downtown because he is so well known. I got him released from jail with two days of grace so that he can help us with the murder investigation."

"What murder investigation? There has been nothing in the newspaper about a murder this week. What the fuck is going on? This could be related to my wife's attack! Even if it isn't, the business community deserves to know."

Holiday moved to the door, "I'll leave Jack to fill you in on the murder. Please give my best wishes to your wife."

The doctor appeared in the Villa's hallway from the master bedroom and Jack left Andy to talk privately with him. After helping himself to a cold Carib beer from the refrigerator, he joined Chad on the outside terrace.

"Twice in one week we are thrown together" chimed Chad when he saw the American walk outside.

Jack waved his beer and answered, "I hear that you are the hero of the day."

"Not exactly, it was the dog. I just happened by... I came to tell Dana about the attack on Marta. They met briefly in my store on Monday."

Jack failed to understand any connection. He quickly sized up the big man as an incredible gossip who now had a juicy story to spread around town. Probably the less he told the jewelry salesman, the better. Jack pulled up a chair and joined Chad in admiring the awesome view before them, not wanting to encourage any more conversation.

After a few moments of silence, Chad could not stand it any longer. "Well, I did cut off the plastic handcuffs and free her. She might have sat out there for hours before Andy came home."

Jack straightened and turned towards him. "Plastic handcuffs? What do you mean?"

"Simple things...you know. Just plastic ties. You see them everywhere. We use them in the warehouse sometimes to secure loose items like wires and cables."

"You mean the plastic cable ties?"

Chad beamed. "Yes! Exactly. I cut them off her wrists and ankles."

"Did you tell the police? Did you tell Andy? What did you do with them?"

"No, I...I put them in the kitchen garbage bag along with pieces of duct tape that I removed from her eyes and mouth. Even though she was shaky, Dana insisted on taking a shower and I waited for Andy to come home. He must have called the police and the doctor. I only did what Dana wanted me to do."

Jack groaned.

"Why would anyone care? Dana is going to be fine. Some nut case attacked her and the dog scared him off. Thank the Lord."

Jack set his beer to the side and reached inside his pocket for his cell phone. He speed dialed Holiday and listened as the man's phone rang without being answered. When the voice mail started, Jack hung up and dialed the number again. After three attempts with the same results he gave up and closed the phone.

Chad stood up. "I need to visit the little boys' room. Do you want another beer? I think I'll check out the liquor cabinet. I need a stiff drink."

"Please, with lime. And if you remember any

more crucial pieces of evidence, let me know."

"Pleeeze! I'm not an experienced cop like you!"

Chad spun around and walked into the house in a huff as Andy came out to the terrace.

"Nice doctor. I can't remember the last house call we had from our physician when we lived back in the states." Andy pulled up a chair and joined his friend. "Now let's talk about this murder that has not been announced in the press."

Jack leaned close and dropped his voice, "Andy, the public doesn't know about the murder. The police have a decoy in the hospital pretending to recover from the attack. If the perpetrator fears being identified by a surviving victim, the scheme may smoke him out. What you do need to know is that something happened to Dana that could connect her to the attack with the dead woman."

Startled by the statement, Andy answered, "What is that?"

Jack looked back into the house to make sure that Chad was out of range. "The dead woman was choked by a common thick cable tie. They are often used by electricians to bind larger wires quickly. Chad just told me that he removed some from Dana's hands and feet when he arrived."

"That seems far fetched don't you think? It doesn't appear that anyone was trying to kill her. Did the jail time the other night throw you into a state of paranoia? I hardly think that there is a serial cable tie killer on the loose."

Jack stood. "Don't be so sure."

"What do you know that I am missing?"

Jack shrugged, "I don't have any magic that connects the dots, yet.. I'm not ahead of you...I was struck by the cable tie connection. You got any in your pocket?"

"Of course not."

"And I don't either. That is the point. Two attacks in one week using the same plastic restraints...let's go and check the trash can in your kitchen. Chad put the cable ties there. The police can compare them with the ones from the dead woman."

Chapter 16

First Aid

After stopping at his apartment for some fresh clothes and washing the blood from his arms, Miguel drove around the island aimlessly. His failure in Guana Bay had put him into a tail spin of emotions. At his home, he had poured peroxide on the gashes from the monster's teeth and almost passed out seeing the depth of the wounds. He was sure that he could see his own bones, but he didn't want to examine himself more carefully. After he wrapped some clean white T-shirts around the cuts until the bleeding stopped, he found some aspirin and swallowed a handful. He knew he could not seek medical attention because of the risk of raising questions about the dog attack. His self clean up needed to work. Besides, he hated to spend the money.

Fuckin' dog almost killed me. Son-of-a-bitch didn't even bark at me...just that evil growl. I wish I had had a gun with me.

After stopping and buying a first aid kit from a Napa auto store, he pulled off the road and wrapped his arms with the new cloth bandages in the box. Feeling like a mummy in a horror movie, he rolled the sleeves down on his shirt and tried to look as normal as possible. He had used all of the gauze in the container to cover his cuts and punctures. The wounds hurt like hell. He checked to see if any blood was oozing through the fabric. He was sure to need a change of bandages after a few hours. Satisfied for now that he was properly clotting and that blood was not leaking through, he returned to the main road to pick up the bypass to the Simpson Bay area. At the bottom of the hill, he slowed at a dumpster and looked for others dropping off garbage. The lot was empty. Relieved, he pulled up and walked nonchalantly to the big green trash container with a used grocery store plastic bag in his hands. Inside was his bloody shirt from the dog attack, the roll of duct tape, and all of the used T-shirt bandages from his attempt at first aid. Miguel was not sure of the police's ability to find finger prints on the silver tape or their skill in matching materials like his duct tape to the tape left behind on that woman with the crazy dog, but he was not going to take any chances by keeping it. He thought about what to do for a brief moment and then reached inside the bag, found the roll of tape and threw it into the stinking heap of discarded trash. After bunching up the plastic bag and tying the top, he threw the bag of soiled rags on the opposite side of the container. He could buy more of everything when he needed it.

The blood on a shirt would surely land my ass in jail... maybe I should light this dumpster on fire?

Before he could consider the act of arson further, a car approached and slowed to turn on the dirt driveway by the trash container. As it entered the area, Miguel was already back in his car with his key in the ignition.

Dumpster rats...you are saved. No fire today. Besides, no one will dig through that stinking trash anyway.

An attractive white woman with a child secured in the back seat of the vehicle jumped out of her car with a trash bag in hand. She could not know that she had passed a few feet on the side of a car driven by a murderer. She caught his eye but then looked away quickly. Her pants fit well and she had a sexy walk. Miguel's stared a little too hard.

Now that's a fine piece of ass. Hey baby...want to fuck? He allowed his car to slow to a stop.

The woman with the baby ignored his obvious gawking, dropped her trash into the dumpster and hurried back to the safety of her automobile. Watching her leave without acknowledging him, Miguel drove onto the hard surfaced road and left the area in the opposite direction. He suddenly felt rejected and angry. Just as he started to make a U turn, his cell phone rang. It was the store number on caller ID.

"Yello?"

"Miguel? It's Kesia. You said Monday night that you would take a rain check for dinner, but I haven't heard from you. Judith said you took time off today because you have to work next weekend, so I kinda expected a call. You didn't find another girl friend on St. Martin did you?"

With lightening speed, Miguel's mind was considering this new opportunity. Without recovering the other rings from Desiree or that woman with the nutso dog he couldn't sleep at home tonight. It was going to be too dangerous. Bucket loved to kick his ass for no reason. Failing today in Guana Bay would give the big bully more than enough reason to go hard on him. It could cost him several teeth or worse when they came looking for him this time.

In his friendliest voice he said, "No, no new girlfriend on this island, yet...I have just been busy with personal stuff at immigration and paying bills. I was going to call you after work tonight. I want to taste your Cuban specialties. Monday at the bar was fun. You were so sexy. I am sorry that I had to cancel at the last moment. You were so...nice to me. You have me thinking about you everyday."

Caught off guard by his positive flirtation, Kesia was encouraged and flattered. Feeling flushed, she took a deep breath. "Okay then. Come over about 7, I just need some time to shop for groceries after work and shower. Do you remember where I live?"

"Yes, Mary's Fancy. I'll be there. This is great timing. I was helping a friend clear an overgrown lot all day and I'm starving. I hope you don't mind a few blisters and cuts on this working man's body. I was even bitten by a stray dog."

"Oh no, Miguel, are you okay?"

"Sure. I kicked the shit out of the mongrel."

"Okay, well. You sound good...and you're sure that you can find my place? I could meet you somewhere first. I'm excited about our date.

You'll have fun, I promise."

"Not necessary…I have your cell number if I get lost. Please, can we keep this quiet for now? I mean…let's not talk about seeing each other. Gossip at work is out of control. You know how Judith and Chad can be. They want us to be professional. Okay?"

"Yes…okay. I understand. Goodbye, Miguel." Kesia hung up the phone and immediately told her best friend at work how happy she was with their plans for tonight.

Miguel placed his cell phone on the passenger seat and slapped the steering wheel with joy. No need to drive through Simpson Bay now. He turned around.

Not only do I have a safe place to sleep tonight, but I'm sure as hell going to get my dick sucked. Motherfucker! My luck is starting to change. Now I just need to figure out another way to get the rings…

Glancing at the car clock, he knew that he had a few hours to waste so he turned into the dump and drove to the whorehouse for a cold beer. He slowed down on the dirt road entrance by a stack of discarded automobile tires and lowered his window. Being careful not to pop open the bandages on his arm, he threw the hammer handle as far into the pile as possible. He could shop for more burglar tools another day. He needed time to think. He needed time to plan another robbery. He just needed a new approach. Returning those rings to Bucket or his ugly side kick would save his butt. The big boss, Mr. G., would be satisfied and give him more work. There had to be a way...he always found a way.

Chapter 17
The Workout

Just as the sun was beginning to rise, Desiree left her home to drive to Dawn Beach and exercise in the newly opened hotel's workout area. The General Manager, a robust and very attractive Italian, had flirted with her during a shopping trip to *Island Ice* a month or so ago and he had extended an invitation to use the facility anytime she wanted. His name was Adolfo something. To her surprise, an electronic pass key had been discreetly delivered a day later to the store allowing her full access to the guest lockers, exercise equipment, spa showers and bathrooms. Included in the sealed envelope marked "Private, for Desiree" were six gift certificates for massages and beauty treatments. A personal note enclosed in the envelope was boldly signed "Hope to see you soon. Adolfo." In preparation for the visit, she had explained to her husband that several of the women working on Front Street were considering joining the spa as a group. She told him that in the hotel's opening promotion, they were given introductory passes as an enticement to examine and consider the benefits of using the equipment in the future with a small monthly membership fee. Desiree considered herself to be adept at dealing with her husband's normal jealousy. Bart did not need to know about the sexy manager, the on going flirtation or his recent gifts to her. As long as Bart was kept informed about where she was spending her time outside work and the home, he seemed satisfied. Plus he had been encouraging her to begin an exercise program for the past year. The opportunity for this possible new romance was perfect. This manager was good looking and his interest in her was apparent. Even if this didn't work out, she still had a small fortune worth of massage and beauty certificates to use or give to friends as gifts. This was a win, win.

Adolfo had called her again yesterday while she was at work and pressed for her to give the gym a try. He wanted her to stop by after work and then to join him for a drink or two after a sample workout and spa treatment. The short notice did not give her time to prepare her husband. She declined and settled on today's early visit. It was best to approach the gym visit casually to assure that Bart would not become suspicious of her sudden booking of the introductory offer at the hotel. She was not scheduled at work until noon and the morning timing was best for an initial visit. Bart had several appointments today starting at 9 AM so the first half of the day belonged to her. Anxious to see the handsome European man again, Desiree's heart fluttered like a school girl in anticipation of hearing the man's soft Italian accent and seeing his blazing blue eyes. She wondered about his skills in the bedroom. Except for one Caucasian high school boyfriend many years ago and some heavy petting with him, she had never had sexual intercourse with a European or any white guy for that matter. Considering the handsome manager's Continental background this might develop into a true around the world experience! Time would tell. If only Bart had not been assigned to that woman's murder. It looked like his police duties over the next few months would tie him to St. Maarten and keep his ass at home.

Why didn't that woman get killed on another island? It's not fair!

As she drove towards Oyster Pond she was glad to be out of the house and away from Bart. He seemed to be in a bad mood for some reason. There was probably a lot of pressure on him at work from the Lt. Governor and the tourism office. Murder on a resort property would make for poison in the headlines. During their love making last night, he had acted irritated and almost distracted at times. The police were the first to be blamed. Bart also did not seem interested in wasting time on her pleasure or her need to climax. To her dismay, he was a bit rougher than usual and more demanding. While she enjoyed an occasional spank on her ass during sex, at one point he entered her from behind and popped her butt with his palm repeatedly until she finally had to ask him to stop. The skin where he slapped her was still sore. Oddly when she kissed him goodbye as she was leaving, he barely acknowledge her and did not get out of bed. His mood was dark but she was determined that it would not ruin her day.

She turned right and followed the narrow road to the new hotel entrance. A security guard waved her into the compound without any conversation.

She wondered if she was expected. Yesterday, the friendly manager had asked what model and color car she would be driving this morning. The answer was clear as she drove closer to the main parking lot. A second security guard stepped in front of her car and motioned for her to turn into a lane marked "Private". She stopped her car and lowered the window.

"Good morning, Miss" the guard said as he stared into the car and ogled her from her breasts to her thighs in the tight fitting workout pants and sports bra. "You will find a reserved spot back here and your pass key will open the door marked Employees only. It is a shortcut to the spa area used by visiting celebrities and your car will be kept out of the hot sun. Enjoy your visit."

Damn, I should have dressed more conservatively for the drive here.

Despite her uncomfortable moment with the leering security guard, Desiree raised the window feeling very special and privileged. The private lane was protected from view by a wall and lush tropical plantings. This was not a service area. It was obviously designed for senior management and celebrity use to keep them away from the general hotel population. She found the right spot and parked next to the only other vehicle there, a new Mercedes SUV. She took a second to check her eyes and lips in the rear view mirror. Grabbing her tote bag out of the passenger seat she slipped out of the car with the pass key in hand. It opened the security door and she glanced inside. It appeared as well furnished as the foyer in a grand villa. Italian marble tile was complimented by a thick Oriental rug. Beautiful wooden tables, island artwork and large mirrors were sparkling clean and highlighted by recessed lighting. Desiree was impressed. This definitely was a secluded entrance for the rich and famous. She stood in the middle of the room, admired the crystal chandelier and checked her makeup in the expansive wall mirror. Preparing for the gym, she had only used some blush and applied lipstick sparingly. Her eyes were another matter. She liked them to look their best even on days at the beach with her kids. Desiree had spent extra time on her eyes for this meeting. She dropped her bag on the rug and stepped closer to the mirror. The only rings she wore were her wedding band on her left hand and her new ring from *Island Ice* on her right. Simple diamond studs in her ears accented her long dark hair. She did not wear a watch. There was plenty of time for this morning visit and she didn't need to watch a clock. Unconsciously she pushed her boobs up in the running bra and then carefully fluffed her hair one more time. Satisfied with her appearance, she turned and noticed the security camera in the far corner facing the door. From her retail experience she knew that it was probably capable of photographing the whole room in crisp digital color. She wondered if the Italian manager was watching her on the security monitor from his office. If so, she would make picking up her bag as good of a show of her body as possible. She did a fashion model's runway turn and bent so that her ass would be a strong silhouette to anyone looking. She decided that wearing the tight fitting workout clothing to the hotel was a great idea, after all.

One of two doors opened and Adolfo stepped into the room. With a broad smile and flashing teeth, he moved to greet her with a light kiss on each cheek. He was wearing casual but expensive slacks and a brand new polo shirt with the hotel logo. "Desiree, I am so glad that you have come to try us out. I'll take you on the VIP tour."

Desiree was speechless. His touch on her shoulders as he welcomed her had been electrifying and his body had an orange and ginger fragrance that made her mouth water. She extended her hand, and he took it along with her bag as they moved together through the open door into a long hallway. She noticed another security camera and several doors with brass plaques indicating each room's use. Art work and palm trees in planters were everywhere. Soft, soothing music floated from hidden speakers and the air carried amazing scents of vanilla and lavender. There were no musky or sweaty smells typical of many gyms. This was not like any gym Desiree had been to before.

"I had hoped that you would come and see this after work but now I realize that the morning is better for your introduction to the facility. We staff the spa from 10 am to 10 pm and most visitors rarely use the equipment this early. Look in here." He opened a door and put his arm around her to encourage her entrance into what appeared to be a comfortable but small locker room with over stuffed chairs, soft lighting, and soothing decorations.

Without removing his light embrace he continued, "Each dressing room is guaranteed seclusion. We have no common locker room. When guests come to workout, have a massage, or use the spa facilities they can change clothing, shower or store personal items in safety and privacy."

Desiree gazed into his sparkling blue eyes. "I see. Are there security cameras in here too?' She heard the door close automatically behind them.

"No, guest demands and Corporate Policy would never allow that to happen. Privacy is taken as seriously as security. As it is, we have so many cameras covering the entrance, the parking lot, the beach, the casino and every main room and corridor that we have to pan selectively during the times of the most frequent guest use. For example, at this hour only the monitor in my office was tuned to the camera located in the private entrance you used. In the private rooms you can take your clothes off with every assurance that no voyeur is watching." Adolfo brushed his thigh against hers as he stretched forward to place her bag on a chair in the corner. They remained standing side by side. He dropped his arm from her shoulder and touched the small of her back on the exposed skin.

"I'll hold you to that." Desiree felt his muscular leg brush hers through the slim material of her pants. She wondered if he was a rugby player. He had the firm muscles. Bart was a bigger man and just as fit, but Adolfo had a more youthful appearance and a certain charisma that screamed success and wild sex.

Bart never should have left me without an orgasm last night...

"Would you like to see the equipment? Or can I get you a cold bottle of water before you start? Please forgive my manners, I was so glad to see you this morning that I neglected to offer you any refreshment."

"Is the bathroom and shower facility behind that door?"

"Yes, it is..."

"Let me have my bag for a moment...you can have a seat. I need to use the ladies room."

Shrugging, Adolfo complied, handing the bag to her and taking a seat.

"Thank you, Sir." Desiree turned away. The tone of voice was matter of fact.

With slight sigh of disappointment, he watched her as she quickly disappeared into the bath area. He wondered if his forwardness had made her angry. A wave of insecurity passed over his emotions.

I hope she doesn't leave. I shouldn't have touched her. Now she seemed anxious to get away from me.

Inside the room with the door closed, Desiree removed her sneakers and socks then opened her sports tote bag. She pulled out a pair of high heeled sandals that she had brought for the trip home and placed them on the floor. She ignored the other clothing, make up, and hair brush in her bag. Turning towards the mirror over the sink, she pulled her sports bra off and folded it neatly. Then she pushed her spandex pants over her hips and down to her ankles. As she stepped out of them, she steadied her body with one hand on the sink, and she slipped into the sandals one foot at a time. With another quick glance, she stepped back to check her hair. Naked except for the high shoes, she opened the door and walked without hesitation into the room where Adolfo was sitting.

A broad smile on the Italian's face greeted her dramatic entrance. "Desiree, you are so beautiful... come sit on my lap. This is a wonderful surprise."

"You mentioned showing me the equipment. Take off your pants and shirt first" she cooed. "I want to see your equipment."

Over an hour passed before Desiree returned to the bathroom, rinsed off lightly in the shower and laid out a pair of conservative shorts and a cotton top with her bra and panties in preparation for leaving. Going home without wearing underwear would not be a good idea. Bart was supposed to be at work, but she didn't want to take any chances.

Especially since her workout had consisted of having several orgasms from Adolfo's probing tongue and fingers, exciting intercourse in several positions in the changing room chair, and finally feeling the warmth of his explosive climax inside her. He had whispered to her in Italian at the end. She didn't understand a word, but the passion in his voice was overwhelming.

During the lovemaking, he massaged her arms and legs, including her left hand but never commented on her wedding band. She liked that. Desiree relished the idea of keeping a lover on the side. She did not need a boyfriend. Boyfriends became too possessive and ultimately would threaten her marriage. Her last lover, Miguel, had become a nuisance. When he showed up looking for her at the restaurant that day she was having lunch with her girlfriends, he stepped over the line. It was time to dump him. Thank goodness she had taken the necessary step that day in her car. Hopefully, he had gotten the message that they were over. She made a mental note to discuss discretion and secrecy with Adolfo the next time she visited for another morning tryst. He could no longer send her presents at the store. He could never again call her there. She would give him her cell phone number and urge him to use text messages. Appearances were everything and Desiree was sure that he would understand. Thank goodness she brought makeup with her. The sweat and tears of pleasure had destroyed her blush and lipstick from this morning. When she told him that it was time for her to leave, he explained that he would dress quickly and exit the room before her. The hotel's day shift office staff would be arriving soon. He said that it would be best if they were not seen together. She agreed happily thinking that he must have been reading her mind! When she finished dressing, she left the gym area alone. Adolfo was nowhere in sight and the entrance foyer remained empty. This arrangement would work out fine, in her opinion.

Outside the building, she felt the warm morning air blow her hair gently on the back of her neck and shoulders as she walked with a newly inspired feeling of attractiveness and confidence. At that moment, she realized that she had sex with a man and did not know his last name! It made her laugh out loud. Her car was still the only one next to the Mercedes SUV in the parking area. She was relieved to find that there were no staff or guards to be seen anywhere in this executive area. Somehow it was better to walk unnoticed after her wild tryst.

Desiree knew that she was probably grinning like a fool and blushing like a new bride after that wild experience. She pushed the release button on her key remote and heard the soft click indicating an unlocked door. Had she bothered to lock it when she arrived? She didn't remember. Not that it mattered anyway. There was nothing in the car to steal except some stale french fries that her kids always drop on the way home from McDonald's. In addition, the hotel property was not exactly in a place where anyone would try to remove the radio or tires. She opened the driver's side door, threw her bag on the passenger seat and slipped merrily inside. As she placed the key in the ignition, she glanced in the rearview mirror to check her makeup again. Noticing that it was askew, she wrinkled her brow with puzzlement... It was facing to the side and she could not see her reflection.

That's strange. Did I bump it with my bag getting out earlier? And this car smells funny.

She reached up to straighten the mirror but was stopped from behind. Her head was pulled hard backwards by her hair and a large cloth appeared over her mouth and nose. Gasping for breath and trying to cry out, she choked on the strange odor. It was sweet yet foul. The powerful hands from behind were all she could see and they were well concealed in latex gloves. Struggling and squirming, she attempted to reach back in defense but could not find the attacker's face or even scratch any flesh. She tried to reach forward for the steering wheel but the pain of her hair being tangled and tugged was too much. She struggled to kick and bring her legs up to push on the horn, but it was no use. Her muscles were weak and she watched her feet extend in slow motion toward the pedals on the floor board. Suddenly she was very tired. She just needed some sleep. A dark peace seemed to draw her in. She closed her eyes, gave up, and slipped into unconsciousness.

Chapter 18

Jack in Paradise

Jack woke up as the rising sun filled his Grand Case apartment with a soft golden glow. Stray cat, his only pet, bounced across the bed and went running toward the kitchen hoping to give a strong hint that it was time for breakfast. Jack let out a long sigh and stood next to his bed. Knowing that his luggage was packed, and that he would not be able to return to his home for several weeks took away his usual joy of the morning. While J.R. Holiday had been able to get the Immigration Head to agree that Jack's passport would not be stamped "deported" it would be best if he remained on St. Thomas for awhile. Then it would be possible to slip back into St. Maarten later. At some point he could take a trip to Guadalupe and then fly back to French St. Martin by way of the small French airport near

Orient Beach. He just needed to remain a tourist and avoid being marked as deported. A stamp in his passport showing a forced exit would mean that he was not allowed to re-enter the island for a period of two years. If caught sneaking in illegally, he could face two years in the Dutch side prison. Despite the fact they had a Prisoner's Union and regular "strikes" by the inmates for cable television and cell phone use, the facility was still a hell hole to Jack. At this point in his life it would be awful to waste any days behind bars. Thank goodness for his friendship with Inspector Holiday. No scarlet letter on this exit. No arguments either.

After opening the French doors to savor the smell of the sea, he walked naked to the kitchen and was greeted by his hungry feline. He opened a can of Fancy Feast chicken and mixed it with a dry food. Stray Cat rubbed against his legs and purred with delight.

He had already paid his housekeeper several weeks in advance to visit daily and feed the cat, empty the litter box, and check on things. She was used to the routine due to his travels to other islands and the United States. However, this unscheduled exit gave his housekeeper concern. Jack was one of her favorite clients and she didn't want to lose him.

Hopefully the Dutch side Government administration would change with the next election or at least other matters of importance would dominate the agendas during the next year. It had happened before. With that, he could apply for residency and hope for the best. For now, it was best to cooperate and leave quietly.

After putting the bowl of food on the floor, he reached for the coffee pot, washed it in the sink and started his next morning ritual. The rich french roast permeated the room as the coffee maker began to brew.

His laptop made a sound like an old fashioned dial telephone ringing and the window for his Skype account popped open on the screen. Jack moved the cursor over and pushed the green answer icon.

"Hello, this is Jack."

A familiar female voice was on the line. "I just broke up with my boyfriend and I'm buying a ticket to see you...am I still welcome? I need to be on the beach this weekend!" It was Fiorella, an American woman that Jack had befriended on a plane ride sometime back when she was visiting St. Martin to attend a friend's wedding. He had given her a ride to Orient Beach from the airport and while their friendship had been filled with personal attraction, it had not become sexual. About twenty years his junior, she was extremely attractive but both of them had been careful not to make a move to raise the relationship to another level. They had spent several evenings together during her visit and when she returned to the USA, the communication through emails and Skype calls had been frequent.

Jack hesitated then said, "Can you give me some time to let you know when to come?"

The phone line was silent.

"Fiorella, are you there."

"Yes, Jack. I am just a bit disappointed."

"No, you misunderstand. It is not that I don't want you here this week. It's just..."

"That's all right, I understand. You don't have to apologize."

"Wait. Damn it. I was caught in an Immigration Raid and the police are taking me to the airport today. I have to return to the US so I bought a one way ticket to St. Thomas. I swear. It isn't about you."

"You got deported? I mean...you're getting deported? How awful. How did this happen?"

Jack reached for his coffee cup, pulled a

container of Half and Half from the refrigerator and continued to talk to the speaker phone in the computer. "Remember when they took my passport at the airport the day you arrived for the wedding? I did not have a return ticket with me. So they made me buy one. I was on the island as a tourist and I overstayed the allowed visiting period. I became illegal. Just like the people that enter the states by crossing the boarder without permission. It's a crime all right. Just ask the Customs and Boarder Patrol Officers that work daily to protect the US boarders."

"But you are on a Caribbean island spending money, Jack. You're like any tourist. You don't work."

"Don't get frustrated. This will work out, I'm sure. In the meantime, I have a state side cell phone so I will email you the number and my location when I get to St. Thomas. My friends, Russell and Ellen, who live there are meeting me at the airport. After visiting with them for a day or two, I'll find a short term rental, let things settle down here and return to the island via the French side airport. Then you can come to visit. Okay?"

"If you say I can visit, it's okay. I think about you a lot Jack. I miss you. I really miss you."

Jack was taken back momentarily by the softening in her voice. Then he thought about the great tattoo she had on her lower back. "I want you to visit. We'll have a great time. Just let me get a few things settled. Or perhaps you can come to St. Thomas."

"Okay. I'll wait to hear from you. Goodbye and tell the police who take you to the airport to go and fuck themselves."

"Now, now. Let's watch our language, young lady. I may have to spank you."

"Promises, promises...goodbye!"

Jack poured a full cup of coffee and watched the cat finish the remainder of his breakfast. He turned back to the computer, then opened the Foxfire browser and clicked on his email link. After scanning the list of spam, he selected a few of the real messages and deleted the rest. He reviewed the news on line from the New York Times, USA Today, and the Drudge Report before opening any personal mail or forwarded jokes. Turning his attention to the regular Inbox, one message caught his eye. With the title "how are ya, sexy" it was from Cheryl, a fortysomething woman who had spent the night with him, along with her best friend Susan, during a vacation visit to the island. Both were divorced and had seduced Jack once they found out that his wife had died from breast cancer. Their visit had been one of the strangest and wildest episodes of his rather boring and lonely life. It made him smile just to think of it.

"When it rains, it pours" he said as he reached for the coffee container to refill his empty cup.

Stray Cat gave him a knowing look from the floor of the kitchen.

"Don't say a word, cat. I have been alone too long and you know it."

An elderly couple walked past his house on the beach holding hands. Watching with envy as they passed, Jack suddenly remembered that he was still naked. He put down his cup and walked into the bedroom to find a bathing suit. Stray Cat followed.

The morning quickly melted into afternoon. Like a condemned man, he lingered over his favorite routines. His flight was at 5 pm, so Jack wanted to savor every moment watching the azure Caribbean Sea from his second floor apartment. He stood and watched the water lap on the beach. He counted sea gulls. He checked out topless girls walking past. He had lost his appetite and had no interest in eating lunch. He wasted time paying bills on line, petting his cat, and checking his travel backpack for his passport, credit cards, and cash. There was plenty of room for his digital camera and his laptop computer. As the hour neared 3 pm he expected a knock on the door soon from his personal police escort. There would be plenty of time to take him to the airport. Holiday and that big guy, Bart Richardson, would use a marked car with a siren to get around traffic. No need to worry about arriving two hours early. He was going to have to go. They would guarantee it.

His cell phone rang with the familiar tune "Take me out to the ball game." Jack searched the room and found it in time to answer.

"Good afternoon, this is Jack."

"Good afternoon, Jack. This is J.R."

"Are you outside waiting?"

"No. Unpack your bags. The Lt. Governor has issued you a three year residency permit. I am holding it in my hand."

Jack sat down. "What?"

"We have a situation. I asked him to allow you to remain. We need your help in a big way. Of course, you have to agree to work with me."

"Are you kidding? Hell, if they let me stay, I'll work for free!" Jack stood, reached in the refrigerator for a cold Carib beer and opened the bottle. "Wow. That is great news. Thank you!" He sipped the beer. "This calls for a special celebration."

"Good news for you, Jack. Not for us. Just before lunch time, the General Manager of the new Westin found a murdered woman in her car on the hotel property."

"I'm listening."

"She was strangled with a cable tie just like the other victim earlier this week from St. Thomas. Not pretty. This European manager guy started screaming in Italian or French. No one really could understand him. His emotional outburst created a big scene and attracted a lot of attention. Security, staff and several tourists ran to the site and saw the body. The press is going wild. We are going to have immediate transparency on this one. We pulled our officer decoy out of the hospital today and now we have to release the information on both murders. This is going to get nasty."

"I can imagine. What else do you know so far, J.R.?"

"Well, it has been chaotic but this is what I have been able to collect during the melee. As I said, she was found with a cable tie around her neck just like the other woman. Dead in the driver's seat...there wasn't a sign of much of a struggle. No gun shot or knife wounds...or at least none that were found yet."

"Was she a hotel guest or employee?"

"No, a local woman. And you know her. At least you know her husband. You just recently met him."

"When...Who?" Surprised that he would know the latest victim, Jack mentally ran through the events of the past few days and the people he had met.

"Her name is Desiree Richardson and she is married to my newest investigative partner, Bart Richardson. Or she was married to him. She's dead, for sure."

Chapter 19
Deja vu, in the Worst Way

Jack stood on the hotel property and examined the dead woman's car in the private parking space. The body had been removed before he arrived. J.R. stood next to him and several police officers kept the curious press and hotel guests behind a line of yellow police crime tape. The smell of the sea and suntan lotion that permeated the area provided a strange contrast to the seriousness of the gathering.

"Looks like your men dusted for prints."

Holiday rubbed his head. "Yes, it was full of prints. But this is a family car used to transport children and friends. We expect lots of prints."

"How is Bart taking the news?"

"I found him in a break room at the station.

When I told him, he cried like a baby. It was hard for me to see a guy bigger and physically stronger than me fall apart like that."

"Where is he?"

"We drove him home and made arrangements for the two boys to be taken from school to Bart's mother's house. He refused any medication from the Government Doctor and is holed up by himself. We gave him the Doc's prescription of valium anyway but I doubt that he will take it."

"Could he be suicidal? He does have guns at home, I assume."

Holiday braced his back against the car and considered Jack's question. "I don't think so. He loves those children and he loved his wife. I don't consider him to be the suicidal type. He's just going through the need to hide in a cave and grieve. I doubt that he would kill himself and leave his boys without a parent."

Jack opened the back door and examined the carpet on the floor. It had sand on the mat. "The killer must have waited on the floor behind the driver's seat out of sight. Usually the perp just wants the keys to hijack the vehicle or wants to grab a purse and run. This was one bold attack. Why was she here this morning, anyway? This is a weekday. Didn't she work or do police officers earn enough money for stay at home wives?"

"She worked. At *Island Ice*."

"No shit?"

Holiday patted the top of the auto. "Cable ties…we have not missed the obvious connection to the first murder. One of my men is headed to see Chad as we speak. Think about it. The store employees may hold the key to solving these attacks."

Jack stroked his chin as he considered the possibilities. "So why was she here?"

J.R. gestured toward the large building in front of them. "Bart explained that she came to the hotel early today to try out the gym and spa. She had the morning off from work and she had been given some kind of a promotional pass that allowed her to test the facilities and then consider a monthly membership. One of those free trial offers to get you hooked, I suppose."

Jack walked around the car and then leaned against the hood of the vehicle. "Random, robbery or revenge? That's the question at this point. Most female victims know their attacker."

J.R. Holiday scratched his head in thought and pushed the sandy gravel around with his foot.

B.D. ANDERSON

"Why was she parked in the VIP section?" asked Jack off handedly.

"I had not thought about that. You're right. This entrance is usually reserved for diplomats, big wigs, and celebrities."

"What did the GM tell you?"

"The guy is not much help at this point. Like many emotional Europeans, he was waving his arms, crying and making no sense. I'm sure that it was the first time he has ever seen a murder victim. We sent him home and will talk with him once he calms down." Holiday looked down and squatted to examine the gravel more closely. He uncovered a penny and cast it aside, then stood.

"You're sounding like a racial profiling kind of guy who likes to stereotype people. I'm surprised, my friend."

"It's just that he was so emotional! Waving his hands and all that stuff..." Holiday answered sheepishly.

"Just poking you...don't worry. By the way, did you get the security tapes?"

"Jack, we may be a Caribbean island but no one uses VHS tapes for security surveillance in this day and time. The recorders are digital and contain huge amounts of data covering many days. We will meet with the IT folks later today or on Friday and see what they have on the recordings. They should be able to burn a DVD for us to watch." Holiday stood.

"Uh huh." Jack pointed at the corners of the building." I don't see a security camera on this parking area. Do you?"

"No. There is one out on the entrance to the hotel property and another overlooking the general use parking lot. Nothing back here. But I did see one inside the entrance, just behind that private door."

Both men heard the giggles of young female tourists walking past on the other side of the dense foliage but they could not see them. Out of sight, a taxi honked at a delivery truck blocking the driveway entrance off in the distance. The sound of a bus accelerating as it exited the reception area made them watch for movement.

"See Jack, the area is well secluded from view, as any special entrance should be."

"Well, try to get the tape...I mean a copy of the recording." Jack corrected himself. He remembered his mother saying icebox when he was a child and he would correct her with the word refrigerator. VHS or DVD, the issue was not important to Jack.

He just wanted to see what had been recorded.

Jack turned around once again in a full circle surveying the area and then walked with Holiday away from the crime scene. "I have more for you to consider, J.R."

"What?"

"When I discovered this, I tried to call your cell phone but there was no answer. So I was waiting to discuss it with you in the car on the way to the airport... when Dana was attacked in her garden she was bound hands and feet with the same type of cable ties. What kind of a coincidence is that?"

Holiday stopped in his tracks. "Wait a minute. Are you sure?"

"Yes, I have them in my jeep. Chad cut them off her when he arrived and put them in the trash. He forgot to mention them to the police officers when they arrived."

"That's an important detail to forget to tell us."

"Not really." Jack raised his hands palms out. "Dana's well-being was Chad's first priority. She had been beaten, tied up and was disoriented from the knock out. Add to that she was filthy and scared. When the doctor arrived she had already taken a shower and laid down to rest. Chad's cleaning up was automatic, I'm sure. He is a tidy kind of a guy..."

"Jack my friend...you've come a long way. Now you're defending Chad."

"How long before we have an autopsy report?" Jack started walking again.

Holiday replied with confidence. "The body is on a plane right now being taken to Curacao and the Lt. Governor has been on the phone with the Medical Examiner. Hopefully we'll have a report late Friday or early Saturday."

"Well, if you don't mind, I think I will go and see my friends in Guana Bay and share my good news. Do you need me for anything else?"

Holiday shook his head. "No, go ahead. We need more information about the body before proceeding. I'll walk you to your jeep and get the cable ties for comparison."

"You can almost bet on a match."

As they approached the public parking area to find their cars, a taxi stopped and three happy couples piled out of the vehicle. All the men had open beers in their hands and the women were carrying shopping bags from Front Street. With a flurry of excited conversation they scurried toward the main lobby.

Jack watched with reflective pathos. "Thank goodness life goes on, even when tragedy occurs close by."

Holiday agreed. "Sadly while millions of folks go about enjoying a happy existence, somewhere there is always a small core of evil people plotting to steal, bomb, or murder...consumed by hate."

Jack looked up at a swaying palm tree and the bright blue sky above. "Or they're just plain fucking nuts."

"You got that right."

Jack took a deep breath. "What makes me crazy is that most men just want to have a decent life, make love with their wife or girlfriend, enjoy a good meal or a drink now and then, and watch their children grow up."

Slowly, Holiday nodded in agreement. "And what do women want, Jack?"

"I live alone and I haven't had sex in too many months to count on both hands. Do I look like someone who knows what women want?"

Chapter 20
Andy and Dana get a clue

In the hours since the attack, Andy had stayed home from work to attend to Dana and watch for problems that might arise from a possible concussion. Dana protested, but he was unyielding. After a busy morning with the housekeeper cleaning and moving them both from room to room, things were now quieting down. They were sitting comfortably on the terrace with cold bottles of water watching as Juan, the pool guy, finished his routine. He disappeared for a few minutes into the pool house, then resurfaced and waved goodbye.

"Thank you, Juan." Dana waved back to him.

Absorbed by the newspaper, Andy did not seem to hear Dana. "It's amazing to me that a woman visiting this island can get killed in a hotel and the story is not in this paper."

"Come on Andy." Dana took another sip from her water bottle. "Didn't Jack make it clear to you that the police had a plan? If it failed, you should see the story in Friday's paper. Don't forget that horrible car accident a few years back...the dead boy driving the SUV was on the front page of the newspaper lying on Airport Road a few hours after his death. The family was horrified. Sometimes no news is good news."

Andy let the censorship issue pass without further debate. "How Jack can be so calm and collected when the police, his friends, are deporting him today escapes me."

"Why don't you give him a call and see if he needs us to do anything. We've been so wrapped up in my attack that we forgot about Jack and his problems with immigration. The poor guy is getting kicked off the island in a few hours. He must be miserable." Dana put down her water bottle. Coby strolled out from the living room and settled with a plop into a favorite spot in the sunshine.

"Honey, the afternoon is passing us by... wouldn't you like some lunch?"

Dana touched the back of her head as if measuring the swelling from the blow. Removing the duct tape from her hair had required a lot of cutting and her long curly hair was now short and chopped in several places on the back and on the sides. Andy thought it best to avoid the subject.

Dana shook her head, "No, you go ahead if you're hungry. There's some tuna salad in the fridge and a loaf of whole grain bread in the freezer."

Andy sighed. Dana's new eat healthy approach to meals and shopping did not allow fresh loaves of his favorite French baguettes in the house. At least she hadn't cut out his beer, so far.

Coby stood and growled then rushed to the front door. He sat down and waited but did not bark. The sound of the brass pineapple knocker echoed through the house.

Dana jumped up. "I'll get it. I need to move around, the doctor said."

"Okay, your boy is guarding the door but please check the peep hole before answering. We have had enough drama for one week."

Dana approached the large wooden door, stood on her tip toes to see through the opening, and pulled the door open with one quick motion. "Jack, come in...What are you doing here? Don't you have a flight today? Where are the police?"

Shocked by Dana's chopped off hair, Jack Donnelly stepped inside and kissed her on both cheeks. "Good to see that you heal fast. How do you feel?"

"Well, I look like an alien when I don't have on this makeup because the damn duct tape pulled off my eyebrows, but I'm good. Aching and still using an ice pack to control the swelling. Time will heal me." Dana turned around and walked to the kitchen. "Come on...let's get you a beer. Do you have time before you have to go?"

"I have plenty of time." Jack grinned, "I received a three year residency permit today from the Lt. Governor's office. Time is on my side for a change."

Andy overheard the comment as he entered the kitchen to join them. "You're fucking kidding us. No one gets a permit that fast. And doesn't Immigration issue Residency and the Lt. Governor's office issue work permits?"

Jack took the cold beer that Dana offered. "It gets confusing...I am officially unofficially working for the police." He guzzled half of the bottle in one thirsty gulp.

Dana touched her head again. "What do you mean? Maybe it is the bump on my head, but nothing you are saying is making sense."

"I will be unofficial in my capacity as an advisor

in the investigation. My name will not appear on police reports...which is fine with me since they are written in Dutch. The Government won't pay me either, but I have agreed to help. There was another woman found murdered today just before lunchtime at that new Dawn Beach hotel. The shit is gonna hit the fan now."

"Oh fuck. That's terrible." Andy pulled a stool up to the kitchen counter and took a seat. "Dana, I think I could use one of the Carib beers now. You need another, Jack?"

"I just left the murder scene. Something about needless cruelty to others makes me want to drink beer. So, yes."

Dana gave both men a skeptical once over. "Uh huh...and sandy beaches make you want to drink beer...and palm trees, and clear ocean water...and"

Andy stopped her. "All right! Guilty as charged. You forgot topless women, by the way!"

Everyone agreed.

Andy continued, "Actually topless women are a reason for living not just a reason for drinking beer!"

Andy and Jack clinked bottles in a toast just as Coby crossed the room, stopped for a drink of water from his bowl in the corner, and plopped down.

"My three dogs..." Dana added. "You are such adolescents."

Andy raised his arms in a mock football referee posture and said, "Visual Viagra...and you get the benefits!"

Dana had to smile at that one. "But enough you two. Jack, you drop a bomb about another murder and leave us guessing. What is going on? This could be devastating to the tourist business once the bloggers and travel forums start blasting away with gory details and relentless rumors. What in the hell is happening this week? Has a serial killer arrived on this island?"

Jack continued to stand and started to pace as he began to review the cases for them. "Nervous energy...I hope you guys don't mind me moving around a bit. The news about the residency permit and the second murder has my adrenaline pumping and my mind racing."

Andy smiled at Dana. "Honey, why don't you sit next to me? Jack's pacing is going to be like sitting at a tennis match."

"When I was sitting outside with Chad yesterday on your terrace he mentioned that Dana was wearing plastic handcuffs when he found her in the garden." Jack continued his walk.

Dana rubbed her wrists. "That's right."

"Andy and I pulled them out of the trash. Chad had discarded them along with pieces of the duct tape when he was cleaning up the house during your shower."

Dana asked, "So what?"

Jack stopped and stared at her. "We had not released news of the first murder and only a few select officers at the scene knew how the victim was strangled. It was a bit unusual. The attacker used a common electrical cable tie exactly the same size as the pieces that I took out of your trash can."

Dana put her hand over her mouth. "Jack, that is soooo creepy. Are you saying that he meant to kill me but was somehow chased away?"

"I'm not finished. Listen to me. Because of all of the witnesses on the scene today the newspaper articles in both papers will report the condition of the body of the second murdered woman. The manager was screaming that she had been strangled. He was quite emotional about it, so I am told."

"Are you saying strangled? Don't tell me...with plastic cable ties? Just like the first victim..." Andy jumped in.

Jack indicated yes with a nod of his head.

Dana rubbed her neck as if feeling for the non-existent cable tie at her throat. "Good God in Heaven." She looked frighten and reached for Andy's hand. "This maniac killed a woman some-time Monday night, attacked me on Wednesday, and killed another woman on Thursday morning. Panic will spread all over the island. I'm surprised that the front courtyard is not full of local reporters."

Jack reached over the counter and touched Dana's other hand. "You have not been connected publicly as of yet. The police have not released any report to the news media concerning your attack. The stories tomorrow will focus on the hotels and the attacks on the two women. One was a visitor from another island and one was a local woman going to a gym that happens to be in a hotel. The murders occurred at different times of the day, and at different locations. Only we know the cable tie connection. Widespread speculation will be the first reaction by locals and tourists. For the most part, people are going to do what we are trying to do...find a common thread that connects the two victims."

"Or they make some shit up…" Andy got up and walked around the counter to the kitchen and opened the refrigerator. He selected a jar of spicy organic salsa and a bag of lime Mexican chips. "I think better with food and beer. Tell us about the women, Jack. What connections have you found?"

Seeing Andy in the kitchen, Coby sat up. Andy pulled opened a lower cabinet and reached for a chicken jerky tender from a shelf of dog food. Coby wagged his tail and waited. "Hey boy...want a cookie?"

The dog accepted the treat and returned to his corner.

Jack walked next to Dana and took a stool at the counter. "Chad knew the two women. The first one, Marta was her name, was a friend and one of his best customers. The second one..."

Dana interrupted. "What? I just met her on Monday at *Island Ice*...I can't believe it..."

Andy chomped on a tortilla chip with a scoop of salsa. "You were at *Island Ice*? I don't remember you going shopping..."

Coby made a soft whining sound and put his paws over his nose while lying on the floor. Jack finished his beer and walked over to the refrigerator for another. Dana said nothing.

Jack broke the tension before the husband and wife could start the shopping discussion, "Chad told us that a ring that Marta purchased the day she was murdered was missing from the personal effects that the police collected from the room. And here is the most interesting part. The husband of the second murdered woman told Holiday that her body was missing her wedding ring and a new ring she just bought at *Island Ice*. When they found her she was wearing diamond studs in her ears but no other jewelry. Her wallet only contained ten bucks. Yet, both murders appear to be triggered by robbery."

Dana shifted in her chair and looked extremely uncomfortable.

"I bought one too" she said softly.

With surprise, Andy and Jack turned to Dana with wide open eyes.

Andy spoke first. "Too? Too? You are saying *two* meaning the number of rings we've been talking about? Or *too* meaning the fact that you bought jewelry that someone would kill to steal? What is the value of a ring like that? 50 Grand? 60 Grand? Why did you spend that kind of money? You know we can't afford that." Andy's voice was near screaming.

Jack waved his hand in the air. "Let's calm down here folks. I've been in that store and know its reputation. They don't sell stuff at that price. They specialize in fakes."

Dana replied, "Manufactured stones, not fake. The gold is real. The silver is real. The platinum is real. But you are right about price. I only paid four thousand dollars."

"Yeh, yeh. I know my wife. She paid four thousand, nine hundred and ninety nine dollars and calls it less. When were you going to tell me, Dana?"

Dana glared at Andy with humorless eyes.

"Time out, children! Let's take a breath." now Jack was hollering. "Save the household budget discussion until after I leave. Right now we need to be more focused on Dana's safety and on helping the police to find a crazy killer that is on the loose. Understand?"

Andy looked sheepishly at this wife, "Sorry baby, I over reacted. It must be the emotions of the past twenty four hours. I didn't really sleep last night. The attack on you yesterday overwhelmed me. I had nightmares remembering that home invasion we had almost two years ago. When Chad called and told me to come home because you had been hurt, I fell apart."

Dana put her arms around her husband and hugged him.

Jack waited for the right moment. "Let's get back on track...Dana is under the radar when it comes to the news people and to island rumors but not with the killer or the police. I told Holiday about the cable ties that Chad removed. Until this wacko is caught, Dana is at risk."

"Jack, the last time we dealt with this kind of a problem there were two men. Two bastards invaded our house and almost raped Dana. Jerks like this seem to travel in pairs. How can you be so sure that the killer is working alone?"

"The answer may be stretched out on the floor in your kitchen" Jack said as he pointed at the dog.

Dana released her embrace of Andy. "What?"

"Think about it. The dog could slam into one man, knock him down and fight effectively. But two men...I doubt it."

"Jack's right, Dana. This guy has to be working alone. Now...can we see this ring that is to die for?"

After flashing her husband an eat shit and die look, Dana left the room and went to the master bedroom. When she returned both men were sitting at the counter enjoying the salsa snack.

"Thank goodness I buy stuff that is heart healthy, you guys. Those chips are going fast." She held out her hand and showed off her dazzling new diamond ring."

"Whoa darling! That is more than stunning. I can't believe that it is a fake...ah, I mean a manufactured stone." Andy took her hand and examined the ring closely.

"According to Holiday, both women had jewelry stolen but not all of their jewelry. Were you wearing anything while working in the garden, Dana?" Jack asked.

"I don't think so...I was so busy trying to get the damn duct tape out of my hair without plucking myself bald headed that I never checked my ears for jewelry. Let me go look. I never wear anything else while working in the dirt. It's too damn hard to get it out of my watch band or rings."

Dana walked back to the master bedroom to do an inventory of her earrings and other jewelry.

Andy and Jack finished the remaining chips and continued to sip their beers as they waited.

Dana called from the bedroom, "Everything is here. Diamonds, tanzanite, aquamarine, emeralds... all my studs are accounted for!"

Andy raised his beer bottle in salute, "Don't forget the two studs in the kitchen!"

Chapter 21
Mr. G's Office above Front Street

Beep, beep, beep...to the sound of the alarm count down, the burly Russian pushed open the door to his office in the parking garage over the Front Street shopping plaza and stepped inside. In his hands were copies of both local newspapers, The Daily Herald and Today. Following his usual morning routine, he dropped the papers on his desk and walked to the opposite wall to disarm his security system before he ran out of time. Pressing in his private code, the light on the white box changed from red to green with an abrupt and final chirp. Even though it was the beginning of the work day, his pants and shirt were rumpled and his wispy and graying red hair disheveled. Personal appearance was a low priority for the business man.

He loved money and the women and bourbon that money could buy. The sun and the beaches on this island meant nothing to him. It brought the tourists and they spent money, lots of money in his stores. His Eastern European partners living in the United States and in Europe obtained the merchandise he sold. Jewelry, electronics, and souvenirs were his stock and trade using a wide network of fencing operations. From hijacking trucks and containers from shipping companies, to buying stolen items in large cities from nameless thieves, the supply was almost endless.

To make his business look legitimate, a small portion of the inventory was purchased through regular wholesale outlets. His profit margins on markups for retail sales were assured by low cost. Desperate thieves would always sell valuable items for pennies on the dollar if they could get enough for their next drug fix. It only took the right organization to keep the supplies coming. His business associates assured this. No one could ever track his real sales volume. Most of the cash from his businesses was automatically skimmed off the top. He paid the Island Government's Turnover Tax promptly on credit card sales and a few small cash transactions to guarantee that the stores remained under the tax enforcement radar.

Adjusting his blinds to allow natural light into the room, he smirked at the sight of six cruise ships jamming the pier and harbor. This Friday was going to be a winner. Even as he walked from his apartment on Back Street, he had seen throngs of casually dressed visitors strolling the streets in anticipation of store openings.

Plopping back into to his leather desk chair, he grabbed one of the papers and opened the fold to reveal the front page.

Police Investigate Murders of Two Women
Robbery Suspected

The headline popped out like an instant headache. He reached for the other paper and saw its attention getting front page blaring out with a large color photo of a body on a gurney being pushed by grim emergency personnel.

Police Officer's Wife Murdered in Robbery

Laying the papers side by side he scanned the text of both articles and felt his blood pressure rising.

Reliable sources within the police force told this reporter that the woman found late Thursday morning at the new Westin Hotel had been robbed of her jewelry. Her wedding ring and a diamond ring were missing.

St. Thomas Visitor Found Murdered

A female visitor from the United States Virgin Islands was found murdered outside her hotel room earlier this week. Police report that several pieces of jewelry recently purchased on St. Maarten were missing.

His concentration was interrupted by a rough tap on the door as it opened. Bucket stood in the sunlight with his sidekick, Brick. Bucket was Haitian and Brick was Jamaican. Neither man was on St. Martin with a legal status. Mr. G liked it that way. He wanted no official paperwork to tie his relationship to these two imbeciles. He paid them in cash or in knock off liquor, stolen watches or phony Cuban cigars and they asked no questions. He needed stolen goods picked up and delivered and they never missed a day. Like the boss, neither man gave a shit about the beaches or the clear water. Environmental concerns were not a focus of their daily existence or conscious thought. They were loyal if the money was easy. Once, a slightly drunk but athletic looking young Greek merchant got in the Russian's face at a local bar with threatening remarks and racial slurs. Mr. G had felt his girlfriend's ass as she passed his table and the younger man reacted violently in public. The older Russian sent these men to discuss the embarrassing offense with the hot tempered Greek. Now, the man crossed the street when he saw the big Russian coming his way.

Both of his employees waited at the door for permission to enter.

With a rude wave of acknowledgement, the Russian directed the men inside. "Close the fuckin' door."

Neither man extended a handshake to the boss or made any attempt to offer any polite island greeting. Instead, they shuffled in and stood near the fall wall.

"Have you seen the goddamn paper today?"

The blank look on their faces showed that reading was not a favorite past time. They kept their eyes on him and did not react. Neither had any clues to why he was angry. There were plenty of ships in port and business would be good.

Mr. G growled, "That stupid ass is killing women to get the rings back...he's out of control. What the fuck is he thinking? What a fucking idiot! Did you see this?" He held up the headline with the photo of the Police Officer's wife being removed from the hotel property in a body bag.

Bucket and Brick knew better than to answer. They could not read the English text and the photo was too far away for them to understand the article. What they did understand was that the boss was mad as hell.

"You have to find him. You have to stop him. If the police get him and interrogate, he is sure to spill his guts and link everything to you. You know that they will make him talk...especially since he killed one of their officer's wives. Find this asshole now! Deal with this. He must disappear. You must find him before the cops or they will find your sorry dead asses floating off the remote ends of this beach. Now get the fuck out of here!"

Chapter 22

A Day at the Beach

Andy rolled over in bed early Friday morning and gazed at his wife, fast asleep. Her hair, framing her face, had been butchered by her attempt to remove the duct tape from her head before the doctor or police had arrived. She had wanted a shower to wash away the trauma, and with only a mirror and sharp scissors, she had chopped away to remove the silver mess. The result from the amateur hair cut was not good. Dana was a creative cook, not a beautician or skilled hair stylist.

The normal routine consisted of Andy rising with the sun without the need of an alarm clock, opening the doors to the pool and back yard so that Coby could go outside and then feeding the cat before starting a pot of fresh coffee. Today, however, he waited for Dana to notice the light and stir. It did not take long. She felt his stare and opened her eyes reluctantly.

"Oh, are you still here? You need to leave. My husband could be home from the night shift any minute."

"Very funny." Andy rubbed her face and played with her hair.

Dana closed her eyes and whispered, "I hurt in places that I didn't know had muscles or nerves. Did we have rough sex last night?"

"Oh yeh. How soon you forget. Let's see... let me review the last 48 hours for you. Someone knocked the shit out of you, wrapped you in duct tape and plastic cable ties, and left you struggling to get free in the dirt. You might have a few physical issues to deal with. Don't ya think?" Andy patted the sheets between them. "You look beautiful."

"And you will never get Lasik surgery to correct your eyesight."

Andy kissed her and held her for a few moments without saying anything more. Coby watched from his dog bed in corner of the bedroom but understood that he was not allowed to interrupt the quietness.

Finally Dana sat up. "I need to use the bathroom. Did you start the coffee yet?"

"No baby. I was waiting for you to wake up. I want to tell you something."

"You're not going to tell me that you are having an affair with one of our pretty young waitresses at our restaurant, are you?"

"Very funny...I have a plan for today. It's going to be a day of healing for you. How are you feeling?"

"I need comfort food."

"No...I mean you need a break. You need a day of focused healing."

"You're right, it is going to be day of healing! I am starting a book by a guy named Putley on St. John called "Sunfun Calypso". I plan to plant myself on the terrace all day." Dana stood and walked towards her bathroom. When they renovated the house, Andy and Dana had added another bathroom off the master bedroom and expanded the original one. The his and hers bath arrangement was their favorite addition to the home. Dana's led to an outdoor shower, and Andy's led through his dressing room into a study, richly paneled in dark woods, green walls and two large flat screen televisions for scanning various shows on his multiple satellite dishes. His desk, framed by bookcases, consisted of two large screen monitors for the desktop computer and a docking station for his laptop.

Andy winked at Coby and announced loudly. "Sorry Baby, but we had a family meeting on today's activities. Coby and I voted to take you to Orient Beach. It's three to one."

"Three?" Dana stopped walking.

"Well, the cat asked for a day of private meditation so she voted too. She says you need a day on the beach. Chevy will be the only girl sleeping on the terrace today."

"You are nuts. Your wife is not going to Orient Beach and be surrounded with all of those hot French girls and visiting sun baked Americans while her head is looking like it was stuck in a pencil sharpener. Forget it. Should I spell this for you? F-o-r-g-e-t i-t."

"The plan is to have fun. We'll get you a nice haircut at the salon next to Bikini, a new bathing suit at the Bikini shop, and then we'll check out a new thong for you at Sexy Fruits near Club O. We'll have lunch at KaKao on the beach and let the young French waiters flirt with you all day."

Dana defended the behavior, "They just like big tips."

Andy countered, "Don't kid yourself. They like

big tits. Yours are the best. A day of topless sun-bathing, great French food, and new bathing suits will heal you just fine."

Dana considered the offer. She liked to buy new bathing suits. She liked to eat at KaKao, be catered to by the young French waiters and take a break from owning her own restaurant. Plus a haircut could include nails and a pedicure.

Absorbed in thought, she carefully considered the carrot Andy was offering, "Let me think about it. Now take the dog out so that I can use the bathroom without an audience!"

Knowing he was in for a bit of a wait, Andy walked into the kitchen and negotiated a path to the door while the cat, Chevy, ran back and forth near Coby's legs. When he opened the door, the dog rushed out and barked at a few birds near the pool. Satisfied that she was now the center of Andy's attention, Chevy turned around and rushed to her bowl. The easy routines of life made for pleasant and wonderful moments to be savored.

An hour and a half later, Dana emerged from the shower looking fresh and ready for the beach. She was wearing a black bikini with a matching see through black sarong. To hide her chopped hair and bald spots from the duct tape, she donned a large straw hat with a wide brim.

She announced the obvious, "Okay guys, you talked me into it. Who am I to go against the wishes of my men? Or to deny my cat a day of peace and quiet. Let's go to the beach! I am feeling the tremendous pull of sand gravity."

Coby wagged his tail in agreement. The word "beach" was special to him. Andy and Dana adopted him at Orient Beach. Flea infested, hungry, and wounded by something that had almost cut his tail off, Coby was more than ready to be rescued. Returning to his old haunts was a big deal to him. The sand and surf gave him a day to play with several of the French dogs that were always there, to swim in the ocean, or simply to lie quietly under Dana's lounge chair. Life is good when you are a dog.

Anticipating her acceptance, Andy was ready. He was wearing a pair of simple blue cargo swimming trunks and a white polo shirt with the Chill Grill Restaurant logo on the left chest. Coby was waiting by the door ready to go. Andy had his back pack stuffed with towels and sun screen on the chair in the foyer. All that was left to pack in the jeep was Dana's beach bag. They would rent beach lounge chairs at Kakao Restaurant, order drinks from the beach attendants, and have a French bistro lunch overlooking the clear waters of Orient Bay. They never took a cooler full of drinks to another business's beach. It was bad for public relations. They had seen a well known manager of a Dutch side hotel do that most Sundays with his family and friends and considered it rather insensitive to others...especially since they all earned their livings in the same manner.

With a cold beer in hand, Andy helped his wife and dog into the jeep and reveled in his successful attempt to distract Dana from focusing on the attack. He started the jeep and pulled out of their courtyard onto the street. As they drove away from the house neither of them noticed the pair of eyes in the bushes about 50 feet away watching them depart. Coby sniffed and growled over the noise of the engine but stayed secure in the back seat.

At the first intersection Andy slowed to turn right. Dana looked at the beer in his hands with a raised eyebrow. "Starting a bit early, aren't we?"

Andy took a sip and raised the bottle, "You can't drink beer all day on the beach if you don't start in the morning!"

Inside Orient Beach resort, they followed the paved road through the villas and townhouses past the small shopping center opposite the Village

Square and turned onto the sandy road toward KaKao Restaurant and Beach Bar. The early hour allowed them the choice of several prime parking spaces across from the Caribbean Riviera condominiums and Alamanda Hotel. Andy parked the car under a grape tree to take advantage of the cooling shade.

As soon as they entered the beach restaurant's entrance and walked between the palm trees and tropical plants, a familiar face greeted them. It was Xavier, one of the beach waiters and a terrible flirt with American female tourists.

The accent was heavily French, "Hello, Dana! Good to see you...how are you? Do you and Andy want lounge chairs on the beach today?" He rushed to her, hugged her and kissed her cheeks.

Andy stood watching the French beach attendant's performance as Coby disappeared behind the watersports shack next to the entrance.

This is exactly what she needs...a day at the beach with French boys slobbering over her.

Almost as an after thought, Xavier stepped back, released Dana and extended a hand shake to Andy. "How are you?"

Andy answered dryly, "Fine. And you?"

"Everyday is beautiful on Orient Beach. Will

you stay for lunch?"

"Absolutely!"

"Well the chef has prepared several additions to the menu for today...A braised duck with a mushroom and port wine sauce on a bed of fresh-ly sautéed spinach, Frog's legs in a cream sauce, and a mixed seafood salad!" He took Dana's beach bag and led them to a waiting set of lounge chairs with a large colorful umbrella.

"Do you have the grilled sardines today?"

"Yes! I had some earlier. They are wonderful."

Dana addressed the waiter, "J'aimerais un verre de Chardonnay, s'il vous plaît" she said with a confident American accent to show off her best French phrase.

Xavier looked exasperated. "Your accent is very nice...but please, speak English. I need help. You always help me. Good English means better tips from the tourists."

With concern and a surprised look Andy said, "Are you sure you can drink wine after the bump on the head you took two days ago?"

"Yes, Honey. I even called the doctor this morn-ing while you got your shower. He said it would be alright, but in moderation."

Andy put down his bag and surveyed the

surrounding sunbathers. "Let's start with a chardonnay for Dana, a bucket of ice, and a Carib for me."

Xavier brushed sand off of the chairs and adjusted the umbrella as Dana spread a beach towel on her chair. "Oui, NFL or WFL?"

"WFL, please."

Dana completed the beach setup routine by removing her sarong cover up and bathing suit top. After retrieving a new paperback book from her bag and placing it on her seat, she dropped the back to a reclining position and relaxed.

"Can I get anything else?" Xavier asked as he pretended not to glance approvingly at Dana.

"Yes, one more umbrella but wait about an hour, s'il vous plait." Dana added with a flirtatious smile. She was feeling better. Still self conscious, however, she pulled her hat tighter on her head to conceal her chopped hair.

The waiter was gone in a flash leaving them to settle and get comfortable. Adjusting his chair back to an upright position, Andy sat down, kicked his feet in the sand to dig a little trench, and leaned over to kiss his wife.

Dana accepted the kiss, closed her eyes, and then looked at her husband with a question, "What is WFL, my bartender husband?"

"With Fucking Lime. WFL or NFL, get it?"

"Sorry that I asked."

Andy smirked. "You speak French, I speak Bartender."

Coby raced past them and dove into the sea. After swimming for a few feet, he left the water, shook off and ran to Dana's chair. Andy pulled out a bottle of water and a bowl from his backpack and poured the liquid. The dog lapped it up, shook off more sand and water from his coat, and settled in the sand next to them.

As the three of them fell into the comfort of quiet beach laziness, Xavier silently moved between their chairs with the drink order which he placed on a small table. Without a comment, he disappeared. The beach began to fill and several other couples found spots to enjoy the day. Most were American and had arrived in rental cars or walked from the hotels and villas nearby. A few of the women kept their tops on, but most took advantage of the European flair and reputation of the resort.

Andy's head was buried in his book. Stretching and adjusting her legs, Dana put her wine glass back into the ice bucket and gazed at her husband. "Honey, do you think they're real?"

"No...a great job, but not real."

"I knew it! You weren't reading that book; you were staring at that great set of tits on the woman to my right."

Andy stood and beckoned his wife to join him. "Let's go into the water...okay? I need to get my feet wet."

"So that you can ogle her tits close up as we walk past?"

Andy reached out and helped his wife stand. "Now that sounds like a plan!"

"Just don't forget that I get to have my hair cut and styled before lunch. I hope you brought plenty of Euros!"

When they reached the water's edge and started to wade into the clear sea, Andy turned to his wife, "Did you see the great nails on that woman's hands? The pink color, the sheen, the way her hands match her toe nails, perfectly? All my male friends always notice a woman's nails first."

Dana popped Andy on the arm as he dove under the water laughing and feeling very smug.

On the beach, Andy's cell phone rang inside the backpack. Coby pulled his body further under Dana's lounge chair seeking more shade and enjoying the cool sand. The cell phone continued to ring unanswered.

Chapter 23
Philipsburg Blues

Most police stations are cold, institutional buildings without concern for customer service. The Philipsburg station was no different. In addition to the unfriendliness that existed in the initial reception window, the small lobby was often full of Haitians, Dominicans, and Jamaicans standing in line hoping to receive their work permits. A "wait and see, come back and check again" policy existed. The result was the gathering of hoards of anxious people salivating for a simple piece of paper to give them legal rights to be on the island. With an arrogant show of confidence, smiling police employees walked through the area all day long, entered the private doors using codes on the locks and ignored the crowds.

J.R. Holiday sat in his small executive office

and ran through the details of the murders in his mind. He reclined slightly in the desk chair and had his eyes closed. It was only 9:30 AM, and most of his co-workers had not reported to work. Holiday had been at his desk since before 8 AM. This quiet time was important to him. The pressure was on. The murder of the St. Thomas woman was disturbing, but the murder of another officer's wife had started a flurry of newspaper, local cable TV, and now international interest. Travel blogs and website forums were full of warnings about the island, and rumors were circulating that 60 minutes or CNN would arrive this weekend. The Leader of the ruling party had called him last night at home asking for answers. The Lt. Governor had called him before 6 AM for an update. Messages were piling up at the front desk and on his office voice mail from members of the press who wanted an interview.

His stomach hurt.

"Hey Boss, got a minute?" It was Joseph Davis, the Officer who shared an office with Bart Richardson just down the hall. He stood at the door and appeared stressed beyond belief.

"Good morning, please come in." His chair creaked as he shifted to a straight up position.

Davis entered the room quickly, closed the door and took a seat opposite Holiday. "My wife is so upset by the murder that she took the kids and went to stay with her mother in Grand Case. The press surrounds my car and asks unending questions, and Bart will not answer his cell or his home phone. You should know..."

Holiday waved a signal of dismissal and interrupted. "I know, it's endless...but just wait. Everything calms down in time. In the interim, what did you find out when you interviewed the staff at *Island Ice*?"

Davis shuffled his feet nervously and tapped the floor. "First off, I didn't get much. The Manager, Judith, was nice but unable to provide much in the way of a connection between the two women. The salesman, Chad, is hysterical. What a loony. Probably gay, but what do I know?"

"Good observation."

"The thing that makes me crazy is that the store sells fakes...the diamonds are not real. Our perp must be stupid as hell to kill for knock off jewelry."

Holiday opened his notebook and scribbled a few notes. "Did you interview all the employees?"

"Yes, except for two. One of the salespeople

was out on her regular day off and the other, some Colombian guy who works in the back, has been out sick or something."

"Okay." Holiday continued to write. "Be sure to follow up with both of them."

Davis shifted again in his chair and held his hands clasped tightly in his lap. "Boss, I'm worried about Bart. Desiree was his life. He bragged about the wild sex life they had, he called her several times a day when we worked together, and then there are the kids..."

"I know. We granted him administrative leave with full salary. He needs to see a shrink...he needs some serious grief counseling. The loss of a loved one is terrible with natural causes...but this was a brutal and horrible murder and he knows all the details. He must be crazy with pain and a need to avenge her death. I feel very sorry for him too. But we have work to do...life goes on. The best way to help Bart Richardson right now is to find the killer. We must find answers. Do you understand your job?"

"Yes sir, but..."

"Joseph. Listen to me. Listen to me." Holiday raised his voice. "Get out there and ask questions. Ignore the press! Turn over every leaf that could lead to a connection between the women. Find a motive, not just the missing jewelry. Do your job."

Davis rubbed his hands together and considered his next statement carefully. "Yes, Inspector. I'll do my best. Would you mind if I stop by Bart's house just to check on his state of mind?"

"Not at all, his terrible loss must be devastating and until the autopsy is complete and the medical examiner in Curacao releases the body, he can't even plan a funeral or continue the grieving process. I feel extremely sorry for him. Any support you can give is sure to be appreciated."

Joseph Davis left the room and left the door open just as the cell phone on J.R.'s desk rang.

"Good Morning. Inspector Holiday. How can I help you?" Secretly he hoped that the caller was not from the press.

"Good Morning. I see you are at work early." It was Jack Donnelly. "How did you sleep last night?"

Holiday stood and walked to the door to close it. "My wife says that I was tossing and turning, but damned if I remember. How did you sleep?"

Jack's voice beamed over the phone. "Like a condemned man who was given a pardon, won the lottery, and found out that several beautiful movie stars have the hots for him."

Holiday returned to his desk chair and sat down with a less than graceful plop. "It is amazing what a simple 3 year residency permit can do for you old white guys."

"You got that right."

"Jack, did you call with any news on the murder investigation? I...I'm dealing with a lot of pressure here to produce something fast. Anything. Even someone we can bring in for questioning. Anything!"

There was a pause on the line. "An ounce of appearance is worth a pound of performance?" Jack asked.

"Jack, don't be a skeptic. You know what I am talking about. It gives the press something to chew on and the public feels like progress is being made..."

"Okay, but you first. I am nursing a hangover from last night's celebration of my new legal status."

Holiday opened his notebook and moved the telephone receiver to his other ear. "Honestly Jack, Bart's tragedy is throwing us behind on the investigation. He was conducting interviews on Tuesday and Wednesday. Now we will not be able to find out what he knows. We'll have to start over."

"Poor guy. It would be rather cold of us to grill him on his findings at this point." Jack agreed. "Any leads from the St. Thomas police or the dead woman's co-workers on that island?"

"No, again those conversations were handled by Bart."

"Shit."

Holiday flipped through his notebook. "I assigned a guy named Joseph Davis to the case in Bart's absence. They share an office in this building. Hopefully they talked enough with each other over the past few days that Davis has a feel for the case. He is a good man and a hard worker, but I'll tell you, he is not an experienced murder investigator. He's a street cop with a specialty in retail theft and tourist relations."

"Great," Jack answered sarcastically. "How about Mrs. Richardson's co-workers at *Island Ice*? Any news since you and I went there after the first murder?"

"Officer Davis is working on it. I believe he mentioned that he only had two more staff members to interview." He checked his notes again.

Jack was pacing in his kitchen as he talked on his cell phone. "How about the autopsy reports?

Are they finished on the two women?"

"Negative."

"Any doctors' reports of someone with vicious dog bites needing treatment?"

"We don't know. There are too many independent doctor's offices on the two sides of the island and two hospitals. Plus, most of the French side locations speak little English. We could waste weeks trying to run that down."

How about retail sources that sell the large cable ties? Any leads from that?"

Holiday shifted in his chair again. "I handled two of the hardware stores myself and Bart was supposed to check a few electrical parts companies. Ace Hardware's manager pulled up three cash sales on his computer records over the past two weeks. No way to know who bought them. A smaller store near the salt pond only writes hand receipts and there is no computer record of sales."

"How do they know what they are selling and what they need to re-order?"

"The manager said that they simply eye ball the shelves."

"Any anonymous tips received on the Crime Line?"

"Negative. But keep in mind that today is the

first day the story will be in the news media."

"You're right...any druggies trying to sell stolen jewelry?"

"Jack, this is not New York City! We don't have undercover cops working that kind of stuff. Besides, we know all of the druggies. You can walk out on Front Street and ask them if you want."

"Then round up the usual suspects."

Holiday groaned, "You have been watching too many reruns of Casablanca, Rick, I mean Jack."

"No offense taken...Louie, this looks like the beginning of a long but successful investigation."

"Jack, I hope so. I really hope so. Because right now the lack of progress is making my stomach hurt."

Chapter 24
Bart in Mourning

B art Richardson rolled over on his living room sofa and looked at his watch. It was already past 9 AM, but he was just waking up from an unsettling and miserable night of broken sleep. Dressed in jeans, a polo shirt and tennis shoes, he had passed out on the sofa in the early hours of the morning. He was in a fog of alcohol and runaway emotions. Not sure how much he had slept, he was not completely sure of the day of the week either. A bottle of rum on the table only had a few ounces in it and there were several empty beer bottles on the floor. There was a full bottle of valium sitting next to a box of cold Kentucky Fried Chicken, both unopened. The Government's Doctor for the Department had insisted that Bart take the pills for the next few days in order to calm his anxiety. He barely remembered identifying his wife's body or the ride home Thursday with the food and medication. He hated to take pills. Bart had no appetite and the sight of the greasy box of chicken made him nauseous.

He tried to stand, and then sat back down to wait for his dizziness to pass. With his head in his hands, he leaned forward and tried to stop shaking. The pain from this hangover was more than he had ever experienced. Fresh thoughts of Desiree hit him hard and tears started to flow down his cheeks.

After a few minutes he picked up his cell phone, examining the display.

17 missed calls

Most of the calls he remembered seeing on the caller ID as they happened. Friends, other police officers, family and of course the press started ringing his cell within an hour of the discovery of Desiree's body at the hotel property. He had spoken with the first five or six of them before deciding that it was more than he could deal with. For no real reason, he scrolled through the list of missed calls. Some of the numbers in the display were unfamiliar to him. Some of the numbers were USA area codes.

I should've cut the fuckin' thing off and let them all go straight to voice mail...

It had been difficult enough speaking with Inspector Holiday while requesting personal leave. Well meaning groups of shocked and concerned people who knew him and his wife were adding to his confusion and turmoil. He needed time alone.

He missed his children, but knew that they were in good hands with their Grandmother. He did not want them around. He simply could not face them. He would need time to grieve before ever again becoming their loving father. For now, they were better off away from him. Both boys had Desiree's facial features and beautiful skin. The mere thought of seeing them anytime soon made his heart ache.

Once he steadied himself, he walked to the half bath in the hallway and entered the small room. He had avoided the master bedroom and bathroom since returning home yesterday. He knew that he was not ready to face those memories. After switching on the light over the vanity, he saw pieces of vomit dried on the toilet seat and vaguely remembered being sick during the night. He urinated and flushed. Turning the cold water on full force, he scooped up the liquid with his cupped hands and splashed it on his face. The tears came again as he held onto the top of the vanity with one hand while he wiped his eyes with the other. His cell phone began ringing on the coffee table where he had left it. Somewhere in the background, a knock on the front door caught his attention and annoyed him. He closed the bathroom door and switched on the exhaust fan to drown out the sounds.

Bart was not sure how long he had been in the small room but he felt better. After removing his now damp shirt, he made his way carefully through the living room. Pausing at the sofa, he retrieved the KFC box and some of the empty beer bottles and discarded them in the kitchen trash. He took a fresh bottle of rum from the counter and pulled two more cold beers from the refrigerator before heading back to the sofa. There was no joy in his movements.

He needed time to mourn. He needed time to sleep. He needed time to weep. He needed time to think. Mostly he needed time to hunt.

There's a murderer out there and I need to find him before anyone else does...

Chapter 25
Miguel and Kesia's Date

Friday morning before the sun came up, Kesia slipped out of her double bed carefully without waking Miguel and walked naked to her bathroom. Two nights together making passionate love had given her a case of honeymoon disease. She was sore but happy. Without cutting on the light, she sat down on the toilet seat and started to pee. When they weren't having sex, they were drinking wine or enjoying cooking and eating in her small kitchen. He had called into work sick yesterday and she had the day off, so everything had fallen into place perfectly. She had left him briefly for her trip to feed her mother's cat while mom was off island, then she made a quick stop at the Grand Marche grocery for more wine. She worried that he would bolt during her absence, but he didn't. As a couple they had not left her house. She doubted that any of the neighbors knew or cared that he was there. The perfect date, Miguel had been her constant and attentive companion. He never once mentioned that he needed to rush off in the morning like so many of her past dates. She wished it could last forever. She sighed. Today was another matter. Both of them were on the schedule to work and with six ships in the harbor, begging off would anger both the boss and her co-workers. Her best friend at the store knew that Miguel was coming to dinner on Wednesday night, so tongues would wag if she failed to show up today.

When he arrived two nights ago, she had greeted him at her door with some apprehension. He was bandaged on both arms and she smelled beer on his breath. While most men on St. Martin stopped for a drink or two on the way home, Miguel had come over slightly drunk. It upset her. She wondered if he had been in a fight outside some brothel. Then again, his clothes were clean. He had put her at ease and explained that a dog had attacked him when he was helping a friend clear a lot over near Cupecoy Beach. Still, even though they knew each other from work Kesia was hoping for a polite and relaxed dinner before jumping into bed with him. As things happened, they never even considered eating dinner until almost eleven o'clock that night. She opened a bottle of wine for them, they sat close together on her sofa and the next thing she knew they were naked and breathing heavily. Of course, she had slept with some men in her past after just meeting them. A girl living alone has her needs. Kesia admitted that she had been making eyes at Miguel for months...so, what the hell? Their sex was wonderful. Despite his protests of having a longtime love back in Colombia, Miguel was ravenous when it came to oral sex with her. She was in heaven. After a series of intense orgasms, she actually had to ask him to allow her to touch his penis. She had never experienced such attention from a man before. Most men had been quick to enter her the moment she spread her legs and then leave once they finished. Miguel was a jewel. He knew how to satisfy a woman. She liked that.

"I was wondering where you were? The bed was so lonely without you." Miguel stood at the door to the bathroom watching her sit on the toilet. His arms were crossed and she could see his wide open eyes as the predawn light from the sunrise started to fill the room.

B.D. ANDERSON

"Miguel. Please, you're watching me pee. Close the door!"

Also naked he stepped into the room and moved against her. Reaching down, he rubbed her nipples between the thumbs and fingers of his hands. She moaned with pleasure. Opening and closing her eyes as she enjoyed his touch, she watched as his erection formed a few inches from her mouth.

Not caring that she was sitting on the toilet, she rubbed his penis and took him into her mouth. She intended to stroke and suck him until he climaxed. Even though she would have loved another episode in bed, she was too sore down there for any more activity this morning.

Sensing her desire to take control, Miguel focused on the pleasure of her wet lips and watched her hair curl around her face as she moved her head up and down. When he exploded in her mouth and she continued to suck on him, he remembered the last time Desiree had done the same thing to him in her marital bed.

Looking up from her seated position, Kesia watched his face show pleasure then serenity. She kept him in her mouth as long as she could.

With a broad smile, Miguel whispered to her. "Oh baby, you are so good to me."

When they finally separated, she stood and grabbed his hand. "Come, let's take a shower and get ready for work."

Miguel seemed suddenly distracted and deep in thought. "Can we just call in sick today?"

Kesia put her hands on her hips and struck a confrontational stance. "You are out of your mind, Boyfriend! There are six ships on the schedule today and we could get in some serious trouble not showing up. Besides, unlike you, I earn commission on sales."

Miguel bit his lip. "I...I...just want us to stay together. This is fun. Can I come back tonight?"

The question was magic to her ears. "Of course, of course! I can't wait. This time we have to have dinner first, okay?"

"Si, senorita. I will only kiss you before dinner."

She thought about the first night he arrived. "Tonight, you wait. No kissing, no touching, until later..."

They stepped into her shower and turned on the water. As the room filled with a steamy mist, they took turns scrubbing each other with a fragrant bath and body gel. This time she avoided touching his penis in fear that they would be hours late for work if he was aroused again. After helping her step from the wet shower stall, Miguel patted her with a fresh towel until she was completely dry. Then he left her to apply her make up while he dressed in the bedroom.

A few minutes later she heard him call out, "I'm off to work and will see you around seven tonight. Let's remain private at work, comprehend?"

She felt disappointment at being reminded of his wish for secrecy, "I understand. Not a word."

As the front door closed behind Miguel, she wondered if the employee buzz about their new relationship would anger him later today. It was bound to leak back to him that everyone knew why he had missed work yesterday.

I hope I didn't mess this up with my big mouth...damn it.

Chapter 26
Read All About It

When the two local newspapers hit the street early that morning all copies were quickly purchased by locals wanting to read about the murders, especially the one at the new hotel involving the Police Officer's wife. Desiree was well known in the retail communities on both Front and Back Street. Strikingly attractive, always impeccably dressed, she attracted the attention of men and women alike. The first murder, now finally reported, of a female visitor from St. Thomas was given some coverage but the attention from the public was pale in comparison to the intrigue surrounding the death of Desiree Richardson. Even before the first store opened for business, the employee lounge areas in the entire downtown area were a twitter. Rumors were flying and speculation over suspects bordered on the absurd at times. From the minute her body was discovered, the telephone lines had been jammed with phone call after phone call spreading the awful news. In the islands, the coconut telegraph works rapidly but not accurately.

With plenty of time to spare before *Island Ice* would open for the day, Kesia drove to her favorite parking spot near the salt pond and cursed under her breath when she saw all spaces taken. She turned the car on the road away from town and resigned herself to a longer walk than usual. It didn't matter to her. Today the palm trees were greener, the sky was a vibrant blue, and the fluffy white clouds all smiled at her like chubby cherubs. She was in love...or at least in lust.

As she dropped her keys into her purse, she noticed that her cell phone was off. Hoping not to be disturbed when Miguel came for dinner, she had shut it off on Wednesday. Caught up in the lovemaking and in entertaining her new man, she completely forgot about the phone. This walk would give her some time to check the voice mail. She dialed the code and entered her password. There were twenty two messages! She covered her mouth and giggled. If only her friends knew why she wasn't answering the phone for almost two days...

The first three calls were hang ups.

Why do people listen to the whole voice mail message then hang up without saying anything? Weird. It pisses me off to waste my minutes on that.

The fourth message was her mom reminding her to check on the cat and clean the litter box.

Delete

The fifth message was from the beauty salon reminding her of a nail appointment on Saturday morning.

Delete...she might be too busy with Miguel to go! Her nail polish could wait.

The sixth, seventh, and eighth messages were all hang ups.

Delete, delete, delete

The ninth message was from Judith, the store Manager. A policeman named Davis had been to the store on Thursday afternoon and interviewed staff. Kesia needed to call him. There was an investigation in progress about some jewelry sold last Monday. Judith left Davis's cell phone and office numbers. She did not repeat them and Kesia could not make out the last numbers.

Save...I wonder what's up?

The tenth message was from Police Officer Davis. He left three numbers including his home and asked that she call anytime at night up to 11 PM.

Save... does he want a date? Who works until almost midnight on a retail store case? No one.

The eleventh message was from her best friend at work and she sounded hysterical.

"You won't believe what's happened. Call me"

Delete, I'll see her in a few minutes.

The next three messages were almost the same.

"I know Miguel isn't out sick...he's in your bed. Call me."

"Call me, call me, stop your fuck fest and get your ass out of bed. I have unbelievable news!"

"I drove past your apartment and saw both your cars. You little whore! Call me." Her girlfriend ended the call giggling.

Kesia was almost to the store so she deleted these messages and dropped the phone into her purse. There would be plenty of time to hear the rest of them during her lunch break. She turned down an ally and took a shortcut to the employee's entrance at the rear of the store. A security guard standing outside spotted her and opened the door with his usual lusty leer at her chest. She pulled her jacket over her low cut top as she walked closer to him.

"Good morning" she announced with a forced sound of pleasantness. "Thank you!"

"Good morning, Beautiful Lady." His crooked smile showed jagged teeth and a bright gold cap.

She ignored the compliment and stepped inside the secure employee's hallway. Once the security latch clicked, she would be able to punch in her code and enter the rest of the building. The guard waited for more of a response to his flirtation but Kesia remained silent. Finally the guard grunted and pushed the door shut. Quickly her access was granted and she headed to the employee lockers and kitchen area. While most stores and businesses designate extra back rooms for Employee use, they are often an afterthought. Most are dingy due to poor lighting and often furnished with cast off items, with very little consideration given for the staff's comfort or enjoyment. This was not the case at *Island Ice*. Extra windows had been carefully placed to capture both the morning and afternoon sun that flooded the room with natural light. Large Italian tiles decorated the floors and coordinated small tiles covered the counters and sink areas. Employees had choices for seating from traditional dining tables in groups or soft sofas in random placements. Mornings were a time to enjoy a quick breakfast with co-workers before the store opened. Retention was excellent. Many of the employees had years of seniority since they had been with the original jewelry and gift store in that location before *Island Ice* took over. For the most part, it was a happy and close knit group.

Kesia walked into a flurry of voices and a sea of bright blue uniforms. Both men and women in sales wore blue coats with tan pants or skirts and crisp white shirts. The laundered uniforms were provided by the company and a quick change was necessary when reporting to work. Dressing rooms were down the hall. Most of the women were talking at once and several were holding copies of the morning's paper. Kesia opened her locker and put her purse inside. As she selected a fresh shirt and her suit from the open rack of garments labeled with her name, she could hear bits and pieces of conversation spinning in the background.

"I can't believe it. How could this happen?"

"I just called her Wednesday night and we talked about the Church flea market donations for this Sunday."

"We were gonna swap days off next week."

"She didn't deserve this."

"It says here that she was strangled."

"I heard that she was raped and stabbed to death."

"Someone told me that she was killed on the French side and her body was dumped at the hotel on the Dutch side."

"It could have been drug dealers. Like in Mexico. They kill the family of police."

"My aunt, she say dat dey found her 'fore she died. I think she named her killer."

"What about that guy from the Westin?"

"What guy?"

"The manager...I answered the store phone and he was asking for her. A lot."

"No. You're joking us."

"That new manager, the Italian guy found her and went nuts...my sister works the front desk and she says he collapsed and hasn't been back to work since."

"Do you think he did it? Italian men are emotional people. Passionate and crazy."

"Why would he kill her? He was sending her stuff by special courier from the Westin."

"How you know dat?"

"I accepted a package and asked the guy. He said it was from the hotel. Private. For Desiree."

"And calling her at the store...I answered two

of the calls. His accent was easy to figure out."

"I can't believe dat she's dead."

"He had the hots for her, if you ask me."

"I can't believe Judith didn't close the store to-day out of respect."

"Shit, what are you talking about girl? With this slow economy and six ships in port. Are you crazy? The dead are dead. I got three grandchildren living with me. The living need to eat."

Not completely understanding the thread of the entire subject at hand, Kesia was nevertheless relieved that she and Miguel were not the topic of this morning's gossip; Kesia scanned the faces in the room looking for her friend. Considering the group's mention of a murder, she suddenly pan-icked. Her friend was not there.

"Where is Wanda?" she almost had to scream over the chatter to be heard.

With her glasses pushed down on her nose, one of the older ladies looked up from a table and said, "She in da washroom."

"Thank God." Kesia thought as she moved closer to the lady and asked, "Who died?"

"Girl, where you been?" the woman sat back in amazement. "Since dey found de body yesterday da whole island's been a buzz. It's all dey been talking 'bout."

Kesia blushed. "I...I...I was busy at home with a new project and cut off my phone."

"Huh. Well you must've stuck yo head up yo butt too if you ain't heard that Desiree was murdered at dat new hotel."

Kesia felt mixed emotions of guilt and shock. Just a few moments ago she had been remembering the great sex she had enjoyed over the past two nights, and now the unthinkable was slapping her in the face. "No. Not Desiree! No. That is not possible. She and I just worked together Wednesday."

"Believe it, Girl. You listen to me. She be stone cold dead. Murdered by strangulation, according to dis paper. Dey sent her body to Curacao for an autopsy. Poor ting."

"Where is her husband? Was he hurt in the attack?"

"No. She was alone. Dat man Holiday..." the woman paused and sipped her coffee. "He no fool. He probably got to the husband fast, took away his police gun and sent him home. Last ting this island needs is a John Wayne policeman out taking revenge for his wife's murder."

"What about her children?" Kesia was clearly

horrified as the news sunk in.

"Wit da Grandmudder. Tank da Lord. Dat man not in any shape now to care for dem children. He worshiped his wife. My friends at da station said dat he fainted when he heard da news from Holiday. Big man like dat. Torn apart by grief."

A soft chime sounded twice alerting the staff to the final twenty minutes before opening. The warehouse and vault workers had finished stocking the display cases and everyone needed to prepare for taking their position on the sales floor.

As the women filed out of the room, Kesia looked down the hall towards the vault hoping to catch a glimpse of Miguel. He was nowhere to be seen.

Damn it. He promised me he would come to work. Where is he?

Chapter 27

KaKao Restaurant on Orient Beach

Andy finished his Carib beer as Jean Paul, another of their favorite waiters, swung by the table with a replacement just in time.

Andy raised the bottle. "Merci" he said with a friendly wave.

With superb efficiency, the young French man hurried to another table. Andy had moved from the beach to the KaKao restaurant after about an hour or so in anticipation of Dana's return from the beauty salon. He knew that the therapy of a soothing head massage and shampoo before her haircut would be helpful in overcoming the trauma of Wednesday's beating. Oddly, the threatening experiences were becoming less nightmarish. He remembered the home invasion they had suffered a few years back and the near robbery at their restaurant after they purchased it. The first event almost caused them to separate, and yet the second put them back into control as a team. It could have been Dana's Army training, but this time she snapped back emotionally ahead of her physical mending. Perhaps they were becoming hardened like professional fighters. He wasn't sure.

The dining area consisted of small tables scattered in random angles with seating for four to six persons under thatched roofs. The walkways, tables and supports were all wooden and very Caribbean. The landscaping was rich with palms, flowering tropical plants, and freshly raked sand. Privacy was achieved naturally without the need for other barriers. Most tables had a full view of the beach lounge chairs, umbrellas, and the clear turquoise sea. Because many of the women were sunbathing topless, a few of the women at lunch also chose to leave the bathing suit tops off.

Andy considered this a good thing.

"Watching the beautiful half naked women and wishing you were single, I see." Dana teased as she returned from her beauty appointment and sat down with a bag from the Bikini Beach Boutique. Her power shopping experience appeared to have been successful.

Caught staring again, Andy was on the defense. "Men can window shop without buying, you know. Unlike women...what you got there in that bag, ma'am"

"My husband promised me new bathing suits, so I took him up on the offer."

Andy groaned as he remembered. "I probably over sold the idea of a trip to the beach today."

"Not at all...where is our dog?"

"Last time I saw him, he was playing Frisbee with a topless brunette on the beach."

"God, he is worse than you are."

Andy agreed. "Arf! I mean...oui. But then again, he doesn't have a beautiful wife."

"Awe, you're so sweet."

Andy motioned to Jean Paul to bring Dana's wine. "Okay. Off with the hat. I want to see what the stylist did with your hair..."

Dana removed her beach straw hat and shook her head from side to side to fluff her hair.

"Okay, baby. That is much better. They definitely layered the locks of hair to cover your duct tape pruning job."

"Thanks for the encouragement. However, I won't be jumping into the sea and getting my hair wet in public for long time."

"You look sexy."

"I am convinced that short hair will be a lot more work than leaving it long."

"Maybe, but now your older girl friends will be happy! They've been pushing you to cut it for years."

"Now would be a good time to shut up, Darling."

Doume, one of the restaurant owners, approached their table with a broad smile and his arms outstretched. After kissing Dana on both cheeks, he extended an American style handshake to Andy.

"How are things on the Dutch side?" he asked.

Andy was honest. "Very busy. As you know, the cost conscious travelers watch the Euro and Dollar values carefully and spend most of their vacation eating on our side of the island because of the exchange rate." He tried not to gloat. It was a fact in the island economy.

"And then the American women are running round topless on our side!" Doume responded playfully. "You get the money and we on the French side get the tits!"

Andy laughed with him. "This argument is

turning against me. I'm winning the unimportant battle and losing the more important war."

Dana kicked him under the table.

Jean Paul returned with a bottle of Chardonnay and three glasses then slipped away. Doume begged off and walked toward Le Village d'Orient to check his other restaurant before the dinner opening.

As Andy reached for the bottle of cold wine, a female arm extended and took it first.

"Here, let me serve…"

The voice was familiar. It belonged to Megan, a woman who had left the island to live in New Orleans. She stood barefoot in a bikini and had obviously come up from the beach out of their view.

Caught off guard, Andy and Dana gazed at her with complete surprise. She looked the same as they remembered from their last meeting in the French Quarter. Her blond hair was slightly longer and she had a few more smile lines, but the sparkle was still in her eyes.

"Seems to me I have done this for you before… did you order three glasses again so that I could join you?" Her distinctive South African English accent was as charming as ever.

Dana responded before Andy, "Please, sit down! We would love for you to join us…"

Megan made a quick show of pouring the wine and slipped into the seat next to Dana. Andy noticed the absence of any engagement ring or wedding band.

They raised the glasses for a toast, as Andy avoided the subject of Megan's return to St. Martin. "Cheers, ladies! Let's look at the menu...Megan, do you have a friend with you today that can join us for lunch?"

Megan sipped her wine and took the lead knowing that her former bosses would have many questions. "I am here alone."

Dana was not as inclined to tip toe around Megan's personal life as was Andy. "So, Megan. What brings you back to the island? We thought the guy in New Orleans was a serious and permanent relationship. We expected a wedding announcement last year."

"Me too, but it was a sham. I found myself in Megan's usual life altering dilemma. You know. Do I stay or do I go? Just like the song. Remember, I entered the United States as a tourist. I worked as a waitress under the immigration radar and avoided detection. I was paid in cash, I lived at his apartment, and nothing was in my name, and I didn't even need a driver's license. We walked everywhere in the French Quarter and it was easy for me to blend in. Then the Casino started discussing a possible transfer to Vegas for him and it was clear that he did not plan to take me."

Dana took Megan's hand in hers. "I'm so sorry."

Andy was more pragmatic. "Love sucks, sometimes."

Jean Paul returned to the table with a large basket of fresh French bread and seasoned olive oil for dipping. Quickly sizing up the table's need to continue their discussion in private, he slipped away without asking for the lunch order.

Sensing that Dana was not going to restrict anyone to whole grain bread today, Andy reached for the loaf and tore off a large hunk. It was his way of dealing with the emotional issue.

Megan's eyes swelled with tears. Dana put her arm around her and hugged her.

Megan leaned into Dana's embrace. "Thank you. I actually just arrived yesterday. I'm staying with my friend, Ingrid, in Philipsburg. I didn't know where to go. So, St. Maarten seemed like a place I could start over. Again."

"Is she still living in the penthouse of the Naked Boy Apartments on the beach?"

"God, yes!" Megan replied cheerfully. "The area has been cleaned up somewhat from years ago, but it still can be rather colorful after dark." She used a napkin to wipe her eyes then discreetly blew her nose.

Andy looked up from his menu and remembered his friend from Canada who had lived in the building. Most nights the homeless drug addicts would steal the battery from his car and then sell it back to him the next day for a few dollars. The social exchange was weird, but at least the battery terminals were kept clean of caustic build up from the salty air near the beach. Plus, the car was always being watched. Steve had called it his security service.

Now composed, Megan asked, "Was that your dog I saw on the beach with some topless brunette? They were playing with a Frisbee."

All three of them broke into laughter and raised their glasses.

"To Coby! Andy's son through and through!" Dana shouted just a little louder than necessary, but everyone felt more at ease with the light distraction.

Megan leaned forward with a concerned look,

"Dana, might I ask you a personal question?"

"Sure."

"Why in the world did you cut your beautiful long curly hair?"

Chapter 28
The Stake Out

The two sullen men wearing jeans and St. Martin T-shirts sat under a tree shaded from the warm morning sun. They knew it was sure to be a hot day due to the lack of wind. If necessary, they would be here for hours. Neither man spoke to the other. Brick and Bucket, fresh from Mr. G's office, were on a mission. The surly Russian had left little confusion about the task at hand. The stupid Colombian had to be found. He was killing women to get the jewelry back and that endangered the whole operation. They did not want to think about the consequences if they failed to stop him.

Groups of happy and sunburned tourists passed in front of them loaded with shopping bags, new cameras and open beers. Several staff workers from the stores scurried by with deliveries to sister stores or with jewelry that needed to be sized at the various gold repair shops found in many second floor offices. With few exceptions, most of the tourists strolling by avoided the men. No one extended a greeting or acknowledgement. Bucket and Brick looked like men who were best ignored. Even the Taxi drivers who trolled looking for fares back to the ship acted as if they did not see them.

Brick punched Bucket and pointed down the street at two of the Special Tourist Police who were approaching them. The man and woman in uniform were smiling and greeting visitors as they walked leisurely through the crowd. Before the officers looked ahead or noticed the two men sitting on the old stone wall, Bucket stood and walked to a display window in front of a jewelry store and Brick strolled nonchalantly towards the bay and the boardwalk. Once the police passed, both men reappeared at the observation spot and resumed their watch for the Colombian. Until they heard of the murders this morning, they had never considered hunting him. The job was to recover the other two rings. Now everything had changed. This man must be silenced before the police questioned him. Too much was riding on Miguel's knowledge of their operation. Police interrogations were known to be tough. If he suddenly had diarrhea of the mouth, the stupid fuck would sing like a canary and ruin everything. They needed to zip his big mouth before he blew the whole deal. They enjoyed their jobs. They enjoyed the easy cash. They also enjoyed the power over others that physical intimidation gives to men with strong muscles and simple brains. Brick and Bucket were professional bullies. They breathed and savored it like others enjoyed the sun and sand of this Caribbean island.

Just a few feet down the street, a local crackhead stepped out to check the tourist scene looking to score a loose bag from an unsuspecting shopper. When he saw the two thugs under the tree, he reconsidered and quickly disappeared back into an ally.

The lunch hour was approaching without a sighting. The Colombian was either staying inside his store or he had not come to work today. Bucket whispered to Brick to go and check Miguel's apartment. After that, he could ride up to Guana Bay and see if Miguel was stalking the woman who bought the third ring. Bucket would stay in place and cover this area alone. Brick did not reply, instead he nodded his head in agreement and slipped away by following a large truck down the narrow street.

Bucket took advantage of his partner's absence and walked a block in the opposite direction to find a street vendor. He would drink with his partner, but he liked to eat alone. After purchasing a hot dog and a beer for two bucks, he walked to Back Street near the *Island Ice* store. Spotting a large empty paint container, he flipped it over and sat down to enjoy the lunch. A stray dog approached and made eye contact. Sensing the unfriendly and evil nature of the man, the dog broke into a run and did not look back.

The dog's flight caught the attention of Miguel who was walking to the same hot dog vendor after exiting *Island Ice* from the back entrance. Luck was with him. Bucket had his full attention on the food and did not look up.

Oh fuck! I don't need to be seen by that asshole.

Miguel side stepped and ducked into the first passageway. He was hungry. That girl was working him to death in the sack and he needed some high carb food for energy. Two or three hot dogs smothered in mayo, mustard and ketchup would do the trick. The buns were always fresh and steamed. Just like his new girlfriend.

Thank God I don't have to go to my apartment tonight. Safe, for now. I just need to stay out of sight.

After leaving Kesia's house this morning, he rode over to the French side of the island, parked and debated his options for the day. Going to work was risky, even though he had promised her. Bucket and Brick were out there and they were sure to be hunting for him to cough up the missing rings. When he had finally reported to work almost three hours later, he had slipped in quietly and unnoticed. Staying mostly in the vault to avoid contact with his boss or the others, had worked well for him. Conversation at the store needed to be minimal while he thought of a new plan for saving his ass. He signed a few routine forms and sent a few emails to the Company Headquarters. He overheard two of the warehouse men and a driver talking some shit in low voices as they walked through the back, but he had no interest in joining their constant and stupid bantering about each other's love life. He thought for a moment that he heard them say Desiree's name, but he couldn't be certain. That was one person that he definitely needed to avoid all association with today. Until he could come up with another approach to retrieving those rings, it was best to keep his head low and stay as invisible as possible.

Walking as fast as he could away from Bucket and towards Point Blanche, he found the next street vendor. This food stand had a more elaborate display of local favorites. Chicken, ribs and hot dogs cooked on fiery coals in a converted oil drum. The owner, a heavy man wearing a white sleeveless T-shirt, stood over the barbecue marinating the meats and controlling the flames. The aroma drifting up and down the street was smoky and savory. Miguel's stomach growled as he crossed the street to make a quick purchase of lunch when one of the ladies selling newspapers to passing cars caught his eye. Sitting comfortably on a large rock, she was holding up a paper and reading it with both arms out stretched. The front page was clearly visible to him and he saw the headline of the police officer's wife being murdered the day before. Stunned, he stood in the middle of the narrow street until a car's horn sounded. Bart Richardson's face was staring at him from the news print.

"Hey lady, can I buy a paper?"

"No, mon. Sold out."

Miguel reached into his pocket and pulled out his small roll of cash. "How about two dollars for your copy?"

"No, mon. I not finish."

He rolled off a ten dollar bill and held it up. "How about ten dollars? I just want the front page. You keep the rest."

Mulling over the offer, she quickly separated the front page and snatched the money from his hands. "You crazy like a white man."

Chapter 29
The One Piece Bikini

The day continued on Orient Beach full of humorous stories, good food and the joy of the reunion. Dana told Megan the little she remembered about the attack on Wednesday while she was working in her garden and the horror of removing duct tape from her hair. Andy boasted about the success of the Former Life Bar and the plans they had set for the future. Megan compared the drunken tourists in New Orleans with drunken tourists in St. Martin. She had experience with all of them. Often they laughed until they cried. All three of the friends avoided any discussion of Conrad, her last boyfriend on St. Maarten, who still lived on the island. In the same spirit, no one brought up a discussion of the murder of one of Andy's past business associates and Megan's boss at the time, Nat. Some ghosts were best forgotten. After she helped Dana finish the bottle of wine, Megan was feeling less lost and more in control of her life again. To Andy, Dana seemed to have recovered from some of trauma of the attack thanks to Megan's companionship. Andy quietly hoped that Dana would become friskier by the time they returned home. Sex healed all wounds in the world of Andy and Dana.

From the garden entrance, a man addressed them with a loud challenge. "I was worried about you! Now I find you with another man!" the voice was a familiar one.

As they looked up, the startled group saw Jack standing with his hands on his hips in mock protest.

"Dana, you have me worried to death about your medical condition and then I find you on the beach, drinking wine, and hanging out with this old guy. I am shocked."

Megan got the joke. Andy and Dana, who groaned in unison, were used to his over the top confrontations in public. Once, he stood in line at the ultra conservative downtown pharmacy with Dana and asked her boldly, "Honey, did you get my double dose of Viagra? It's been weeks since we had sex and I need your love..."

Dana almost killed him outside in the parking lot.

He had defended himself by explaining, "At least I didn't ask you if you needed more Depends."

"May I join you?" Jack asked with a devilish grin as he took the seat next to Andy and across from Megan.

Looking directly into Megan's eyes, he waited for her response or at least an introduction by his friends. She turned away slightly and placed her hands together on the table. Jack took the opportunity to appraise her figure in the small bikini she was wearing.

Andy, missing the exchange between the two singles, grinned as he spoke. "Once again, Jack, your alimony payment to Dana is late and you expect us to buy you a beer. Have you no shame?"

With his gaze still focused on Megan, Jack asked, "I'm sorry. Did I take your husband's seat? I didn't mean to barge in..."

This time, Megan held his stare then looked at Andy and back at Dana. "No, I'm alone. My old bosses were kind enough to invite me to lunch."

Dana interrupted before anyone could continue. "Megan is our former employee. That makes us her former bosses. Not her *old bosses*. Besides we are about to offer her a job."

Instantly Megan glowed. In less than twenty four hours since she returned to St. Martin with some trepidation, she was not only accepted by Andy and Dana; now she was offered employment.

Something about Megan was familiar to Jack, but he couldn't quite put his finger on it. Of course, he was a regular at the Chill Grill since Andy and Dana opened it, so he could have seen this young woman in passing. How he could have missed those dazzling blue eyes puzzled him. Her voice was soft yet firm, and the English accent was charming. She had to be in her mid to late 30's given her emerging laugh lines, and except for the diamond studs in her ears, she was not wearing any jewelry. No wedding or engagement ring. He felt a spark of interest. He hoped that she was feeling the same.

Dana spoke. "**Hellooo**, Jack. Are you there? You seemed to have drifted off for a moment."

Jolted out of his daydreaming thoughts of Megan, Jack straightened up and said, "Sorry, I was wondering when Andy would finally get the hint and order a cold beer for me."

Jean Paul walked near by to serve another table

and Dana caught his attention with a quick raise of her hand.

"Jean Paul, a Carib beer for our friend please and some dessert menus!"

"It's time for me to visit the bathroom" Andy announced as he stood up.

Dana joined him and held his hand. "Me too, you guys get to know each other better and we'll be right back."

As they strolled hand in hand down the wood planked walkway towards the restaurant's bathroom facility, Andy discreetly said "Do you think we should leave those two alone?"

"Depends on what you mean?"

Andy waved hello to the bartender as they passed the crowd at the bar and then leaned closer to his wife's ear. "Well, the last time she was on this island, Jack was hunting her."

"Hold that thought. Right now, your wife has to pee."

Husband and wife disappeared into side by side stalls in the unisex bathroom.

Andy was the first to emerge and stop to wash his hands. Dana joined him at the sink.

"Are you concerned that I offered her a job without asking you first?" she said as she pulled off a sheet of paper to dry her hands.

"No honey. We are partners and you are the expert in handling the staff, not me. I pay the bills and keep the government requirements current. Besides, we are short of workers at the moment."

Dana shrugged. "Thanks for reminding me that I haven't been to work in three days!"

Their conversation was interrupted by a large black woman in a full sun dress carrying a new beach bag entering the toilet area. She looked puzzled as she moved her head from side to side and examined the room.

"Excuse me. Where is the Ladies Room?" her accent was strongly Northeastern USA.

Dana waved nonchalantly and pointed to the various doors to the stalls. "You are in a French style restroom. Men and women together...pick a door, pick any door."

The woman's hand moved immediately to her mouth in a kneejerk reaction of self consciousness. "Oh my! I don't know if I can do this" she replied as if talking to herself.

Andy stepped out of the area and left Dana to console the shocked and rather anxious lady.

"Don't worry. You'll be fine. After all, you're in a foreign country. The culture is different from home. Are you in a hotel or visiting on a cruise ship?"

Dana's obvious American accent momentarily soothed the woman's concern.

"On a cruise ship...my husband read the day excursions and picked this half day on Orient Beach. We have never been to the Caribbean before."

Dana stepped back as two topless women speaking French entered the room and separated to enter side by side stalls. "I wonder why he decided that...has he always been a beach lover?" Dana asked slyly.

This made the visiting American laugh out loud, "You must be kidding. He didn't even own a swim suit that fit him until I bought one for him in the ship's mall of stores yesterday. Now I see why he booked this day at the beach. What an adolescent. Men! They're so damn horny."

Dana agreed with a nod of her head. "Yes, they are. Thank the lord."

"I'm gonna kill him."

Dana flashed her latest ring purchase from *Island Ice*. "Oh, I don't know...it seems like a great opportunity for you to take him jewelry shopping before the sun sets."

"Damn, woman. You are a wise one."

The two women separated with grins on their faces as Dana returned to the restaurant bar area to find Andy. She spotted him sitting on a bar stool with a slightly grey haired black man toasting cold beers.

"Dana, meet my new friend from New Jersey. Walt, this is my girlfriend and wife, Dana!"

Walt extended his hand for a shake and Dana stepped forward. As he looked up, she leaned over and kissed each of his cheeks in the traditional greeting.

"Wow! I like this place" he exclaimed. "It's been a long time since I was kissed by a pretty woman that I don't know. Nice to meet you Dana...did you see my wife in the ladies room?"

"It's a fun story. I'll let her tell you when she comes out. Nice to meet you too, Walt."

Walt caught the attention of the bartender. "Would you like a drink, Dana?"

"Thank you, water would be great. We have been celebrating this fantastic day with food, wine and friends. It's nice to add more. Friends, that is."

"Ice water for the pretty lady!" Walt looked at Andy as a cold bottle of French water appeared in front of them. Andy stood and Dana took his seat. As he raised his beer bottle to toast Dana, Walt spoke again. "Speaking of stories, your husband tells me that you guys live here. It must be nice. What a life. How did you talk Dana into this, Andy?"

"It was easy, actually. We all have a dream of someday...you know. Someday I will do this, someday I will do that...then you wake up and check a calendar."

Walt was confused but polite. "I don't understand."

"Sure you do. The calendar has Mondays, Tuesdays, Wednesdays etc. but there is never a Someday. Then something happens to make you prioritize your life and follow your dreams."

Walt sipped his beer and became serious. "Strange you should say that. My younger brother and I told each other for years that someday we would take our wives on a cruise. He died recently from a heart attack. He had just turned 44 years old. Within the next month, I booked this cruise."

"Makes sense to me. Sorry for your loss." Andy raised his beer in salute. "To your brother."

Both men took another sip.

"Once I read a quote by former President Jimmy Carter. He said that we are old when regrets replace our dreams."

Walt's smile returned. "Here's to dreams!" Looking behind Andy, his attention was drawn to the two topless women prancing out of the rest-room area with his wife walking a few feet behind them. "I could get used to this place!"

Across the restaurant, Jack and Megan were quiet as they watched Andy and Dana disappear into the covered dining room. The beach waiter swooped by and dropped off a beer for Jack, along with four dessert menus. Relieved, Jack grabbed the frosty bottle, pushed in the piece of lime at the rim, and opened a menu. More time passed. Megan remained silent.

"Megan, are you a chocolate fan? They have a wonderful cake with a soft center."

"I'll pass, I'm afraid. The closer I get to forty, the harder it is for me to keep my weight under control. But you go ahead."

"No, I'll save myself for that famous island dessert."

"Which one is that?"

"Rum and coke."

"Jeeze, I should have known! You and Andy are friends. I've heard him use that line a hundred times in the bar." Megan adjusted her position in the seat and pulled up her bathing suit top. She caught Jack's eyes on her breasts but was not annoyed. There was something nice about him.

Jack was warmed by her relaxed attitude and suddenly found himself at a loss for words. He wanted to be charming and witty but was feeling a strange twinge of embarrassment that was unfamiliar to him. His years of detective work had always given him plenty of confidence. After all, he had met and interviewed hundreds of strangers. Now he could only stare at Megan and feel a bit lightheaded. *"I wish Andy and Dana would get back already"* he thought as he took another sip of his beer.

Megan took the lead. "I remember you from my last time on St. Maarten. You used to come into Andy and Dana's restaurant often. I didn't get to know you because you never sat in the dining room where I served. You were usually alone at the bar."

"Yeh, that's right. I have never felt comfortable eating alone in a restaurant. Bar seating is more of a safe haven for me."

"Then again, I remember you sitting between those two American women at the bar once. Both of them were rubbing your legs under the ledge.

They thought that no one could see, but I did."
Megan gave him a wicked and all knowing grin.

Red faced, Jack remembered taking Cheryl and
Susan to the Former Life Bar a long time ago. "You
must be mistaken. A lot of guys look like me."

Megan responded with a skeptical gaze and a
playful tone. "Deny, deny, deny...now you sound
like my last boyfriend in New Orleans."

She relaxed Jack with her comment and he felt
his face return to its normal color.

"Did you get a visa and a green card for the
US?" he asked. Now was a good time to change
the subject away from his ménage a trois and Jack
took it.

"No, I stayed under the immigration radar. My
boyfriend gave me a place to live, a friend of his
owned a restaurant in the French Quarter, and I
worked for cash. But when we broke up, I knew
I needed to leave before I was discovered and deported by Homeland Security."

"Ahhh, I see. You and I have much in
common."

"We do? How?" Megan asked with growing interest in the man across from her.

"Well, just a few days ago I was scheduled
to be deported by the Dutch side police for
overstaying my visit."

Megan was now completely fascinated in the common story of adversity. "No shit! Did they arrest you and everything?"

"Yes, I spent the night in the exciting iron bar hotel in downtown Philipsburg."

She covered her face with both hands. "Oh God. Was it as bad as everyone says?" Without residency, Megan knew that it could happen to her at any time.

Jack watched her animation and was no longer missing Andy and Dana. "It's okay. I have been in worse places and this jail was not dangerous. My cell mate was not a murderer or rapist. Just another guy from Trinidad picked up because he didn't have a work permit. I suspect that someone was sending him a message. In my case, I was in the wrong place at the wrong time. They grabbed me at the Get Wet Bar. However, I won't be reporting the sleeping accommodations with any recommendation stars on the Travel Adviser webpage."

Her reaction of caring for another who had faced the issue of jail and ejection from the island was natural to her and she reached across the table and took his hand. "Well, I am glad that you dodged the bullet. How did you get to stay here?"

Andy and Dana returned at that moment. Both

noticed the couple was holding hands. Dana returned to her seat next to Megan and Andy slapped Jack on the shoulder as he sat.

"Old guy! Are you stalking pretty young girls again?"

Jack released Megan and held up his hands. "I knew that I should have helped the cops find you and lock you up that day when you fled from the police...you have a mean streak."

Both men savored their simple attempt at humor while Dana and Megan stared at each other without joining their banter. Megan reached for her wine glass and drained the bottom. Then she stood and looked at the table.

Jack was suddenly disappointed. "You're not leaving?"

"I just need to stretch. We have been sitting and eating...plus, I barged in on their lunch. Can I pay my share?"

Andy waved his hand. "No, you're our guest. Jack on the other hand owes me for his beer."

Jack stood and reached for Megan's hand. "This is turning ugly." He looked directly at Megan. "If you don't mind, when you do decide to leave, I would like to walk you back to your car."

"A friend dropped me off earlier. I'll take a taxi

home later. I have a beach towel on the sand and this bag with all my essentials. If you want, let's take a walk on the beach."

Andy and Dana watched as Jack stood and the two moved close together. They had mixed emotions about this match. Then again, Jack was a big boy.

Megan looked at Dana and asked, "Can I leave my bag with you guys?"

Dana nodded, "Of course, and don't worry about a taxi. I'll drive you back to Philipsburg."

Jack didn't want to miss this opportunity to continue to talk with Megan. "We're going to walk this incredible beach for a while. If you guys leave to return to your chairs in the sand, make sure you pay the bill."

Everyone laughed again and Megan followed Jack's lead into the soft white sand at the water's edge. Megan turned back and mouthed the words "Thank you" to Andy and Dana. Andy put his arms around Dana and hugged her.

"A short time ago, Jack might have put Megan in jail, now he is in lust. Ironic, don't ya think?"

Dana slapped his arm. "Shut up. Just shut up. We know nothing."

On the beach, Megan sighed with pleasure at

the warm afternoon sun on her shoulders and quickly removed her top as they moved away from the restaurant. Jack pretended not to stare, but he snuck a glance at her profile every chance he had. He walked along as if they were just another vacationing couple enjoying the sand and sea. However, his heart rate was increasing to lift off stage.

"Can you put this in your pocket?" Megan asked as she handed the small bikini top to Jack. "I want to get some sun. New Orleans is not exactly a topless beach community. I really missed this island, and I hate tan lines."

Jack made another effort to look straight ahead as he debated how to gracefully accept half of everything she was wearing without slobbering like a dog.

Megan waved her top in front of his face and then slapped his arm playfully with it.

"For goodness sake, please take it."

"Megan. You are almost naked in that tiny bathing suit bottom and I'm starting to drool like a lonely guy watching porn on the internet. Give me a minute to recover, okay?"

"Jack, you're so sweet. That is one of the nicest things a man has said to me in quite a while." Megan hugged his waist, "Are you a lonely guy?"

"Not at the moment, that's for sure."

"What's up with the wedding ring? Dana told me long ago that you were one of their single friends."

Jack took her top and slipped it into his front pocket. "After my wife died, I could not bring myself to take it off."

Megan side stepped a few children playing in the sand leaving Jack to walk alone for a brief moment. They rejoined after passing the group and continued to walk towards the hotel at Mont Vernon on the far end of the beach. Jack pointed toward the CoCo beach bar as they passed. "Do you want to stop for a drink on the way back?"

"Yes, that would be nice." Megan watched as a small wave covered her feet. "Jack, you didn't finish our conversation earlier. I asked you how you were able to remain on the island."

A small group of tourists passed in the opposite direction. The men stared at Megan from behind reflective sunglasses. The women with them were wearing full coverage swimsuits and glared at the couple with obvious disapproval. Megan flashed a broad smile to all and Jack gave the men one of his shit eating grins.

"I'm a retired police detective. From time to

time, I help the local government with murder investigations, unofficially of course. This week the Government and Police resources have been challenged by the murders of two women. The Chief Inspector negotiated with the Lt. Governor on my behalf...and I received a residency permit in exchange for assisting with the investigation."

Megan stopped walking. "You help the police solve murders?"

"You seem surprised. Bad guys are my business. I don't cause the problem. I just try to help fix it. Are you okay?"

Megan looked at the sand and held her hands in front of her body. "I'm okay. Just surprised. I thought that you were a retired stock broker or something." She tried her best to deadpan her expression and not appear so startled.

Jack laughed and laughed. He stopped when he realized that Megan was not joining in the fun.

"Jack, how long have you been helping the police with murders?"

"Over the past two years, a couple of times. Why?"

Megan took his hand and turned them back towards the CoCo beach bar. "Oh, you know...I was just wondering. Could we get that drink now? Just give me my top and I'll stop in the restroom and enjoy a quick shower to cool off a bit."

Jack pulled the bikini top from his front pocket and reluctantly handed it to her. "Actually I was feeling the need for more sun. Could we walk just a bit more?"

"Nice try, voyeur guy. Let's get a cold drink." Megan turned and ran towards the restaurant without putting her top back on. "I'll meet you at the bar, I'm going to stop in the ladies room first."

Jack stood in the sand and admired her from behind as she disappeared behind the building.

Within a few minutes she was back and they were sitting on bar stools with their backs to the ocean. Megan had put on her bikini top and her skin sparkled with small water drops from the outside shower. Jack was bare-chested in his favorite designer bathing suit, and was wearing a continuous smile on his face. Megan was impacting him in a big way.

"Jack, did you help with the murder of the Front Street merchant found on the French beach awhile back?" Megan asked as she sipped her frozen drink through a straw.

Jack looked at his beer and considered his response carefully. The experienced police officer in him was always reluctant to talk about cases, especially the ones that were never solved. Plus he never liked to brag or pound his chest to impress women.

"Yes. I did. Why do you ask?"

"I worked for him."

It suddenly made sense to Jack. "You were one of the workers in his store without a work permit that disappeared after the murder?"

Megan touched his arm. "Yes, sorry for that. But most of us were illegal on the island. When Nat was killed we ducked out of sight."

Jack watched the tension build in her face and the muscles pulling her attempt to smile into a slight grimace. His training and experience told him that it was a good time to listen and not interrupt her.

"Jack, if I seem strange it's just that Nat is the first person I have ever known who was killed. The shock sent all of us who worked for him into hiding. I'm sorry."

Jack nodded and looked ahead. "I understand. Most people are spared the horror. That case was, without a doubt, difficult."

"Why?"

Jack brushed salt or sand from the bar surface

absentmindedly. "The initial forensic examination had some errors. And the investigation became haphazard once semen was found in his rectum. Suddenly the sense of urgency in finding the killer cooled off dramatically. There is some discrimination against gays in this culture, I'm sorry to say."

Megan pretended to be surprised. "He was gay? He never acted like that in the store." Again she hoped that Jack was not reading her real reactions to their conversation.

He played with his beer bottle. "It actually got worse. When a maiden aunt surfaced before his remains were returned to St. Maarten, she claimed the body and had it sent to Texas. Totally focused on solving the murder, she had another autopsy and x-rays done in Texas. The results produced more confusion."

Megan drained her drink and motioned for another from the bartender. Jack looked at his beer and realized that he had not consumed even half.

"The second autopsy in the states included several x-rays of the head. It turned up something that was missed in the first report we received."

Megan leaned closer to Jack and touched his arm. "What?"

Jack cleared his throat and looked into Megan's

blue eyes. Her interest in the former boss's murder seemed genuine and her rapt attention was flattering. He decided to throw caution to the wind. After all, the case was not being pursued by the local police.

"Well, I guess it won't hurt if you hear this. His head contained two bullets, not just one as we originally assumed. It seems that a first shot did not cause serious damage and the bullet lodged in his mouth. He had been smoking weed and drinking heavily. He passed out. The second shot from the same caliber weapon was fired much later. It went into his brain and definitely caused his death. But the two bullets did not come from the same gun. How weird is that? I'm thinking that this guy had a few enemies."

Megan had a confused expression on her face. She remained speechless and she did not let go of Jack's arm. He liked that.

Two men walked up from the beach chatting loudly and stood a little too close to Jack as they ordered four frozen Guavaberry drinks. Megan glanced at them briefly but did not start a polite bar conversation, so the men took the hint, quickly paying for the drinks and left.

As the bartender disappeared into the back

area, Jack continued. "We heard several rumors about the murdered man's unnecessary conflicts with locals, abrasiveness in business, and weird personal behavior but this theory is over the top. Two different people shoot him in the same night? What is the likelihood of that happening to someone? Even if several people had reasons to kill him. Hell, even my friend, Andy, was the prime suspect at one point. Then we developed a long list of possible murderers. There were plenty of people ready to ax this guy. Then the murder of a young woman drew all the media attention and finding Nat's killer was placed on a back burner. The gay issue, as I said earlier."

Megan's eyes shifted from side to side as her mind raced with the memories of the night that Nat died. Nothing made sense.

Finally, Jack spoke again. "Are you alright? I hope that I didn't upset you by bringing this up."

Megan's hand moved from his arm and held his wrist, and then she began to stroke his fingers. "No Jack, actually you've made me happy. No time to explain today, but..."

"I hope that means we will be seeing each other again after today, Megan, because that would make me happy too." Now it was Jack's turn to touch.

He placed his arm on the back of her bar stool and lightly rubbed her back. Megan had Jack's full attention.

"Could I drive you home?"

Megan turned and stared directly into Jack's eyes. "I already accepted a ride home with Andy and Dana, but I'm available for a dinner date. How about this weekend?"

Chapter 30
Autopsy Upset

Officer Davis sat in one of the seats across from Judith's empty desk and waited patiently for her to return. She had left him in the room alone to find her employees for the interview. He had returned today so that he could question the last two on staff that he had on his list for *Island Ice*. One was a salesperson and the other was a vault controller. Judith had already told him that the salesperson was a local woman and that the vault worker was Colombian with a work permit.

Davis had had the unpleasant experience of driving Holiday and Richardson to the funeral home before they took him home last Thursday so that Bart could officially identify his wife's body. Every moment had been charged with emotion. Thank goodness when the funeral director pulled her out of the cooler, she was still dressed. Standing and gawking at another officer's dead wife's nude body would have been horrible. This formal identification was bad enough. Both Davis and Holiday knew Desiree well and could have confirmed the identity, but procedure was procedure. An immediate family member was required for the records. They almost had to carry Richardson out of the room once his wife's face and torso were uncovered. The sight was gruesome. Plastic electrical ties were cutting deep into her skin at the neck. After he regained some composure in the waiting room, Bart was cooperative but barely coherent. They gave him some coffee and Holiday asked Bart to examine her personal effects which he did. The only items that he could determine were missing consisted of her wedding ring and a new ring that she bought this week using her employee's discount. Her bag found in the car contained some workout clothes, make up and tennis shoes which would be normal considering her morning.

The silence in the room was interrupted by the sound of his cell phone playing the Pink Panther theme.

"Good Afternoon, Davis here."

"Good Afternoon, Officer" it was Holiday.

"Where are you at the moment?"

"*Island Ice*, hopefully finishing up the interview with the two employees that I missed earlier. Any news from Bart? Is he okay? I stopped by his house and knocked. He did not answer the door or his cell phone."

"I'm not surprised. This has been a very rough 24 hours for him."

"Yes, it has. Poor guy."

"I just got off the phone with the Medical Examiner in Curacao. Given the VIP status of a Police Officer's wife, they went to work on Desiree Richardson as soon as the body arrived." Holiday sounded uncomfortable with what he was about to say.

"Sounds reasonable."

"Yes, time is of the essence for us...and luckily they know it."

"Did they find anything useful for us?"

"They called me because they found semen in her vagina." Holiday spoke the words with a hint of trouble and unpleasantness in his voice.

Davis was momentarily embarrassed; he shifted uncomfortably and looked behind him to make sure no one had entered the room. "Not surprising, she was a married woman."

"That's true. However, the initial tests on the sample indicated that she might have had sex with more than one man during the final 8 to 10 hours of her life."

"Oh god, was she raped?" Davis put his hand on his forehead. "Bart will be devastated."

"No, they do not believe that she was raped. Other than the contusions on her neck from being strangled, there were no signs of any other injuries. No definitive wounds, or cuts and abrasions from brute force on her body. She may have been slapped on her ass during foreplay, however. They found some sight bruising. But no tears in her vagina or anus as would be typical in a rape. It appeared to the doctor doing the autopsy that consensual sex occurred."

As his stomach began to churn after hearing this news, Davis shifted the cell phone to his other ear. "What about the robbery? Bart said that she left the house wearing a wedding band and a new ring she bought at *Island Ice*. The sex thing might just be coincidental."

"We still suspect robbery in both murders. There was no jewelry on her hands when we found her and certainly none in the car or her gym bag."

"What else?" Davis was relieved to change the

subject from any hint of sexual impropriety. He just didn't want to go there.

"Someone may have administered a form of ether or some similar anesthesia to her in the car."

"To knock her out?"

"Or to at least make her weak or disorientated... there were traces of a cloth material in her mouth. Used with chloroform or something like it, I don't know...we didn't find a rag."

"Any drugs in her bloodstream?"

"They say that initial tests are negative...but then they usually look for hard stuff like coke or heroin. Sophisticated drugs require other tests."

"hummm..."

"Can you think of anything that we are missing? Can you think of any times when you were with Bart that would indicate problems at home?" Holiday was firm.

Immediately uncomfortable, Davis feigned surprise. "What are you saying?"

"I'm saying that we have to figure out what happened to her during the last days of her life if we are going to find the murderer. Given Bart's mental state when we left him at his house, any questioning will be difficult. But this sex thing may shed new light on her death. Or maybe not.

Perhaps he and Desiree were into swinging and
mate swapping with another couple. It wouldn't be
the first time it has happened on this island."

"No way. I know Bart. He was too possessive
to have allowed another man to have sex with her.
Even if he was screwing the other guy's wife."

"Or she had a boyfriend."

"Impossible, Bart kept a tight reign on her. He
would even follow..."

Holiday's cell phone rang in the background
and he missed the end of Officer Davis' sentence
as he answered it and left Davis's comment hanging in mid air. The Police Officer waited for his
boss to re-enter the conversation.

"I apologize. It was my wife on the other
phone. Good thing that I took the call. I'm getting
enough pressure at work. I don't need trouble with
the woman at home."

Davis was not offended. He needed a moment
to process the overwhelming information.

"No problem, I understand." Davis assured
Holiday. "Still my point is that Bart and his wife
would never be into anything kinky like that."

Holiday was skeptical. "Well, for now forget
about those two remaining interviews and come
back to the station. I'll call Jack and the three of

us will put our notes together and review what we know so far."

"Yes sir, I will be there in a few minutes. Inspector? One thing?"

"What is it?" Holiday sounded grim.

"We have to help Bart. I want to find this murderer...Bart deserves it. His children deserve it. Let's find this son-of-a-bitch!"

"I understand Joseph. Bart is a good man. As painful as it will be, we need to talk to him at some point. Something he knows may be the key to solving this."

Davis considered the statement. "Okay, but please... let's give him a few days to calm down. His emotions are raw and her body is not even in the ground."

"I don't know if we can waste a minute given this new twist. Let me think about it. Goodbye. I'll see you in a few minutes..."

The door opened and Judith stepped inside with a female employee and started to introduce her, but Officer Davis was already on his feet.

"Ladies, something has come up, and I must leave unexpectedly. I hope that I did not inconvenience you. I will be back again on another day. Do you work Saturday?"

Not waiting for an answer, he rushed out of the room and closed the door behind him. Judith and Kesia gave each other puzzled looks.

"Well, that was strange" Judith said with a flip of her hair. She walked behind her desk. "You can go back to the floor and make some sales."

Chapter 31
Miguel's Lunch Break

With the newspaper in hand, he hurried away from the woman as she shook her head in disbelief. Disorientated and anxious, Miguel walked briskly until he found an empty space between some buildings and ducked into the alley. He stepped over some trash and moved to a clearing. His head was spinning and he held the paper as if it contained a snake. His appetite was gone. Slowly he unfolded his purchase and studied the headlines. While he spoke English well, the language of his home country was Spanish and reading English was difficult. He stumbled over enough of the text to comprehend. Bart's photo in the story seemed to reach out and grab his throat. He started gasping for breath. The events over the past few days made it clear that his life was spinning out of control.

Two murders in a week would put public pressure on the police to step up investigative activity. The Dutch police or Marechaussee might be called in to help. He saw the letters "FBI" in print but did not understand the full text. Instinctively, he knew that a fire storm was coming. Dropping to his hands and knees, his mind reeled with confusion. Tears rolled down his cheeks. Then he froze as he heard steps behind him.

"Hey dirtbag. I been lookin' for yo sorry ass."

The sound of Bucket's voice sent shivers of terror through Miguel's body. He was trapped. Bucket stood above him and used the opportunity to kick him hard in the side. Miguel rolled over in agony.

"Ya tink ya gonna kill dose women and not get caught? Ya stupid fuck! Mr. G wants ya off dis island."

"I'll get the rings! I promise. I...I..."

Bucket bent his legs at the knees and lowered himself close to Miguel's prone position. Grabbing his hair with a sudden jerk, he popped the Colombian twice in the face with his open hand and snarled, "Forget da rings. Yo takin' a boat ride with us and stay outta sight for a while. Ya need to hide. That cop gonna kill you, mon, if he find yo ass."

"Let me call my boss. I'm working today."

Bucket slapped the back of his head and made Miguel see stars. "Listen up, asshole! You need to go with us today. Forget yo job. We take care of you. You be safe from da police. Now get up and clean yo ugly self off."

Bucket stood up and pulled a cell phone out of his pocket. He punched in some numbers and said, "I got him. Meet me at da boat."

Alarmed by the conversation, Miguel steadied his nerves, and tried to stand. Just as he pulled himself into a semi-upright position, Bucket kicked him behind the right knee and sent him dropping to the ground. Miguel groaned and curled into the fetal position writhing in pain.

"Dat's so you don't try to run." Bucket raised his shirt and showed Miguel a large fishing knife stuck into the waistband of his jeans. "See dis? If I gotta chase you, I be cutting off yo balls. We walking. Understand?"

Miguel slowly nodded in agreement but remained on the ground expecting another blow. "I don't like boats. I get sea sick. I don't swim."

"Too bad." Bucket pulled him up with a powerful tug of his arm and moved closer to his captive. Miguel smelled the man's foul breath and choked down his own rising bile. Without further comment, Bucket pushed him forward and started the walk down Back Street away from the shops and tourist areas. The woman seated to the side who had sold Miguel the newspaper front page noticed the tension between the two men as they passed. Miguel stumbled slightly in front of the larger one, so she quickly averted her eyes and ignored them. Something bad was about to happen and she wanted no part of it.

"Can I take a flight out? I have plenty of cash at home for the ticket. I told you, boats make me seasick and I can't swim."

"Shut up and walk. I don't fly no planes." Bucket made a mental note to find the cash later in Miguel's apartment. "No way we gonna let dem cops see you at da airport."

Once the men had cleared the parked cars that lined the outskirts of Philipsburg, they continued on the sidewalk toward Bobby's Marina. Delightfully lined with palm trees, the passageway had been newly embellished as a welcome for the visiting cruise passengers. Today, however, the purpose for this walk was more menacing. Bucket guided Miguel quietly and firmly to the docks. With several boats in sight, he motioned to Brick who was already waiting next to an old 30 ft. Grady White with a small forward cabin. The outboard engines were running and the sputtering noise from them frightened Miguel. He had only been on a boat once in his life, and he hated the rise and fall movements. This boat was smaller, and the thought of being on it in deep water to reach another island was more than he could stand. He quickly scanned the dock and nearby businesses for a way to escape. Bucket sensed his panic, and reached for his shoulder. Almost hugging the smaller Colombian, he raised his voice in case anyone was watching or listening as they boarded the boat.

"Come, my friend." Bucket extended his other arm outward as if he was issuing an invitation to a special event. "You gonna love fishing today!"

With Bucket pushing him onto the boat and Brick now in place to receive him, Miguel had no options for flight. He stepped aboard without protest.

"Get below. And don't chuck yo cookies or ya be cleaning it." Bucket said with a scowl. He led Miguel forward and motioned for him to enter the small space. As Miguel stepped inside, the bigger man's body blocked the daylight. "Ya be safe soon." Miguel heard the hatch close and a lock turn.

Brick busied himself by releasing the lines from the pier and the boat started to drift away from the dock. In the cabin, Miguel tried to steady himself and remain standing but the motion of the boat was making him nauseous. Resigned to traveling by sea, he sat down and held onto the old wooden cabinet near him. The room was hot and dark. The carpet was musty and the sounds of water lapping on the hull did nothing to calm Miguel's fear of the sea. There were portholes on each side of the bow, but old moldy curtains covered the openings and very little sunlight filtered through.

Within minutes of leaving the dock, Miguel heard the engine noise increase and he felt the pounding of the boat as it cut through the water. He knew little of the nearby islands and hopped that the trip would be short. Friends who had visited Anguilla's beaches often told him that the entire trip could be accomplished in about twenty minutes, so he was hopeful. St. Barts and Saba, on the other hand, were further away and the seas could be treacherous for the novice sailor. He also knew that the American Virgin Islands were about eight hours away but he prayed that he would not be forced to go that far. He closed his eyes and started reciting every childhood prayer he could remember.

Almost an hour passed before the boat slowed and the slapping of the waves on the hull died down. Luckily, he could see that it was still light outside. Traveling in the dark while at sea would be even more terrifying. He tried not to think about all of the creatures that swam below the boat. He saw that shark movie as a child, and never forgot the message. The haunting music from the film still played in his memory when he was near the sea. People could be food for the monsters. An eerie silence took over when the outboard motors were cut off. Miguel shuttered and strained to hear the men on the deck above him. Naively, he hoped that when he stepped outside he would be able to see land within a few feet of the boat. He had heard that human smugglers often stopped within sight of an island then made the poor immigrants wade or swim to shore. Swimming was not an option for him. And he hated to get wet wearing jeans. Poor desperate immigrants…he could not imagine how they could start over in a strange land without family or friends waiting to greet them. From time to time, they were even dropped on the wrong island and simply left to figure things out for themselves. They were wet, disoriented, and carrying few personal belongings or cash. Miguel, on the other hand, had immigrated to St. Maarten by plane as a visiting tourist and then was met by his uncle. There was no stress. He knew how to blend into the background of a Caribbean community. Bucket's plan to move Miguel off St. Maarten without planning ahead was crazy, he thought. It made no sense to him. They should have let him pack a bag and take a plane to another Netherlands Antilles island. His work permit would get him into other islands within the Dutch Kingdom as a tourist. Then he could disappear. This boat trip was too hasty. It was insane. He listened carefully, but heard no words exchanged between the men on deck. Then he heard what sounded like a beer bottle top being opened.

"What in the shit could they be doing? Where am I? Come on you fuckers! Get me to someplace safe. Get me out of this hell hole."

Chapter 32

Dana and Megan take a ride

After dropping Andy and a sandy and salty Coby off at their house, Dana and Megan drove towards Philipsburg and the Naked Boy Apartments where Megan was staying with her friend. Megan seemed withdrawn. Dana could not imagine what might have happened on the beach with Jack that could account for the sudden mood swing. Staring straight ahead as she drove, Dana waited for her passenger to speak first. There was plenty of time due to the heavy traffic as they approached the busy streets surrounding the town. A line of tourists walked purposefully towards the waiting vessels in anticipation of the usual 6 PM cruise ship departures. The scene was a blur of shopping bags, video cameras and sunburned legs.

Without looking at Dana, Megan spoke. "Dana, thank you for the job offer. That was most kind."

"You're welcome. This time you will have a work permit. No more hiding from Immigration."

Megan dropped her head into her hands and burst into tears.

"Hey, I didn't mean to upset you. Andy and I just thought that..."

"That's why I'm crying! You guys think that I murdered Nat, yet you're still willing to hire me."

Dana considered the contradiction of the job offer before she answered. "Megan, the only evidence we had was a weak assumption. You were wearing what looked like Nat's diamond stud in your ear when we saw you in New Orleans, remember? That's all."

"I know."

"You also know that Andy was a suspect. Hell, even I could have shot the worthless bastard. Most of my close friends back in the States thought that I did, considering how badly he had treated Andy."

Megan mulled over the comment. "Here is what happened today...when I went walking with Jack. He told me that he had worked on the investigation into Nat's murder. I almost peed all over myself right there on the beach, I got so nervous."

Dana imagined Jack and Megan for a second as they took their stroll this afternoon on Orient Beach. "You need not worry about Jack, I think. He is interested in you, that's obvious, but not as a suspected killer. He has horny guy written all over his face."

Megan started to deny it then she decided to fess up. "I accepted a dinner date for this weekend from Jack. Now I feel guilty."

"Why would you feel guilty?"

"You need to know that I didn't kill Nat...someone else did. I swear to you! Jack told me stuff today...but he might think that I am manipulating him or something. I don't know...I like the guy and my past experiences with younger men have been a disaster. Jack is mature. Thoughtful...funny. He doesn't take himself so seriously. I like that."

Dana was quick to respond, "Jack's only a few years older than you, actually." She slowed the jeep as a tractor trailer truck passed them like a bat out of hell with a 40 ft. container. Hot dust swirled around their vehicle.

Meagan waited for the noise to diminish. "Still, if he ever connects me with being at the murder site. If he ever gets suspicious, I will look like some cheap conniving bitch that was just trying to use him."

"Megan, there is no evidence to connect you to the murder. In fact, the whole murder is off the police radar screen. You have nothing to worry about. Or is there something else you need to tell me?" The traffic ahead of them was stopping and they slowed to a crawl.

Megan suddenly blurted out, "I shot him, but I must not have killed him. Can you fucking believe it! Someone else came to the car after I left and fired a second bullet into his head."

Dana felt her pulse quicken. "Where did you hear that?"

"From Jack, just today…he said that a family member took the body back to the USA and had an extensive autopsy with multiple X-rays. Curacao only did a cursory one. There were two bullets in his head. The first one did almost no serious damage. It was the second shot, fired from a different gun that killed Nat."

Dana clutched the steering wheel and stared ahead at the backed up cars and trucks. Her head ached and she could feel sweat on her brow. *Did Andy do it?*

Megan rattled on with excitement. "I might have given Nat a bad toothache, but I didn't kill him! You have no idea how relieved I feel. My nightmares have been horrible."

Finally Dana spoke, "Are you sure Nat was not shot before you arrived?"

Megan contorted her face with disgust. "Yes. I'm sure. He was busy getting fucked in the ass by his boyfriend. I saw it. Then they kicked back and smoked a joint together like any familiar lovers after sex."

Dana believed her story, but was feeling strange about the information. The topic of this conversation was bizarre, to say the least. "What happened next? Did you confront Nat and his lover? After all, we found you in New Orleans wearing a single diamond stud just like his."

Megan motioned toward the side of the road. "Dana, pull over. You need to watch me when I tell you the truth. Pull over, please."

Dana stopped the car on the side of the road and took a deep breath. "Okay, let's hear it." She watched Meagan's expression carefully.

Tears rolled down Megan's face. "I was so angry. He humiliated me over and over and I was too stupid to know it. We never had intercourse.

Instead he would push me down to give him blow-jobs. I should have figured it out. I was so fucking dumb. I was his beard."

Dana stroked her now short haircut. "I'm showing my age...or my years as a married woman. What in the heck is a beard?"

Megan leaned over and touched Dana's arm. "You are not old or stupid. You are lucky. You don't have to deal with this shit. A beard is a cover. A way to hide reality by offering a diversion. I was Nat's beard when he was out in public. Just like his purchase of a Harley. Macho. Just like his constant conflicts with other men in business. Everyone except him was a fucking asshole. It was endless. You know...you know."

"I hear you. But you stole the earring. Did you steal anything else from him? Where was this other guy during your conflict?"

"I know. It looks bad. On that night, I found them at the beach spot where Nat liked to park with me. The younger French guy saw me, I think, but he can never come out of the closet because of his family. He'll never tell the story of that night. His father is a big deal in St. Maarten business and a real womanizer. He would kill his son if the boy's sexual preferences were made public.

It was dark...I can't be sure what he saw. Once he left I approached Nat. We had words. I told him what I saw. He denied it. He said some awful things to me. He said that no one would believe me. He called me a crazy bitch. He dismissed me as insignificant. I shot his sorry ass in anger. I had been drinking. When I saw the two men having sex, I was confused, rejected in the worst way...I was nuts. I wanted the police to think that it was a simple robbery so I took his money, the diamond stud from his ear and anything else that I could find. Besides, he owed me salary from working and I knew that it would never be paid."

Dana decided not to debate the morality of Megan's rationalization. "Well, the presence of semen in his butt when the autopsy was done probably ruled out a woman as the murderer in the minds of the police. Just my guess..."

"So you believe I'm safe from suspicion?"

"Yes, I think if there ever was a cold case that lost the public's interest, this is it. No one cares about that dead bastard."

Chapter 33
Miguel's Boat Ride

After cutting off the engines and allowing the boat to drift slowly in the calm sea, Bucket and Brick opened a cooler of beers and settled back on the deck to share a freshly rolled marijuana cigarette. The day was coming to an end, and they wanted to return to the Philipsburg marina in the dark. If someone had watched three men leave to go fishing, they didn't want any witnesses to see only two return. They had traveled out of the shipping lanes and away from Cruise ship routes in an effort to achieve the necessary privacy they needed for dealing with Miguel. Bucket hoped that even the Coast Guard would not be out here. Bucket was not a qualified captain, so he really had no idea where they were. He had carefully followed the compass heading away from St. Maarten, and would reverse course going home. One thing he did know: he could no longer see land and the water was very deep.

Almost an hour passed and the men topside remained silent. As they shared the last puffs of the joint, they switched to chain smoking cigarettes. Neither man offered to share his pack with the other. This was self-serve. They pulled their own beers from the ice chest independent of each other's empty bottle. Brick and Bucket were not concerned with social graces. As if watching for visitors, they studied the horizon and the setting sun but not each other.

After a while, Brick broke the silence. "Heard a good joke last time in jail... wanna hear?"

Bucket grunted.

"Dare was dis man drivin' past a field. He stopped to pee on the side of the road and saw a farmer under dis apple tree wid a pig in his arms."

Bucket threw his empty bottle in the sea and opened a fresh one. He belched loudly.

Brick continued, "The farmer was liftin' da pig up to eat apples. Da mon say to the farmer...whatcha doing? Ya can save time by puttin' dat pig on the ground to eat apples dat fall."

Bucket looked at Brick with empty eyes.

B.D. ANDERSON

Brick smiled and showed one gold tooth and a few missing. "Yeh, say da farmer. But time don't mean shit to da pig."

The punch line hit Bucket with an unexpected wave of amusement. He had done time. First, he spent several months in a men's prison as an adolescent then again for 2 years in his 20's. Time was a joke to him and to his fellow prisoners. The dumb courts thought that it was harsh punishment and that it was feared by the convicted. Instead, Bucket learned to ignore it, to use it, and to beat it. He coughed up some beer and snickered with snorting sounds. Time don't mean shit to a pig. How true. Brick joined in with a hearty laugh, and the two men high fived each other.

The laughter up on deck did little to calm Miguel's anxiety as he huddled impatiently in the small cabin. He was hot, uncomfortable and now his own sweat was mixing with the stench of the moldy carpet. He wanted off the boat and to be back on dry land as soon as possible. The sun was beginning to set. Wherever they planned to hide him, darkness would make his task of settling in that much more difficult.

Don't these assholes understand shit?

At least the seas had been flat and the amount

of rocking during the trip had been minimal. There was little wind, thank God. Miguel had not become seasick. Throwing up would have added to his misery, big time. After the long day, he was getting thirsty and having missed lunch, was starving. He considered banging on the locked door then decided that it would only anger Bucket. It was best to stay quiet.

Brick stood and moved to the cooler for another beer, then stopped and squinted into the setting sun.

"What you see?" Bucket asked without standing.

He framed his eyes with both hands as if holding binoculars and scrunched his face in puzzlement. "Not sure, somting move, somting shiny."

Bucket threw another beer bottle over board, stood next to Brick and grabbed his own crotch absentmindedly. "What you talkin' bout? I don't see nothin."

"Dere...in da wadder, see?"

Bucket shook his head from side to side in disbelief and slapped the back of his accomplice's skull. "Dumb mudderfucker. We got nothin' but wadder around us. What you mean in da wadder? It all wadder!" He turned his back and found a seat on the side of the boat.

"Naw...naw. Somting be out dere, I know."

"Damn sure of dat. Sharks, fish, maybe a whale. Monsters from da sea."

Brick's gaze remained fixed on the horizon and the multiple colors of the setting sun, determined to prove himself right. Waves slapped lightly against the hull but there was no other sign of movement. As he was about to sit on the opposite side of the boat, another flash of light caught his attention.

"See, see! Somting shiny! Over dere..." he pointed off the starboard side with excitement.

Bucket moved quickly behind the captain's chair and started both engines leaving them in neutral.

"What it be?"

Brick again strained to see in the distance but was not able to be sure what was there. "I donno...a sail, I tink."

Bucket turned the wheel to port and pushed the throttles into forward. "Just watch. We move away slowly."

"Where we be?"

The boat was not equipped with expensive electronic equipment. There was a simple VHF radio and a basic compass. Bucket shrugged. "I donno. Way off shore."

One of the engines sputtered and spewed out a thick cloud of gray smoke. Then it cut off.

"Fuck!" Bucket slapped the instrument panel with the back of his hand and tried to restart the engine. More smoke billowed out as it turned over, but the motor refused to start. He switched the key to off and continued to move the boat forward with the one running engine hoping that the puffs of gray were not noticeable by whatever other vessel might be out there. He scanned the sea, looking for any movement on the horizon. The last thing that he wanted was an attempt by some Fucking Good Samaritan who might try to help a fellow mariner. Of course, he would wave them off if they came close. However, the Colombian might start yelling for help and cause a real problem. He regretted trying to restart the second engine. For now, it was best to simply put distance between the boats. Without increasing speed, the boat would not create much of a wake and would be less likely to be seen. Bucket was counting on that. Slow and steady would be his best course, he decided.

"What you see, now?" he asked Brick after a few minutes.

"Nuthin" Brick replied as he moved to the stern of the boat and surveyed the water for as far as he could.

Bucket moved the operating engine's throttle into neutral and switched the key to off. "Let's do it. Ice the mudderfucker. No more fuckin' around," he mumbled under his breath.

Unable to understand the conversation above except for an occasional expletive, Miguel could only hear the foot steps of both men on deck. Something was upsetting them. In the back of his mind, he hoped it was the Coast Guard from St. Thomas. He would think of a believable story to get away from Bucket and Brick. The U.S. Government would at least give him food and water before sending him back to St. Maarten by plane. On the other hand, if the boat had entered a hidden cove or dock without causing attention, that would be fine too. Ready to get off the boat, he felt his pockets and tapped lightly on the small wad of money that he had with him. His back pack was still at *Island Ice* in his locker. He had removed all the cash from his apartment when he went to hide at Kesia's home and left it in his employee locker for safe keeping. It had always been safer for him to stash money at the store instead of in his rental. Twice, he had been broken into and his home trashed while he was at work. Unfortunately, he needed that money now. Bucket was not likely to have brought any cash for him so he would just have to figure something out later. First things first, he thought. He had enough money in his jeans to hold him over for several days. Once freed from this awful boat, he would find a place to buy a beer and a burger, and then would worry about his next step.

The door opened and Miguel lowered his head to avoid banging it as he cleared the small hatchway into the fresh air. Slightly stiff from the close quarters, he moved awkwardly onto the deck when suddenly his arms were grabbed from both sides. His feet barely touched the deck's surface when he felt himself propelled into the air and over the side. The shock of the cool water as he entered it momentarily took his breath away and he instinctively held his mouth closed as he disappeared below the surface. Kicking and flailing his arms, Miguel managed to pop up out of the water like a cork despite his inability to swim. Automatically he began to scream and twist his body wildly. The salt from the sea burned his eyes. Aboard the Grady White, the silent men watched intensely for a moment, shrugged nonchalantly, and then turned away. Scared and confused, Miguel could see the frightening distance grow as the boat drifted from his grasp. A small wave broke over his head and he choked from the taste of the salty water.

Without looking back at the struggling man in the sea, Bucket started the one engine that worked and put the control forward. Checking his compass, he realized that he would have to turn almost 180 degrees to set course for St. Maarten, so he increased the engine speed and allowed the lopsided propulsion of the single engine to turn the vessel. With one last glance around the area he satisfied himself that no one had seen them, and he followed the compass heading for home as the sun light continued to fade.

Brick looked back. "We gonna check him? Make sure he dead? I tink we better gaff him like a fish. Make the asshole weak. Blood will draw da shark."

"No. Mr. G say no scars, no bullet holes and no ropes around his arms or feet. No matter. Dat man can't swim." Bucket concentrated on the compass heading. He was well aware of his own limited boating skills. Returning to Philipsburg quickly as darkness set was important. Lights from the harbor would be visible from the sea. They would guide him back to the marina. "He gonna drown for sure. Dumb fuck. Killin' dem women. Hope a shark eats his balls."

Brick laughed half heartedly and turned away from Bucket. With wide eyes, he peered down at the water in fear. He could not swim either.

Chapter 34
The Nude Cruise

Captain Richard Allard tacked the large catamaran and continued on his course back to the island of St. Martin. As he watched the nine naked women sitting or reclining on the forward trampoline enjoying the last warmth of the setting sun, he glanced about for any other vessels in the area. He did not want to be boarded by the local horny Coast Guard men. For a moment earlier he could have sworn that he heard an outboard engine start or sputter, but the sound had been drowned out by the laughter and chatter of his female passengers. The calm seas today along with the soft wind had been perfect for this day charter. His position on the raised helm station provided him with a sweeping view of the attractive female bodies, and he had to admit that his concentration was not exactly on the sea as it should be.

The 48 ft. South African built cat had 4 state-rooms and 4 heads and showers, complete with a modern galley and salon that offered air conditioned panoramic views from inside. Richard lived aboard with his girlfriend in the Marigot Harbor. When they were not in weekly charter with 3 couples sharing a live-a-board experience, they offered the day cruises for larger private groups. Usually at least eight to ten couples would split the cost for a look at the magnificent waters off the island and a chance to party naked off shore. The Captain insisted on couples or families. He had experience with wild singles and fights breaking out among jealous testosterone charged males. People could be out of control at times and he did not need that.

The sunset portion of each cruise was among his favorite times of the day. His girlfriend, Coco, who doubled as the First Mate and Chef, was below preparing sushi while surrounded by the nine men who had accompanied the women. Some of the couples were married and some were not. It didn't seem to matter. Just like any other social situation in an average backyard, the men would congregate as a group separate from the women.

Richard had seen it happen many times. Because Coco was a striking brunette with a shapely body, and was preparing the sushi naked, it was easy to understand why the men were huddled in the boat's salon. Word of mouth and internet forums touting the interactive sushi presentation on board kept them busy most of the year. Slightly uncomfortable with the nudity, Richard usually kept a pair of swim trunks on at the helm in the event of unexpected visitors. Today he was wearing his signature black thong bottom and his back up shorts were one quick reach away.

Coco had once dated a Japanese sushi chef and she had learned well from the master. She was a pro when it came to the selection of fresh fish at the open market in Marigot, and then preparing and freezing the cuts. The result was an exotic blend of what could be award winning sushi to the delight of the cruising tourists.

The presentation of the food was the real crowd pleaser. Each group of women was asked if they had seen the sushi scene in the movie "Sex and the City". Invariably at least several of the women remembered the display of the tasty morsels by Samantha as she awaited the return of her lover from work. Coco only had to ask once for a volunteer and one of the female guests always agreed to give it a try. Tonight's first volunteer was Cheri, a bubbly blonde, whose husband beamed with approval.

Richard was sure that once the group saw Cheri's performance on the main salon table several of the other women, if not all, would join the fun. For Richard and Coco the rewards were many. Since the day they started this unusual and interactive Happy Hour, their tips at the end of the cruise had more than doubled.

Up on the deck the women were suddenly summoned by Cheri, tonight's first volunteer sushi presenter. "Look over there! See it?" she asked as she pointed into the water from the bow.

Several of the women jumped to their feet and strained to see where she was pointing.

"See, over there. It's black and white. Something is floating...oh my God...I think it's a man!"

Once he had landed in the water and surprised himself by bobbing up on the surface, Miguel remembered the words of his younger sister, Maria, who was an avid swimmer. "Caribbean water is salty and easier to swim in, Miguel. Don't be afraid. Just lay back and pretend that you are a butterfly. Slowly move your arms and kick just a little so that you can float. It's easy."

As he calmed down and got past the initial panic of being overboard, Miguel began to float backwards, even though he was terrified, not knowing how far from land he might be at the moment. The sun was setting and that made matters worse. He closed his eyes and tried to pray for help. His head bumped something and the panic returned. His first thought was that a shark might be behind him ready to devour his head. Then he realized that it was a large branch from a tree floating behind him. He easily grabbed the snarled mass and held on for dear life. It even enabled him to free one of his arms to cross his chest and utter a quick prayer. But it was still hopeless. Surrounded by nothing but water for as far as he could see, and hugging the wood like a young child sleeping with the family Golden Retriever, he peed in the sea from fear. A flash of light caught his eye and he turned from side to side looking about wildly. A silver mast was near, and he raised an arm in a frantic attempt to wave at the passing boat.

"Yes, I see him now! He has dark black hair and is wearing a white shirt! See him! Over there! Richard, bring the boat around to him!" Cheri yelled as she dove from the forward bow into the water and began swimming to the floating body.

With some effort due to the distance, Cheri reached the frightened looking man clinging to a large piece of wood. Cautiously, she swam around him. Then she made her approach from behind. She hoped to avoid any wild clutching or dangerous body hold that often occurs with a panicked, near drowning victim. She knew that a frightened man might pull her under and kill them both. She needed to stabilize his emotions first, and then get them both back on the catamaran. She treaded water so that he could see her face and hear her talking to him while she maintained a safe distance.

"Hello handsome, whatcha doing out here by yourself?" she said softly as if they were standing at a bar on the beach. She could see in the clear water that he was fully dressed in jeans and not a swimming suit.

Looking over his shoulder at the woman, Miguel brushed his running nose and took a deep breath. Clearing his vision by wiping away his salty tears, he realized that the woman was topless. "Are you a Mermaid?"

"No, sorry... I have legs just like you."

"I can't swim. Help me, please."

"Of course, just relax and wait a minute. The

boat I was on is coming about to pick us up. What's your name?"

"Ah…Juan. I live on St. Maarten."

"Alright Juan, from St. Maarten…how did you get here?"

Miguel paused and wiped his nose again. "I…I'm not sure."

"Don't you remember anything?"

"No."

"Should we search for other survivors?"

"No, I'm alone."

Cheri wondered why the man was confused at one moment, but then in the next, he was so sure he was alone. Something was not adding up. Or he might be in shock. For now, her priority would be to get them both to safety. The Captain could deal with the issue of Juan's being out here alone under suspicious circumstances.

The boat was slowing and drifting towards them. The back swim platform was populated by the other eight naked women holding lifejackets and a life ring to throw to Cheri as Captain Richard expertly pulled it along side the man and woman in the water. He had started the engines as soon as Cheri jumped into the sea. The smooth approach and his calm composure during the ordeal had not alerted the men below of any problem.

Not seeing the male Captain at the helm, Miguel stared at the group of all naked women in disbelief. "Am I in heaven?" he asked.

Chapter 35
Monday, Monday

"Yes, I hear you, I understand Lt. Governor...Yes...I will...Yes...I know it is important." Holiday hung up the phone and leaned back in his desk chair as he released a large amount of air from his lungs relieved that the conversation was finally over. He reached into his desk and found a package of Tums. Gulping several, he groaned again as a knock sounded on his door.

"Come in."

Jack Donnelly smiled broadly as he opened the door and entered J.R.'s office in the Philipsburg Police Station. "Good Morning, I'm here at exactly 10 o'clock as you requested, Boss...How's your Monday so far?"

"Don't ask. Or better yet, let me stand up so that you can check to see if I still have an ass left.

It was just chewed off by the Lt. Governor."

Jack acknowledged the drama. "Yeh, I get it. The media and the internet forums are brutal when you have two unsolved murders in a week and you still haven't issued any details or arrested a suspect. Folks like closure."

Holiday nodded. "You forgot the Hospitality and Hotel Association. Several bookings have been cancelled due to the alleged massive crime wave we are having. An emergency meeting was scheduled today at 4 PM, so I am expected to attend on behalf of the Government. There is also a public outcry from Amsterdam in Holland to send in the Dutch Police and bypass us entirely for the investigation. No one is happy. They even discussed closing the schools until the killer is found. Can you believe it? You and I need to get serious here, Jack. What are we missing?"

"I know what you mean..."

"One other thing, Jack. You arrive this morning looking like a man returning from a six month vacation. Happy, almost beaming. What are you up to? It seems every time I see you now, you're grinning like a Cheshire Cat."

Jack took a seat across the desk from Holiday. "I admit it. I just had a wonderful weekend with a terrific lady. Things in my personal life are starting to look up."

Holiday finally smiled for the first time today. "Now I know why you failed to show at the Sunset Bar and Grill on Sunday afternoon! How did this lady enter your life? Were you scamming on lonely tourists again? Or did your two favorites from the U.S. arrive for another threesome?"

Jack dismissed the kidding from his friend. "No, just one. This woman is special. Can I have some coffee, please?" He gazed around the room and noticed that J.R. had brought in a large white board so that they could review all of the known details and connections between the murders.

Holiday picked up the phone and dialed an extension. "Good Morning, Joseph. Jack's here. Could you please join us and ask someone to get several coffees and some muffins from across the street? Take some petty cash. And bring all your notes from the investigation. We need to spend a few hours in a comprehensive review. Okay?"

Jack raised his head. "This may sound insensitive, but is there any chance that Bart Richardson could attend? I know that it has only been four days since his wife's murder, but..."

"Come on, now. You see what I'm saying to

you? I don't expect Bart to return to work for a few months after her funeral, given the circumstances." Holiday said with a brush of his right hand in the air. "I wouldn't. I couldn't. Would you?"

Exasperated, Jack looked at the lead Investigator. "I would be hell bent to find my wife's killer. Probably to the point of obsession...how he can grieve at home is a puzzle to me. He's a policeman. A professional. He has the training and skills to help with the investigation. I don't get it."

"You're a cold son-of-a-bitch, Jack."

"Maybe so, but you asked if we were missing..."

Jack was interrupted by the door opening and the entrance of Joseph Davis. "Excuse me. Did I interrupt you? I'm sorry."

Both Holiday and Jack stood. Holiday pointed to an empty chair. "Not at all, we were expecting you any moment."

As Davis took a seat the door opened again with a soft knock and a policewoman entered with the coffee order. "Louis just brought this to the front reception area and said that it is for you." She leaned over the desk to place the package down and lightly touched Jack's leg with her lower body as she turned to leave. For a quick second their eyes met and she smiled. "Is there anything else I can get you?"

Jack blinked and cleared his throat. Holiday took the lead and replied formally, "No, Officer. Thank you. Did Louis leave the bill?"

"No, he said that he would see you later. You owe him lunch!" She slipped out the door and closed it quietly.

Jack gazed at both men after watching her leave. "Well, I must say that you guys have difficult working conditions!"

"Enough Jack." Holiday glared sternly. "Let's get to work. Coffee anyone?"

While Jack and Joseph opened and fixed the coffee as they liked it, Holiday moved to the board and opened a black marker. He quickly listed the Monday evening murder in Philipsburg of Marta and the Thursday morning murder of Desiree in Oyster Pond. Under each he wrote "Common elements" and "Differences" then he turned to the men. Under the common section, he wrote "Island Ice" and "cable ties used to strangle the victim."

Jack sipped his coffee and concentrated on the details as he knew them. "You forgot the connection to my friend, Dana. She was attacked on Wednesday by someone who used cable ties to bind her arms and legs."

J.R. nodded and wrote "Dana" on the board. Then he turned to the men, "Sorry, but everyone is so damn focused on solving two murders that I over looked the obvious."

Officer Davis added, "One thing's for sure. If our perp is responsible for all three attacks, he must not work a regular job."

Holiday turned with a question, "Why do you say that?"

"Look at the time differences. Most employed people do not have that much flexible time. We're locked up in details and responsibilities 40 hours a week."

Jack answered in his usual speculative fashion during a review meeting, "He could be a delivery-man. They are out and about without supervision." He paused, then added, "Unless, of course, the boss has installed one of the new GPS tracking systems on the truck."

Holiday and Davis stared quizzically at Jack as if he was speaking in a foreign language.

"You know...GPS. It allows the truck, boat, car or cell phone to be tracked by position."

The local policemen looked at Jack in disbelief.

"Honest guys, I haven't been watching too many spy movies...I go boating from time to time. Someday all the cell phones will be equipped with GPS. You'll see."

Holiday brushed off the comment and pulled the discussion back on track. "Let's get back to the victims. Okay?"

J.R. picked up his marker. Under Marta's name he wrote "No sex activity" and under Desiree's he wrote "Sex with two men before death." Then under common elements he wrote "jewelry missing but not all." Under Dana's name he wrote "not wearing jewelry at time of attack." Next under differences he wrote "struggled and hit with object" under Marta and "drugged, not hit" under Desiree. Under Dana he wrote, "hit with blunt object and bound with cable ties." Under the names of all three women he wrote, "Chad."

Officer Davis spoke first, "Do you suspect the big salesman as our murderer?"

"No, not really, but we can't ignore the connection. All three of the women were in his store on Monday. They each bought new rings from Chad."

Jack studied the white board. "Officer Davis, did you ever complete the interviews of all employees at the jewelry store, *Island Ice*?"

Davis hesitated for a split second feeling guilty that he had taken most of the weekend off. "I'm almost finished." Of the two remaining employees to interview, he still had not found the Colombian vault attendant to talk to him. He looked at his boss and expected more questions. Fortunately for him, Holiday was absorbed in his notebook and missed the detail.

"What did you learn this weekend?" Jack asked as he shifted in his chair to see the younger man's face.

Davis opened his notebook and turned a few pages. "First, I heard the strangest news from the Manager, Judith. She was upset that Miguel Martinez, the vault manager that I had been waiting to meet, had disappeared on Friday when he left the store for a bite to eat around midday. She was pissed. It was out of character for him not to return or at least call, and very disturbing to her."

Holiday put down his marker. "Okay, go on... did he show up for work the next day?"

"No, he was dropped from the schedule due to Friday afternoon's unexplained absence. But there's more..."

Now Officer Davis had Jack's full attention.

"Let's hear it. Did you find him at home?"

The door opened and the policewoman who had come in earlier smiled at the men. "Excuse me, the Chief Prosecutor has been calling for you, Inspector Holiday, so I informed him that you were in a meeting."

Holiday was feeling the mounting pressure of the investigation and slumped in his chair. It was going to be a long day. He stretched his shoulders and rubbed the back of his neck in an effort to relieve the stress.

The door closed with a soft click. Distracted by the interruption and the involvement by the Chief Prosecutor, no one continued the earlier train of thought, so Jack brought the subject forward once again. "Did you find the vault guy? What's his name, again?"

Davis shook his head no as he looked through his notes. "Miguel, his name is Miguel Martinez. Judith told me that the employee lounge was abuzz with news that Kesia, the last salesgirl I needed to interview, and Miguel had recently hooked up as a couple. Kesia had been quite upset during the afternoon Friday when Miguel failed to return from lunch."

Jack was skeptical of the information. "Let's

see...boy meets girl...girl is fun, sexy and probably cooks great. They have sex. Now she owns his ass. With lightning speed, marriage bells sound. She wants him to cut his hair, buy a ring, and find a nice family styled van to drive. He freaks out and runs for the nearest exit. Is that it? He's probably hiding from her on the French side."

Joseph laughed, stood and paced the room in front of J.R. and Jack. "Here's what I know. When I went back Saturday, Judith called the girl, Kesia, into her office for me to interview...she knew little about Chad's sales to the three women. She was shocked by her co-worker's murder, that was evident, but she seemed to know little that would add to our information. I asked her about this guy Miguel. Once I brought up his name, she glowed like a new light bulb. He had called her on Friday night from a bar in Philipsburg long after dark. He told her that he had eaten some food from a street vendor on Back Street and had become seriously ill and was unable to return to work. Since his backpack and cell phone were in the employee's locker room at *Island Ice*, he could not call her for help or to explain his absence from work. He claimed that he had slept it off on the beach. It took hours for him to feel normal again. Later, he walked into the sea fully clothed to shake off the dizziness."

Holiday spoke after making a few notes of the story. "She believed him? Sounds like he just got drunk on the job and stayed away from work to hide from his boss. It happens a lot on Fridays around this island."

Davis was now ready to sit down. "You could be right. She confirmed that when he arrived at her apartment later that night, his clothes were still wet from the beach. Part of his story must have been true. He probably got drunk and dove into the water to sober up."

"Well it sounds like a bunch of bullshit to me." Jack said loudly for emphasis. "Joseph, did you ever get to meet with him and interview him?"

"No. That's it. All my information comes from the manager and his saleslady girlfriend, or whatever she is to him..."

"All right then," Jack pointed at the white board. "Let's add the name Martinez to our board and talk to him next. I have a funny feeling..."

Davis raised both hands for emphasis. "Wait, there's more. Judith spoke with me privately after the young saleswoman left my interview. She told me that last Sunday she and Chad had discovered money in a bag under the front register desk. It had been placed there by this guy Miguel in the early hours before the store was scheduled to open for business."

Jack sat up straight with a quick snap. "How much cash?"

"She told me confidentially that it was over eight thousand dollars. She also told me that she confronted Miguel on Monday and he explained away the cash saying that it was borrowed. He took a loan because he needed to send it to his family in Colombia."

Holiday crossed his arms and gave Davis a skeptical look. "I don't see anything unusual. Half the earnings of foreign workers all over the Caribbean get sent back to their home countries. It's a common thing. Have you ever driven past Western Union on Friday afternoon?"

Jack spoke, "Maybe so, but it's my opinion that the name Martinez should be underlined on our story board. That's a lot of cash. Drugs? Human smuggling? There is something going on..."

Davis suddenly began to play the devil's advocate. "Let's just not jump to any conclusions, okay? The manager stressed that this guy had been a responsible and loyal employee in the past."

Jack tapped on the desk top and played a little

drum roll with his fingers. "Cash and crime, dance together. I don't have that kind of cash at home, do either of you?"

Holiday was quick to point out Jack's lack of cultural understanding. "Jack, most workers on the island don't have checking accounts. Paychecks are cashed as soon as they get them and the money goes home in their pockets. This guy could have saved the money, or borrowed some of it ..."

Jack did not want to argue the issue and allowed Holiday to make his point. "Okay, I get it. There is a large cash economy in the Caribbean. But let's try to find Miguel this afternoon and interview him. Sound good?"

Holiday motioned towards the door as a signal for the men to leave, "Whatever. Thank you, men. Let's see what we can find..."

Chapter 36
Miguel's Escape

As soon as Miguel heard the front door close, he jumped out of bed and headed to the window. Staying out of view, he watched Kesia's car back out of the driveway and turn towards Philipsburg. Relieved that she and the manager at the store had believed his story of getting food poisoning on Friday, he had used the weekend to think and plan. He stretched the fake illness out and took today as another sick day. Now he was ready. He entered the living room and went to the desk where Kesia chatted with her friends on the telephone. He pushed the books from side to side and found a copy of the yellow pages. Turning to the section for "Airlines" he scanned the ads for island to island travel. Lifting the receiver, he noticed that Kesia had switched off the ringer.

He chuckled and dialed the number for Air St. Maarten to check departure times.

Thank God Kesia had retrieved his backpack on Saturday from the locker at *Island Ice*. He needed the cash hidden inside it in order to make his escape. Trouble was piling up like garbage. Her story about the Police Officer's visits and interview was the last straw. He had to disappear. The police were fishing for information but one thing was for sure, he couldn't show his face in town and risk being seen by Bucket or Brick. For now, they would think that he was dead and he needed it to stay that way.

After the rescue, the Captain of the catamaran had reluctantly agreed to divert the course from the Marigot harbor and drop off Miguel in Philipsburg. Miguel had been more than ready to get away from them. They asked too many questions. In his jeans, he had his car key and the soggy dollars. He offered all of the cash to the Frenchman, but it was refused with a brush of his hand. Instead, the Captain seemed more concerned about getting back to the French side of the island for the final leg of the cruise. Miguel thanked Cheri over and over for pulling him to the boat and the group of women and men for saving him. Not one of the cruising vacationers seemed to believe his amnesia story, but he didn't give a shit. They did not know his real name. Promising to report the incident to the police and Coast Guard on Saturday morning, he waved goodbye to the boat as they left Bobby's Marina. Once underway, the party animals on the catamaran turned their attention back to the planned fun and their bathing suits were once again removed before they were out of sight of Philipsburg. Laughter from the boat could be heard in the harbor as they returned to the prepared and waiting sushi presentation. Miguel shrugged as he stood on the dock. Americans were an odd lot for sure. They ate beef rare and fish raw. Miguel could not understand it. He liked his hamburgers and steaks dark brown and well done. Fish, on the other hand, he avoided. Food from the sea repulsed him. As for the lack of modesty, Miguel knew that he would never allow his woman to be naked in front of other men.

The weekend had given him time to figure things out. His escape from St. Maarten today would be under the cover of tourism. He planned to board a plane for Curacao, which was within the Netherlands Antilles group of islands. The officials would recognize his work permit status and allow his passage. Hopefully in short order, he would find a way to Trinidad, then Venezuela. He would return to Colombia only if it was his last option. It was time to go. Bucket and Brick's attack at sea Friday assured him that St. Maarten could no longer be his home. The police visit to the store Saturday asking to interview him had shaken his confidence. Then there was the issue of Desiree's murder. Miguel was sure the monster of a husband would be out for blood. Even with Kesia as a cover, he had to go. His time had run out and danger was everywhere.

Earlier that morning before the stores opened, Bart Richardson sat near the Courthouse in Philipsburg eating a Burger King Breakfast sandwich. The warm bread and the tasty meat were making him feel almost normal. He was dressed in typical tourist attire: cargo shorts, a Nike polo shirt, expensive tennis shoes with short socks, and a souvenir baseball cap with St. Maarten stitched on the front. Several days of unshaven beard growth and dark sunglasses helped to disguise his appearance further. Local St. Maarten men simply did not wear shorts. Period. No one would give him a second look. He was near the *Island Ice* store and wanted to find that sneaky Hispanic bastard.

After seeing him in the brothel talking to that bad dude, Bucket, and then seeing them pass something between them, he figured out that they were involved in some way with the killing of the first woman or they knew who did it. When he saw that bastard getting into Desiree's car outside of Peg Leg's restaurant, that was all it took. The guy was no fucking good. Whatever was going on, Bart was going to finished it. He needed to make sure that the murderer was never captured or interrogated. There could no press coverage. There would be no public questions. Not once he ended it. Bart felt his temples ache from a continuing hangover as he took another large gulp of coffee. Various groups of retail workers appeared and moved to their respective stores. Cars full of Indian men stopped, they got out with bag lunches, and disappeared into jewelry stores. Local women wearing the uniforms of many different stores passed, but Bart kept his head down and tried to avoid recognition or any casual conversation.

In the background, three cruise ships sounded horns as they docked. Bart stood, walked out on the pier where the Water taxi would later dock and watched as the white sands and decorated boardwalk on the protected Bay came alive with people. Workers from the hotels and restaurants set up lounge chairs and umbrellas on the beach. Locals living downtown strolled to work smiling in the morning sun. A lady with a small dog walked the animal to the water's edge then headed away from the pier. This was his first venture outside of his home since Inspector Holiday and Davis had taken him to identify Desiree's body. Except for several pizza deliveries, some women from the church bringing more KFC chicken and leaving it on the porch, and talking for a few quick minutes to his children on the telephone, Bart had been grieving. Being inaccessible was a good thing for him. He had time to think. There was so much to consider and work to be done. He reached into one of his pockets and removed Desiree's cell phone. He opened the menu and scrolled through her address book and recent calls. It might be a good time to call one of her friends at *Island Ice* and chat. Sometimes people will tell lots of important stuff in idle conversation...especially when they are concerned for you. Under his breath he chuckled as he remembered the police term, "diarrhea of the mouth." It might be a good time to phone some of these women. He might find that spic a lot quicker that way instead of sitting here waiting. That guy was out there. Somewhere…

Reaching into his other pocket, he pulled out Desiree's wedding band and the new ring she had purchased at work last Monday. Without ceremony he pulled his arm back and flung them into the sea with one powerful pitch worthy of a professional baseball pitcher's best strike ball.

"Fuck you, Desiree" he whispered. Then he patted the 9mm gun hidden in his waistband and turned back towards the historic courthouse area of Front Street.

Back at Kesia's apartment, Miguel showered leisurely and prepared to leave. It could be several days before he had hot water and a roof over his head again. No need to hurry. Mistakes are made when people are anxious and move too quickly. As he collected his belongings, he picked up the clothes she had laundered for him and tucked them into the backpack. She had taken his clothes to a coin laundry last night. Now the few items that he carried were clean and fresh. He was going to miss a few things about Kesia, but he had to go. This island was too dangerous for him. Inside his backpack he had a new roll of duct tape and a small pack of cable ties. Without any weapon for his travel, they might come in handy. He checked his cash again. There was plenty for this trip. He knew that the work that Mr. G had given him was an opportunity to save money. His salary at the jewelry store would never have allowed him to accumulate this kind of cash. If only Bucket and Brick had not been such assholes. One small screw up on last Sunday had changed everything. If only Chad had not found the extra shipment and put those rings out for sale! If only…he had better luck. That woman's death was not his fault. He knew that if she had just shut the fuck up, he could have walked away. Now he had to run. Not from the police, but from the men who had worked along side him. It just wasn't fair!

The sheets on her bed were still rumpled from their last night together. He wondered if he should leave a note for Kesia, then decided that it was a bad idea. He would miss her. Maybe he would call her someday…after things settled down and he was forgotten by Mr. G.

Miguel hated not being able to sell his car. It wasn't worth much but still he could get several hundred dollars of quick cash for it. The license and insurance were paid for several more months and any illegal worker would jump on the opportunity. Reluctantly he realized that the risk was not worth it, given his need to get off the island without leaving behind anyone to remember where they saw him last. He would not leave his car at the airport, that was a given. Any slight clue might lead to his death. For now, it was better that the bad guys considered him drowned. They would never suspect his plane flight out.

Feeling just a slight bit of hunger, Miguel walked into the kitchen and made a sandwich. Bread and meat would carry him a long way. The choices for lunch foods were limited, but he was not in a position to complain. After all, her Cuban dinner recipes were the best he had ever tasted. Add to it, the wild sex...he might miss her. He found a cold beer in the refrigerator that he missed last night and opened it. Now he needed a bag of chips and he would be set. The first long gulp from the beer forced him to belch loudly.

After finishing, Miguel made another check of the apartment before making his getaway. He made no attempt to clean up his food preparation or the dirty dishes. Momentarily he considered wiping off his finger prints from the kitchen and bathroom counters, glasses, beer bottles and other items he touched then rejected the idea as foolish. TV detectives would not be combing the house for evidence. Kesia was not suspicious of him. She would return to an empty house and call his cell phone over and over long before she figured out that he was not coming back. It might take hours. It might take a day or two. She would be pissed. Mainly because he knew that she would never keep her mouth shut at work about the new love affair. The save face explanation of his disappearance with friends would be embarrassing and painful for her, but he had too much to risk by hanging around any longer. There were other girls for him out there. It was time to move on and start a new life.

With a full stomach, a freshly showered body and a confident attitude, he grabbed his backpack, opened the front door and stepped out into the warm sunlight only to be surprised by a taller man blocking his exit. He squinted to adjust to the light and focus on the larger figure. Bart Richardson was standing on the porch smiling strangely with his gun pointed directly at Miguel's eyes.

Chapter 37
The Quiet Neighborhood

J.R. Holiday paced the small area of his private office in preparation for the meetings and abuse he was about to endure. The Chief Prosecutor, the Lt. Governor, the Hotel Association, and the media wanted answers. He had none.

I love my job, I love my job...

His self talk was interrupted by his cell phone ringing. "Good Afternoon, this is Holiday."

"J.R. this is Jack. You may want to sit down."

"With no ass left for anyone to chew on, sitting is not an option."

"Then put on your super hero costume. You are about to become a rock star on this island."

"Jack, don't fuck with me, okay? I am in no mood."

Jack breathed heavily in frustration, and then

continued, "I mean it. Officer Davis and I went back to the store and talked with that salesgirl. It took awhile but she finally admitted that Martinez was staying at her house. And get this, Inspector... she told us that he came to her last Wednesday night bandaged from dog bites!"

"No shit?"

"Yep. He gave her a bullshit story about working with a friend doing gardening and being attacked by a dog out near Cupecoy Beach."

"Sounds reasonable. Stray dogs are everywhere on this island, Jack. They bark. Sometimes they bite."

"She also admitted that the employee rumor mill in *Island Ice* was speculating for months that Desiree and Miguel might be doing the down and dirty whenever husband, Bart, was off island. Martinez denied it to her, of course."

"Jeeezus! Can you pick him up?"

Jack waited for a second then said, "Inspector, there is much more. Officer Davis finally told me that Bart had suspected his wife might be unfaithful."

"Why would Davis keep that from me?"

"Come on J.R. You understand the code of silence that exists between police officers. These two men worked closely together..."

"Jack, I am a bit stunned and I'm not process-ing the information as pragmatically as you are."

"Let's do this...Davis and I are on our way to the girl's home to see if Martinez is still there. Can you meet us in a few minutes?"

"Absolutely, just hand your phone to Officer Davis so that I can get directions..."

Holiday arrived in the neighborhood driving a marked police car without turning on the lights or siren. As he turned onto the street that Davis had given him earlier, he could see their police car parked next to a small sedan with local plates. This was a working class area and no other cars were on the street. The children were in school and the adults at work. The area was dotted with older homes, some appearing to have been con-verted to apartments. The established landscaping was colorful and lush from age, but most plants were not well maintained. Thick low lying palm trees, mature hibiscus, and overgrown bougain-villeas shielded the homes from each other and provide natural privacy. He pulled across the street and parked a few feet down the road. Hopefully, their suspect would not have seen the police car arrive and run out the back door. As he exited his vehicle, he checked his waistband for handcuffs and adjusted his gun holster for easy access if he needed it. He put his uniform cap on, but left his sunglasses in the car.

Jack appeared from in front of the small sedan and gestured for him to cross the street. His focused look and rigid stance gave J.R. pause. Something was amiss.

He hurried across the road. "What? Spit it out man, tell me!" Holiday said as the stress of the moment got to him. "Did he get away?"

"Not hardly. Up on the porch is a young Hispanic man shot to death, backpack in hand, and holding a car key. There are two shells near him from a 9mm pistol." Jack turned and pointed. "I would say there is a good chance that we just found our suspect."

"Good God. Another murder! You said that I needed to call the Chief Prosecutor and the Lt. Governor and become a hero. Now I have more bad news for them. Shit. This is getting out of control."

Jack shook his head. "No, wait until you hear the rest of what I found. His backpack is full of money, some clothes, a passport, work permit and guess what? Cable ties and a brand new roll of duct tape. At least we can be sure that this was not a robbery. Someone wanted this guy dead. My guess is that raw passion and revenge was the motive. Given some of the details I have pried out of Joseph Davis, I think it was the work of an angry husband."

Holiday moved closer to Jack so that their words would not be heard by any neighbors if any were listening from nearby houses. "What details?"

"Davis admitted to me that recently Bart had been shadowing his wife. She always told him where she was going, and it was easy for him to watch her from a distance. He liked to keep tabs on his wife. After the first murder last week, Bart had become secretive and stopped talking to Davis about Desiree. At first, Davis assumed that Bart was totally focused on helping you with the investigation. When he asked if anything was wrong, Bart told him to just mind his own business. It gave Officer Davis a bad feeling. He's been a nervous wreck debating what to say to you since Desiree's body was found last Thursday."

Holiday scratched his head in confusion. "What are you saying? Bart didn't attack his wife and he sure didn't have anything to do with the murder of that first woman. That was robbery. Hell, they were both robbed."

"You're correct about the robberies, I think. However, Bart was one of the few people other than the murderer, you, me, Davis and the medical examiner who knew about the cable ties used to strangle that woman from St. Thomas. Suppose Desiree's murder was a set up? A copycat, trying to link the two murders to avoid suspicion."

"I'm having trouble wrapping my head around this one. I don't know what to say, Jack. Bart? Bart? I've known the man for years. He is a good officer. He is a good father. I can't imagine...he fell apart when I found him at the station and told him that Desiree had been attacked. It couldn't have been him. I just know it."

"I understand. Let's take it one step at a time. First, call the Chief Prosecutor and the Lt. Governor. You can give them this information on a silver platter. They are sure to want to be here when this body is removed since he is our prime suspect for the first murder and the attack on Dana. Dog bites, cable ties, duct tape, and cash. It is starting to fall together, don't you see?"

"Then what? By the way, where is Officer Davis?"

"I sent him around back to keep watch until you arrived. As soon as we saw the body on the porch, I figured that we should cover both exits."

"Good idea, but somehow I doubt that the shooter is inside. With spent shells outside, the action was here." Holiday pulled out his cell phone and started to speed dial from his address book. "I'll make the call."

Jack stood silently as Holiday explained the scene to his superiors. When he finished, he had a relieved expression on his face. The news that there was a suspect in hand and that the man was dead had obviously been well received.

Holiday put his cell phone back in his front pocket. "I guess we can search inside first, then leave Davis here to monitor the crime scene while we go find Bart Richardson."

Jack patted his friend on the back. "I know it's hard for you. But we need to find him and bring him in for questioning."

"You're right. Besides, he could be completely innocent. He may have a great alibi for today...after we take a look at this apartment, Davis can come out front and put up some crime scene tape. My bosses like to see that when they arrive."

Holiday started to walk towards the building

when Jack called out, "One other thing, Inspector."

"What is it, Jack?"

"Could you borrow Officer Davis' service revolver for me, please?"

Chapter 38

The Whole Truth

During the drive to Bart's house, Jack could sense the conflict that his friend, Holiday, was feeling. On one hand, there was a murdered man lying on the porch they just left who may have been sleeping with Bart's wife. On the other, the victim was involved in some skullduggery that had not only increased his cash flow, but may have led to his murder. The cable ties in his backpack were rather conclusive. How many young men carry cable ties as they walk around on a normal day?

Jack watched J.R. grip the wheel purposefully. When they almost sideswiped a parked truck on the side of the road, Jack decided to bring the Inspector out of his deep thoughts. "You know, in my years of police work, I was only shot once."

Holiday peered at his passenger then back at the road.

"Yep. My wife always worried about the risks. I knocked down doors with warrants in hand, I chased bad guys down dark alleys, and I even walked into an armed robbery by accident at a convenience store, but no one ever fired their weapon at me...until I answered a domestic call on a bright and sunny Sunday morning."

Holiday became interested. "They shot you or they shot at you?"

"Shot me." Jack stared out the side window as he remembered the details. "It was a he. The husband. My partner and I parked in front of the house so that everyone could see us arrive. Neighbors had called 911 because of a loud argument between a man and a woman inside. One neighbor was sure that she had heard a woman's scream. Another neighbor heard crashing noises like glass or dishes breaking. But all was quiet when we got there. What a contrast...the house was nice. The grass neatly mowed and there were comfortable chairs on the porch. You didn't see a lot of folks sitting outside on a porch in that part of New York. At least you didn't see it often back then. This setting was tranquil and the atmosphere welcomed us like a Norman Rockwell painting. We both checked the address again on our sheet thinking we were in the wrong place. My partner stayed in the car to report our location to dispatch and I got out. My first thoughts were to ask the guy what type of lawn fertilizer he had used and how often he watered. The grass was beautiful. I started walking up the driveway when he stepped out of the front door holding a Magnum 44 pistol and shot it before I could react. He never said a word to me. He didn't appear to be angry or crazy. He was just a normal, plain old kind of a guy. We were less than twenty feet apart. The bullet hit my left arm and knocked me down. Damn scar still aches in cold wet weather."

Holiday examined Jack's face for an instant and decided that he was reliving every cop's nightmare. "Damn, he could have killed you."

"Yes, I figured a hit about eight inches over to the center of my chest would have been fatal. We didn't wear body armor on sunny mornings. It's weird, don't you think? A team of officers sent out late at night on a drug bust would mean everyone was in Kevlar. We tended to be more on guard. Then when you least expect it, bam! Some guy with a gun surprises the shit out of you on a pretty day."

"What happened next? Did your partner return fire? Did the shooter flee? Had he killed his woman?"

"No. The guy just dropped the gun and stood there. My partner, Dole, ran to me, and then ordered the shooter on the ground so that he could cuff him."

"He gave up easily?"

"Never said a word or resisted in any way...it was surreal. I was in the Twilight Zone."

"Was his wife alive?"

"Oh, yes. When Dole stepped back to call in on his portable radio for back up assistance, the woman ran out of the house and attacked him. She was screaming to let her husband go and not hurt him. Her dress was torn, her nose was bloody and she had a busted lip. Can you imagine? I am on the ground bleeding like a stuck pig and she is defending her shit of a husband. Dole had one hell of a time subduing her and he finally had to punch her out. She just would not give up. I ended up calling the dispatcher while he dealt with her."

Holiday slowed to make a turn and put on his left signal. "Let me guess, someone forgot to read them their rights, the couple was released and they ended up suing you both for brutality."

"Not this time. He got some prison time, and she received a suspended sentence for assault of a police officer. The court cases cost them their jobs once they were convicted, and she had to sell the house to pay all of the attorney fees. While my arm healed, I spent precious time at home with my wife then worked at a desk job until the doctor decided that I was mentally fit to return to the streets. It's probably why I was first noticed for the promotion to Detective. Ironic, isn't it. If the bullet missed, I might have still been in uniform today."

"Did you notice that on this island we like to wear uniforms? I like to wear them when I work. Mine has the insignia of my rank." Holiday replied with a slight sound of defensiveness in his voice. "Our promotions are ceremonies that give the right to wear the uniform. Being in uniform gives us a special sense of pride."

"Oh, don't get me wrong. It's just a cultural difference, that's all. When I got promoted to Detective I was told not to wear a uniform, and I was even given a clothing allowance to buy some suits and sport coats."

"I see. I missed that." Holiday slowed the car and stopped in front of Bart Richardson's house.

Jack agreed. "We all learn from each other's differences."

The house and the neighborhood were similar to Kesia's. Mature plants and fencing separated the homes and provided the intended privacy. Again, most of the cars and children were gone. The first thing Jack noticed about Bart's house was that the automobile that Desiree had been driving on the day of her murder was not parked in the driveway. Since it was the murder scene, he wondered if it was being held for evidence or if Bart had decided that he could not bear to see it again.

Holiday cut off the engine and removed the key. "Should we call him first or just knock on the door?"

"Your decision."

"Knowing Bart like I do, he will probably ignore both the phone and the knock on the door. The word is that he is holed up and grieving."

"Do you think he has been drinking a lot?"

Holiday nodded yes. "For days now, I guess."

"So what's your plan? Do we try to talk him out by standing outside the door? Do we try to break into the house and force him to go to the station with us?" Jack kept his eyes on the house and watched for movement.

Holiday studied the front door. "Tell you what...I'll go up there while you wait in the car. If he see's me alone, he might be more likely to open the door and talk. After all, Jack, I only need to know where he has been today."

"And if he has been at home alone with no witnesses, what then? Will you ask for his gun and take him downtown for a gunpowder test on his hands?"

"I suppose so. I don't want to..." Holiday opened the car door and leaned back inside. "If it were my wife, I might shoot some bastard too. I don't know..."

"I'll wait here if you want, but if you need me I'll be there with Davis's gun as fast as I can."

Holiday pushed the door closed with a soft click and said, "It won't come to that. Mark my words."

Jack watched J.R. approach the house and reach inside the gate to open the latch. Before he could enter the yard, there was a flash of fire from a window on the left side of the home as the rear passenger window in the police car shattered into a thousand safety glass pieces. Jack ducked down into the driver's seat and waited for a second shot. There was none. Instead Jack heard Holiday's footsteps run around the car and take cover on the passenger side.

Holiday was breathing heavily as he said loudly, "What the fuck?"

Jack reached over, opened the door and slid out of the car. He noticed sweat on his friend's forehead and dirt on his trousers. His hat was missing. Both men had their guns drawn as they crouched side by side and watched for any sign of movement in the house or yard.

"I guess that eliminates the need for a gun powder test," Jack said dryly. "This reminds me of a Robert Redford movie, somehow."

Holiday rolled his eyes. He was in no frame of mind to indulge in any reminiscence of Jack's favorite movies. "Why did he shoot at the car and not at me?"

Jack peeked over the hood and scanned all of the windows of the home. "Dunno...I have little training in psychology, but my guess is that he wanted to drive us away rather than be confronted by you. In his mental state, who knows? He certainly could have tried to hit you if he wanted. What's plan B, by the way?"

Holiday pulled out his cell phone again. "I wish you had not told me the story of how you were shot. I think you might have put a voodoo hex on us." He dialed Bart's home.

"I agree. Remind me to avoid any late night goat sacrifices, snake dances or other dark rituals...I'm feeling a bit superstitious now too. By the way Inspector, welcome to the club."

Holiday looked at him blankly. "At least you and I are consistent in daytime police work."

"What do you mean?"

"Just like the day you were shot, neither of us are wearing a bullet proof vest today either."

"Good point."

With no answer on the house phone, Holiday made another attempt to reach Bart inside the house by dialing his cell phone. After several rings, a pleasant recorded female voice advised him that the phone was either turned off or that the owner had travelled outside the calling area. He was urged to try the call again later.

Holiday grimaced at the inane sound of the cheerful default message given the circumstances.

"Are you going to call for backup? We can cover the front and rear doors until more officers arrive. It's better than trying to take him alone, don't you think?" Jack asked.

Holiday shrugged. "This is going to be strange, at best. Most of the men in the Swat team that will be sent have been trained or commanded by Bart."

"We can't just leave him, so let's separate and you make the call for help. I'll follow the old stone wall on that side and try to get a clear view of the rear yard. You remain behind this car and watch the front."

Before Holiday could respond, Jack was gone. He moved away from the car silently, down the street and back to the side of the house near the wall that would offer some cover if the shooting resumed. When he stopped and looked back, he could see J.R. talking on the cell phone. He was barely 30 feet from the front porch.

Jack froze when he heard a noise. The front door opened and Bart appeared. He was dressed in full military camouflage, heavy boots, and was carrying a semi-automatic 9mm pistol in one hand. In the other, he had what appeared to be a small silk item. Jack could not be sure. It appeared to be a pair of women's panties. He gazed with empty eyes at Jack and seemed to look right through him. With no sign of aggression to either of the men waiting for him, he walked calmly into the yard and dropped the cloth in some dirt and then ground it forcefully into the soil. With a satisfied grin, he raised his gun to his mouth and fired it once, destroying the back of his head.

Chapter 39
Local Newspaper Coverage

Philipsburg--Netherlands Antilles authorities have an-nounced a dramatic breakthrough in the murders of two women last week. In an unexpected appearance, the Windward Islands Chief Prosecutor and the Lt. Governor for St. Maarten issued a statement at a special called meeting of the Hotel Association to announce that the case has been solved. A love triangle involving a popular and well known Police officer had spurred a double murder-suicide in which the officer killed his wife's lover and his wife in a fit of rage. When surrounded by police officers, he then turned his gun on himself according to official reports. When asked about the robbery-murder of the first woman, a visitor from St. Thomas, the Chief Prosecutor was quick to explain. "It seems that the lover was a minimum wage hourly employee who wanted to impress his married girlfriend with gifts that

.D. ANDERSON

he could not afford. He resorted to theft to acquire expensive presents. Unfortunately, when the robbery of the woman at the hotel near Great Bay went bad, he was recognized and he killed her outside her hotel room to hide the crime. Conclusive evidence of the murder weapon was found in his personal belongings."

Friends and neighbors of the deceased Policeman, Bartholomew Richardson, expressed great sorrow for his immediate family.

Chapter 40

The Talk

Still wet from his morning swim, Jack walked from the water's edge through the sand to the staircase leading up to his apartment terrace. He was the only person anywhere on the beach, and he paused to pick up a discarded beer can in front of his building. It was a perfect day. With the exception of a few passing dark clouds, the sun and sea had the usual picture perfect postcard appearance. The smell of bacon cooking greeted him before he reached the top step. The kitchen door was open. Megan must have returned from her quick trip to the Dutch side of the island. She had borrowed his car. They had reached a point in the dating relationship where a few of her personal items had found a home in Jack's bathroom. Often she needed to pick up one more thing to wear from her girl friend's apartment or she needed to buy more makeup to add to her cosmetic supply. Jack's medicine cabinet had previously been limited to toothpaste, shaving cream, aspirin, a bandage package, and aerosol sunscreen. Things were changing. Now the shelves in the bathroom were looking more like an Estee Lauder display at the best department store. He did not mind at all.

At the top of the wooden stairs, he stopped to brush the sand from his feet, and then opened the door and stepped into the kitchen. Megan gave him a quick once over, and raised an eyebrow at the sight of the beer can he was carrying. She was dressed in skimpy cotton shorts with a bare midriff croptop from the Former Life Bar. Like Jack, she was barefooted.

"Starting a bit early with the beer, huh big guy?"

"You can't drink beer all day if..."

She threw a dish towel at him. "I know, I know... you and Andy have got to learn a few new lines. I better sign you up for Twitter or Facebook."

Responding with a non-committal grunt of acknowledgement, he dropped the empty can into the trash bag by the counter. With sparkling eyes, he turned towards Megan to kiss her. She moved quickly away from the stove and their lips met. Touching each other by mouth only, they lingered then moved apart. After finally taking his eyes off of her, he noticed copies of the two local newspapers, Today and the Daily Herald on the table next to a steaming cup of coffee and a frosty glass of Welch's grape juice. Both front pages showed car wrecks from the day before.

"Oh, thanks. You got me the news. Where was the wreck of the day?" Jack took a seat and sipped the aromatic coffee.

"Union Road, heading towards Marigot, like usual. That straight-away claimed another life, adding to this island's record of one car accidents." Megan answered as she placed the bacon on a paper towel and dropped two whole grain English muffins into the toaster. "Do you want one or two eggs?"

"Just one, thanks." Jack opened one of the papers and scanned the headlines. "You're spoiling me, ya know. I started drooling when I smelled your cooking. Of course, it might have been your washboard stomach..."

As she placed the warm muffins on a plate surrounded by fresh tomato slices and added the cooked Applewood bacon and a single over easy egg, she pointed at the newspapers. "Any more stories about that policeman's double murder-suicide you solved?"

"I don't see any and I don't expect any. My involvement will never be discussed or acknowledged officially. It's better that way, I guess. Marta James, the first woman murdered, was the most tragic of the victims, in my opinion. She happened to be alone in the wrong place at an opportune time with some valuable jewelry. That guy, Martinez, probably wanted her Rolex the most. Something happened to spook him, so he killed her and ran, leaving behind most of her stuff. I doubt that he went there to kill her."

"It's awful, Jack. They shifted all of the focus to the love triangle and none to the tourist who was robbed and murdered. It's horrible!"

"I believe that they wanted the whole mess to go away fast, and the spicy extramarital affair became the talk of the town, anyway. Most local folks knew the married couple, but not the visitor from St. Thomas. Naturally their attention was on the forbidden sex and the husband's horrible acts of revenge."

Megan sighed. "But I feel so sorry for the children. The policeman could have simply asked for a divorce once he suspected his wife of cheating. He didn't have to do those terrible things…"

"That cocktail of passion, anger, and humiliation propels some people to commit acts of violence that are way beyond what we have come to expect from them. The out of control emotions few of us ever experience produce the behavior of monsters. That probably is why attorneys use the temporarily insane plea, don't you think?"

Megan's face paled and she turned away from Jack to hide some tears that were welling in her eyes.

Unaware, Jack casually flipped more pages in the newspaper. "Oh look, here is another car that ran off the road yesterday…no injuries, just another wreck."

"You would think that these local drivers would understand that speed and islands don't mix. After all, where are you gonna go? We only have two stoplights on the whole island."

After composing herself, Megan brought the food to the table and sat across from him. Jack immediately noticed that she was not going to eat.

"You're right, but then some of the tourists do a great job of speeding too." He looked at his plate then back at her. "You're not having anything?"

B.D. ANDERSON

"I..I snacked on the bacon while I was cooking it. You're lucky you even got a single piece." She avoided his eyes.

Jack ground fresh pepper over the egg and took a bite. "Delicious...thanks! I should have known that you were a closet eater. Any other secrets to share this morning?" he added jokingly.

Megan's expression was serious. "Jack, we have to talk."

"Oh shit, the four words that put fear into the heart of every man." Putting down his fork, he tried to break her sudden dark mood. "You're not going to tell me that you used to be a man, are you?"

Megan's blank stare quickly convinced him that there was no way to avoid whatever was on her mind. He quickly reviewed her comments since he returned from the beach but could see no connection between car wrecks and the dead policeman. Something was up and he did not have a clue.

"*Not knowing your crime, is your crime*" he thought to himself as he waited for her to start The Talk.

"Eat, please." She motioned towards his plate.

Jack squirmed slightly in the chair then he picked up his fork and continued the meal.

— 414 —

"Do you want any hot sauce for your eggs?" she asked.

Jack didn't really want any but he debated his answer. If she stood to get a bottle from the refrigerator, it might lesson the growing tension. He decided to give it a try. "Yes, please. That would be great."

She rose and walked across the kitchen but she only made it halfway. Putting her hand to her eye and brushing away a tear, she stood motionless. Jack could see she was trying to pull herself together. He did not know what to do.

Turning back towards him she said, "Jack, I have fallen head over heels for you." More tears appeared and she began to shake.

He started to stand but she waved him back down.

"No sit. Please listen."

"Okay."

"I have done some terrible things. Things that evil people do…things that monsters do. You need to know…"

"Megan, we have all done some terrible things and made huge mistakes. You don't have a lock on human frailties. There is nothing that you've done that will change my feelings about you or chase me away. You make me happy and I haven't felt this way in years. Sooner or later, everyone screws up. Get over it."

She grimaced and lowered her voice, "No, I can't let us go forward without telling you something. I am not the person you think I am..."

Jack kept silent.

She wrung her hands and looked at the tile floor. "That guy I worked for...Nat. The murder that was not solved...I fired the first bullet into his head." Turning to him with wet eyes, she watched for Jack's reaction.

The shock must have shown on Jack's face. Megan cried out and ran out the open door to the beach steps.

"I'm sorry, Megan. Come back, please" Jack called out to her. He watched her pause before descending. She took two steps down and surprised him by sitting.

Without another word, he joined her and sat beside her. The water lapped on the beach as a passing dog barked at a pelican that had just dove after a fish. Jack's leg brushed hers, but he did not put his arm around her.

"I have so much to tell you, Jack. I believed for a long time that I killed him. I believed it until you told me on the beach that someone else also shot him that night. I was not sorry. I was not torn apart by remorse. Then somehow, you shook up the whole emotional mess for me. I was glad that I wasn't a murderer. On the other hand, sometimes I feel angry with myself that I missed the shot...I'm slightly crazy, I think. Then there is you...you might have caught me back when it happened and sent me to prison...you can't just brush this off. I saw the look on your face. You have been sleeping with a woman who is capable of murder."

Jack put his arm around Megan. He was still bare-chested and in his swim suit. Any passer-by would assume that the couple sitting on the wooden stairs was simply enjoying the view and a beautiful morning instead of talking about the attempted murder of her former boss.

Megan cast a quick glance at him then turned her head back towards the sea. "I only pretended to be shocked that he was gay when you told me about the autopsy. I saw him having sex with another man the night he died. It humiliated me. It made me crazy with anger. There was a time when I wanted him to love me. We were intimate but we never had intercourse. What a fool I was. I didn't see the forest for the trees. He used me. Everyone in Philipsburg thought that he was fucking me. I was the fool. Whatever happened to him that night, I'm glad the son-of-a-bitch is dead. Have you ever wanted to piss on someone's grave? I do. Given the chance, I would."

Jack bit his lip and kept his arm around her.

"Even if I didn't kill the bastard, I stole his shit. I took his money and a diamond stud from his ear. I thought that it would look like a robbery... or something. I know I am rambling. Listen to me. I tried at first to put this behind me. I don't even know why I returned to St. Maarten. Maybe I wanted to be caught and locked up. Maybe I just wanted to return to the scene of the crime to gloat or whatever criminals do. I did this morning when I borrowed your car to go to Philipsburg. I went to the beach where he died. No sign of car tracks now, just more trash from late night parties on the beach. A few cigarette butts and stubs from joints littered the sand. There was a fresh condom and I wondered if it had been used by a gay or straight couple. Weird. I'm weird and I know it. You should ask me to leave you alone. I'm nuts. I must be."

Jack pulled her closer with his arm and took her hand in his. He cleared his throat but remained silent.

With her free hand, she gestured in the air. "I drank too much the night of the murder. I was crazy. I know now that I was out of control. Sorry? No, I'm not sorry. Do you hear what I'm saying, Jack? I'm a horrible person. I can be a dangerous person."

Jack finally spoke. "We can all be dangerous people given enough passion and rage. Can I ask you a very serious question? I only want a yes or a no answer. Someday we'll analyze our feelings and talk some more about what you just told me, but not today."

Confused but feeling relieved from the emotions of purging her story, Megan wiped a tear from her eye with her hand. "Sure Jack, what is it?"

"Megan, will you move in with me today? We can go right now and get your stuff from your girlfriend's apartment. I want you here, permanently."

Chapter 41
The British Virgin Islands

Cutting across the clear blue water at full speed, the gleaming new boat performed beautifully. With the island of Tortola fading in the distance behind the boat, the sea ahead was calm and the view clear of any other vessels. Enjoying the balmy breezes, Lisa and Dana sunned on the front of the big Moorings power catamaran as Andy enjoyed a fresh Dominican cigar on the aft deck. Capt. Carl was at the controls and was pushing the twin Cummins engines to their maximum rpm's and highest fuel consumption. They were crossing the Sir Francis Drake channel to spend the next day or so visiting Cooper Island. There were no formal plans or cruising schedule. Each day they would simply organize in the morning and make a decision to explore in the dingy, swim and enjoy the beach, or move the comfortable live-aboard boat to another piece of paradise.

"Caaarl...slow down! I want to see the water!" Lisa hollered back at the fly bridge.

"I only have about 500 gallons of fuel aboard, so I'm testing fuel efficiency at full throttle..."

"Caaarl...I mean it. Slow down! We can't talk up here."

Andy listened to the banter between the husband and wife without concern and propped his feet on the rail. Everyone had arrived the day before; they provisioned the boat for seven days and were ready for summer vacation. Because their last charter trip together had had perfect weather and few mechanical problems, Andy was totally in a mindset for doing a lot of nothing. For fun, he had a surprise gift or two ready to add to the memories. On the last trip, Carl dove under the boat repeatedly to cut loose an obstruction on the props using a kitchen knife. Then a few days later there was an incident when Carl caught a barracuda that used its razor-sharp teeth to chomp through the fishing line and free itself. Andy was prepared with memorabilia. His luggage contained a pirate's cutlass suitable for mounting and displaying in Carl's study, a book on barracuda fishing and skimpy halter tops for the women with "Carl's Diving Team" printed on them.

Andy heard Lisa scream again and the engines slowed. Perhaps a death threat had been issued.

Time passed in comfort as the cruise took a slower pace. As they entered the protected area of Cooper Island, Andy came up on the bridge and looked happily at the charming clean beach and lush palm trees of the Cooper Island Beach Club. Their timing was excellent because most of the mooring buoys were still vacant at this time of the morning. They would have several nice choices with privacy but easy access to the dingy dock and restaurant. This was a great place to start the vacation and one of the group's favorites.

Once the boat was at secured, the women dove over the side and began an in the water exercise program while Carl and Andy opened some beers and return to the bridge to enjoy the view. A 373 Power cat entered their line of sight and moved through the calm water towards them. At the helm was Jack Donnelly, grinning like a baboon as Megan stepped forward on the bow wearing only a tiny bikini bottom.

"That your friends?" Carl asked. "Nice one piece bikini."

Andy waved to the smaller cat but it was unlikely that Jack noticed. He seemed to be focused on his date. "Yes, that's Jack and Megan. They've been down here for four or five days now."

"They should have joined us. We have lots of room for more couples on this one." Carl offered in his usual generous manner. He waved across the water to them and yelled, "How ya doin'?"

"Not for a newly hooked up man and woman in the throws of lust. I'm afraid that being with two married couples for more than an afternoon would drive those guys into madness. You'll see. They can't keep their hands off each other."

Still watching the nearly naked Megan, Carl replied sarcastically, "Disgusting, just disgusting."

The men watched as Megan pulled the mooring buoy line aboard their boat and Jack shut down the engines. They were close enough to each others position in the anchorage that Dana and Lisa swam over to greet them.

Carl watched the women board the other boat. "Your friend Jack looks happy enough."

"He has good reason. Not only does he have a new girlfriend after being alone for some time, he hit a major home run with the Dutch side Government."

"By doing what?"

"He solved two murders that were haunting the tourism industry. Both murders occurred at hotels."

"That is scary."

"Actually he solved three murders, it gets a bit complicated. There was a love triangle, stolen jewelry smuggling, marital infidelity, bags of cash, jealousy, lust...you name it."

"Sounds like Rhode Island."

Andy laughed. "Okay, we don't have an exclusive on any of that in the Caribbean, but it was a bit stressful...Dana was even slightly involved in some way and was attacked at our home while working alone in the garden. The guy duct taped her and that's why she is wearing her hair short."

"You're kidding...you both haven't said a word."

"It causes her some nightmares, so we avoid it."

"Is she okay?"

"She'll be fine. This is just what the doctor ordered. We might even talk her and Lisa into jumping naked off the Willie T in Norman's Island this trip." Andy added, "I really want one of those free T-shirts."

"I heard that they outlawed the nude diving at dinner and stopped the restaurant from encouraging tourists with the free T-shirt deal."

Andy rubbed his chin. "Damn, just when you start to believe in something..."

"Everyone needs to believe in something... and I believe that I'll take a quick shower." Carl mumbled as he dropped down to the lower level.

"Don't fall asleep on us! We'll leave you here to starve." Andy called after him.

Carl yelled back from below, "Oh yeah, starve. We have enough food for two weeks in this galley and Lisa will insist that we eat out every night."

Andy saw that Lisa and Dana were back in the water swimming to their boat. He reached for some dry beach towels and went to the rear platform to help them aboard.

"Where's Carl?" asked Lisa as she pulled her firm and tanned body on to the swim platform.

Andy leaned over the water and pretended to search the surface carefully. "I think he saw a barracuda go by... so he jumped in with a kitchen knife to spear us some lunch."

"Funny, very funny, he damn well better not be trying that deep diving trick again."

Unaware of the conversation as she came on

board, Dana looked around and asked, "Where's Carl?"

Lisa dried her hair with the towel and replied, "Don't encourage Andy. He'll have Carl wrestling sharks any moment now..."

"Sharks, where?" Dana took a towel from Andy. "I hate to swim with sharks."

Andy loved this opportunity. "Good, because Carl and I will keep that in mind when the two legged ones start circling you girls."

"They thought that you guys were our fathers." Lisa was quick to add. Both women broke into laughter from the memory.

"How many times are we going to hear this story?" Andy groaned.

The Blackberry phone in Dana's bag chimed signaling the arrival of an email. Dana reached over and examined it. "Hey, it's from Chad...he says that he might fly over and meet us in Tortola the last day or so before we leave."

Andy tapped his cigar ash in a glass ashtray. "That would be fun. We can take him to the Willie T to dive naked and win us a T-shirt."

"Stop already...don't encourage bad behavior. These are English islands. Proper." Dana countered.

Lisa saw Dana's ring from *Island Ice* for the first time, "Oh my god! Your ring is gorgeous! Where did you get that? Andy, you must have gotten some serious kinky sex for that one!"

Andy replied with a wryly smile, "There is a long story behind that ring."

Dana went into the boat's salon and returned with a bag of mail and magazines. "Here, while we shower and get ready for lunch you can make yourself useful and sort through the latest batch of mail we received from our U.S. mail service. I stopped by St. Maarten Mail on Back Street before we left and picked up all of our local and our stateside mail.

"You brought mail from home on our trip? That's crazy. What were you thinking?"

Lisa heard the beginnings of a marital disagreement and quickly excused herself to join Carl below for a shower.

Dana watched the door close to the salon. "Sure, why not? It's full of the latest Boston Proper and Victoria's Secret catalogues, some magazines, and there may even be a check or two there."

"90% of this stuff is junk mail. Why do companies still send this crap? No one reads it, do they?"

"At least banks got smart and went paperless with on line accounts."

"Only because it saves them money, Sweetie."

"Just check everything before we pitch it at the next trash drop."

"Yeh, yeah...wait a minute. There is a fancy hand addressed envelope to you. Nice stationary. Impressive."

Dana took the envelope and started to open it. "Look it even has a fancy courier stamp on it. Hand delivered to our box at St. Maarten Mail. Marked personal, I might add."

"Good. I hope that it has a winning lottery ticket in it." Andy was preoccupied with sifting through the huge stack of junk mail and placing new magazines on the center table of the deck.

Dana took a seat and pulled several items from the envelope. "Oh my God, Oh my God! Look! Look what I have...a pack of gift certificates for days of beauty, massages, nail appointments and use of the fitness center at that new hotel in Oyster Pond. There must be over a thousand dollars worth of freebees here! I love it!

Andy peered over one of his favorite boating magazines with a puzzled expression. "Who did that come from? It's not your birthday and you only had lunch there with your girlfriends for the first time last week."

"Well, the Italian manager who stopped by our table was a bit of an outrageous flirt. I was flattered. I hope I didn't encourage him. Wait! Here it is...a note with the certificates..." She unfolded the paper, read it with a devilish smile and handed it to Andy.

The boldly written man's signature made Andy raise an eyebrow in disapproval:

"Lovely Dana, I hope to see you soon, Adolfo."

Acknowledgements

Many authors and public speakers screw this up and overlook someone, a group, a business or an organization that was very special in the creative process. Many people made suggestions, provided inspiration, read sample chapters, and gave enthusiastic support to the authors. We are going to try to get it right this time, but we recognize that we may forget someone. Please understand. This list is random and no rank of importance has been assigned or should be assumed. Inspiration, like love and the other mysteries of life, can be hard to measure or explain. It simply carries with it our never ending gratitude and humble "thank you" for the encouragement you gave or the creative spark you provided.

Belton Jennings
Bryant Nix
Jay Nelms

Barbara Leary

Paula L. Anderson

Aarica Bezanson

Gerrit Koellers

Denis Boulet

Kim Parks

Mickey Fritzinger

www.Traveltalkonline.com

Contessa

The Fallers (Monsieur Bob and Madame Joan)

The Weinbergs (Monsieur Carl and Madame Lisa)

Tony and Cheri (Wow)

Linda Ascherl

Tim Barry

S. D. Freeman

www.orientbeach.com

Our friends at Kakao Restaurant and Club O

Robert S. Ricks

Robbie Ferron

Jack and Linda at Peg Leg Pub

Carl Johansen

Arnie Craven

Bob Gilbert

J.W. Montoya

About the Author

B.D. Anderson

B.D. Anderson is a pen name for Bill and Debra Anderson, an American couple who decided to set aside successful management careers in the United States and live their dream by moving to the Caribbean Island of St. Martin. When they are not working, they enjoy bareboat cruising, reading, raising island rescue animals and experiencing the Caribbean culture. They have explored many of the American and British Virgin Islands and the Bahamas by sea. More conventionally, they have traveled by plane to visit other Caribbean islands including Anguilla, Antigua, Barbados, Grenada,

Aruba, Curacao, Trinidad and several of the family islands of the Bahamas. Their Caribbean adventure continues...

www.WetFeetTheNovel.com

Which island was the setting for this novel?
Learning to say "SXM"

The authors of this book are often asked, "Is this the island of Saint Maaatin or Saint Marteen or Saint Maartin that you used for your setting in the Novels?"

The confusion is partly rooted in the history of the island and the governments that have controlled it for 400 years or so. The Netherland Antilles spelling often used is Sint Maarten. However, the French side of the island often uses Saint Martin or St. Martin. Air France, for example, lists the destination as Sint Marteen. We have seen many variations from Maartens, Marten, and even Martan. Our readers might find many others. The diverse cultures of the island and the many variations of English usage create several more examples.

Our point is this: who cares? The beautiful white sand, the consistently sunny skies, the clear blue water and the friendly people will be your reason to visit. Just search SXM, the airport code, when finding a ticket from your nearest airport, and you will understand. Yes, visitors need a passport. And, no, it is not too hot there during the summer months.

Call it what you want. We call it "Paradise."

No matter how you spell it...or say it...or dream it.

See you on the beach!

Bill and Debra

B.D. Anderson

"O sweet Saint Martins Land"
Where over the world, say where, You find an
Island there,
So lovely small with nations free,
With people French and Dutch,
Though talking English much, As thee St. Martin
in the sea?
Chorus:
O, sweet Saint Martin's Land So bright by beach
and strand With sailors on the sea And harbours
free; Where the chains of mountains green
Variously in sunlight sheen; O, I love thy Paradise,
Nature beauty very nice
"The St. Maarten Anthem"
Composed by Father G. Kemps
Circa 1958

LaVergne, TN USA
08 January 2010
169370LV00001B/8/P